FEEDING

Various thoughts flicked through Layla's head as she scrambled away from the opening, two rising from the torrent of panic with singular importance: *Feeder. It heard me.* The wreck was a dozen feet away, and she had spoken barely above a whisper. But whatever lurked in that wreck had heard her.

Heart thumping, she regained her feet and fled back to the cavern, the rats scattering before her. *Have you ever seen a feeder?* Taxo had asked her. *Now I have.* The thought provoked a laugh, short and shrill, until she clamped her teeth against it. She looked back at the archway and the dim light within, watching for any change. The sight of the tattoo on the thing's skin loomed large, demanding more notice than she wanted to give it. *They don't move in daylight*, she reminded herself. But still, the sense of being observed lingered.

THE FEEDING

A. J. RYAN

A list of the Orbit imprint
orbit-books.co.uk

RUN FOR IT

First published in Great Britain in 2025 by Run For It

1 3 5 7 9 10 8 6 4 2

A CIP catalogue record for this book is available from the British Library.

ISBN 978-0-356-52642-3

Typeset in Bembo by Palimpsest Book Production Limited, Falkirk, Stirlingshire
Printed and bound in Great Britain by Clays Ltd, Elcograf, S.p.A.

Papers used by Run For It are from well-managed forests and other responsible sources.

MIX
Paper | Supporting
responsible forestry
FSC
www.fsc.org
FSC® C104740

Run For It is a list of the Orbit imprint.

Orbit
An imprint of
Little, Brown Book Group
Carmelite House
50 Victoria Embankment
London EC4Y 0DZ

The authorised representative
in the EEA is
Hachette Ireland
8 Castlecourt Centre, Dublin 15, D15
XTP3, Ireland
(email: info@hbgi.ie)

An Hachette UK Company
www.hachette.co.uk

orbit-books.co.uk

To the late Sir Christopher Lee – war hero, monster, assassin, Sith Lord, wizard and, of course, vampire.

"What a curse, to be immortal."

From the far north they heard a low wail of the wind, and Uncle Henry and Dorothy could see where the long grass bowed in waves before the coming storm.

The Wonderful Wizard of Oz by L. Frank Baum

Chapter One

She heard the sirens at the same time as she heard the dogs. Ignoring both, she continued to strain against the pipework, reaching for the length of shiny metal inches from her fingertips.

"Layla," Dresh said, keeping to a whisper as they always did in the Undercut.

"I know," she grunted back. Angling her body, she managed to squeeze herself deeper into the gap until her fingers touched the cool, smooth surface of the shiny metal tube. About a yard long and only as thick as her thumb, yet still so very precious.

"Gotta go." The whisper faded from Dresh's voice as sirens and dogs continued to echo through the surrounding maze of tunnel and ruin. The yap and growl of the dogs was louder than the deep-throated wail of the sirens. "Now," he added, poking her ankle for emphasis.

Layla's reply consisted of a garbled obscenity, her face being squished against a something leaking a steady stream of liquid she hoped was water. She shut her mouth against the acrid taste and contorted her slim frame for one last grab at the length of shiny metal. A gasp of triumph and relief escaped her lips as her hand closed on her prize, the flare of success dwindling when it refused to budge.

"Layla!"

"OK," she sputtered, releasing the copper pipe and squirming free of the gap. "It's stuck. We'll have to come back."

A spasm of frustration flickered across Dresh's narrow, grime-flecked face before he cast wary glances at both ends of the tunnel. "Can't tell if they're coming from left or right."

Closing her eyes, Layla tried to parse the distant wail of the sirens from the babble of a rapidly approaching pack. Sound played tricks in the Undercut, and so did the dogs. Hatefully smart, sometimes they'd make a big noise in one direction so you'd go in the other, guiding you to a dark nook where the rest of the pack lay in wait. They weren't big, these Underdogs, named years ago by some forgotten comedian. Products of a hunting ground that favoured viciousness over size, generations of subterranean existence had produced something that resembled a pale, overlarge rat. But lack of bulk didn't make them any less vicious, especially when angered by incursions into their territory.

"Both," Layla said. Looking up, she played the beam

of her headlamp over the interweaving matrix of pipe, rebar and concrete. "We have to climb."

Dresh's shoulders sagged as he swallowed a groan. When they had first begun exploring this dangerous but lucrative playground, his scrawny frame allowed him to navigate its constricting passages almost as easily as she did. The intervening years had transformed scrawniness into lean athleticism while adding a fair amount of muscle to once wiry limbs. These days, it was clear he found squirming his way through the constricted maze of the Undercut difficult. His arms bore the scars of numerous scrapes and cuts, evidence of his determination not to let her scavenge alone.

"You first," he said.

Layla didn't argue. She had the best eye for finding a path in the Undercut, anyway. Adjusting her pack, lighter than she would have liked thanks to the meagre pickings today, she leaped, grasping a rebar and hauling herself into the jagged chimney of tumbled material. She climbed with a fluid ease Dresh could never quite match, long honed instincts seeking out the least obstructed route that also offered the firmest hand-holds. After ascending a dozen feet or so, angry yelps and growls echoed from the tunnel below. Layla had grown attuned to the dogs' vocal repertoire and heard a note of real anger in the chorus that chased them as they continued to make good their escape. Fearsome as they were, the dogs were poor climbers.

As they neared the upper levels of the Undercut,

the sirens gradually smothered the song of canine frustration. The sound wasn't constant, each ululating blast lasting for three seconds, followed by a pause of equal length. Everyone in New City Redoubt knew what it meant, and many would already be crowding the wall to view the imminent spectacle. Layla felt the sirens' lure as keenly as any, and would soon take her place among the audience. Yet, as always, the prospect filled her with as much dread as it did anticipation.

"Come on, come on," Dresh urged as he held the great steel door open to allow her to crawl out. "Got three chits riding on Drucker being the only one to make it back."

"Three?" Getting to her feet, Layla brushed accumulated grit from her clothes, shooting him a disparaging squint. "You pissed away a week of meals on a long-odds bet?"

"Long odds mean big wins." He let the door clang shut and started off at a jog, eager to get to the wall.

"Wait," she said, kneeling to gather up the chain and padlock. "Gotta seal this first."

"What's the point? No one ever comes down here." He didn't say this every time, but still did so with enough frequency to make it annoying. *Thorn never said it.* The thought came with a guilty sting. Dresh wasn't his brother and the comparison unfair. Also, for all that she had loved about Thorn, he had been by far the more damaged of the two. The eldest of their trio by a couple of years, he could remember the Feeding with a clarity they never could. The kind of clarity that made him bottle it all up when awake and scream it out at night. She still bore a scar on her arm where he had scratched her in his manic thrashing. His abject self-recrimination at the sight of that injury made him withdraw further. She always wondered if his guilt over her scar had led him to a singular and unwise decision, and later, over the wall. With Thorn gone, she started taking Dresh along when she went scavenging. It was more an obligation than a kindness.

"No." Layla looped the chain through the steel braces on the door and drew it tight. "They never come here when we do. No rust, see? Means it gets changed regularly." She didn't add that the crushers had an inspection schedule which she had memorised and he hadn't. Although kindly by nature, Dresh could exhibit a mean sulkiness when reminded of his limitations.

Layla snapped the padlock shut and worked her key in the hole. Next to picking it, fashioning her own key for this lock was one of her prouder achievements, not that she could ever boast about it. "Besides—" she straightened, offering him a bland smile "—wouldn't want the dogs getting out, would we? Or anything else."

Dresh just scowled and resumed his jog, fixing a scarf about his face. They were downwind of what City Administration referred to as the "Sanitation Complex" and everyone else called "the Tip". Mounds of waste formed a constantly shifting range of hills obscuring the entrance to the Undercut from curious eyes. According to Strang, it had once been a collection of roadways and elevated junctions interspersed with fuel and electrical charging stations. The gateway to the mix of suburbs and industrial estates that had formed the basis for New City Redoubt, it had been bombed midway through the Feeding to block the western approaches to one of the few defensible places left. After the wall went up, City Administration made efforts to pave over the ruins, but the surface remained unstable and unsuitable for building. Now it was another no-go area, visited only by the likes of her and Dresh.

The stink of the Tip provided additional discouragement for casual onlookers. Anyone seeing them would assume they had come to join the dozens rooting through the mounds for something to sell or eat. Layla had done so herself once, before realising that the real treasure lay beneath their feet, if you were willing to risk your neck to get it.

They made their way through the rows of houses bordering the Tip, mostly empty since few could stomach the smell. Shiners called out to them from hollowed-out buildings, more in hope than expectation. Upon being ignored, some hurled insults with varying degrees of passion, but none tried to obstruct or pursue. The shine they drank had a bad effect on both eyesight and mobility.

Nudging and occasionally shoving their way through the throng, they reached the stretch of wall facing the shortest span of wasteland separating New City Redoubt from the great, ruined sprawl of the Old City. The wall itself was sixty feet high and twenty thick, a solid barrier that circled the city and remained the sole reason for its continued existence. Scaling the switchback stairwell to the top, Layla paid dutiful attention to the iron plaques set into the concrete, each bearing the name of a Special Construction Battalion and listing those lost in the feverish haste to raise the wall. Strang had led one of those battalions, and she retained dim memories of him from those days, yellow hard hat on his head, casting out an endless string of orders to his work crew. He stood a lot taller then.

Atop the parapet, rows of tiered benches ensured all present got a clear view, reflecting the abiding popularity of these occasions. However, wary of the rickety construction, Layla always preferred to place herself at the balustrade. Return days invariably produced an air of excitement, but today was different. Layla saw plenty of people clutching their betting chits, eyes alive with greed and hope. But plenty more stared at the Old City in silent, hard-faced desperation. Their hands were mostly empty, although their stake in the outcome was probably highest among the audience. The last two crossings had failed to return, making this the first such occasion for four months. The worsening weather added to the weighty mood. A thick bank of grey cloud filled the sky and Layla could see distant curtains of rain obscuring the deeper reaches of the ruins. In between siren blasts, she heard the phrase "a feeder's sky" repeated several times.

"Any idea how many?" Dresh asked a man in the crowd. A spindly, bearded character with a stack of betting chits clutched in both hands. He wore a pinstripe suit that was far cleaner than he was, and loose enough to make it plain it had once clad a more substantial frame. Layla assumed he only wore it on return days. His gaze barely flickered from the dark sprawl of Old City as he jerked his head towards the guard post. A trio of crushers were on the roof, bulky figures in patched body armour that gave them a motley appearance and led some to refer to them as "the clowns", although rarely in their hearing. One crusher peered through a bulbous telescope on a tripod, while another held a clipboard in one hand and a walkie in the other. The third crusher was in the process of settling herself behind a scoped rifle that was longer than she was. The siren would have blasted at the telescope's first glimpse of the crossing party, summoning those with the keenest interest in the outcome.

"They're not saying," the man in the pinstripe suit grunted. His eyes darted to the chit in Dresh's hand. "Who'd you pick?"

"Rucker."

The bearded man clicked his tongue. "Just one? Bad tactics, son. Odds too long. Went with Rucker, Lukaz and Slatt. Even money. She's done six before this one . . ."

His voice was smothered by another siren blast. This time, it went on for a few seconds longer before falling silent. When it did, a frigid hush settled over the crowd, broken by the terse shout from the crusher with the rifle. "Crossers in sight! Counting two!"

"Shit!" the bearded man hissed to himself, clutching his chits tighter. "Still in it. Rucker and Slatt. Rucker and Slatt . . ."

Variations of his mantra were echoed by others in the crowd. Different names, or combinations of names. Most Layla had heard before, since it only took a few successful crossings to acquire notoriety in the Redoubt. She thought it said a lot for Dresh's judgement that he was the only one repeatedly muttering, "Rucker."

The crusher at the telescope spoke then, a rapid tumble of words Layla almost didn't catch: "Feeder in the open!"

"Sending!" the woman with the rifle snapped back. The weapon boomed a split second later, the recoil shoving it hard into her shoulder. Layla scanned the jagged line of buildings opposite for some sign of an impact, or any movement at all, but saw nothing. Crushers typically reported a kill, but the sniper wordlessly levered the bolt to eject a long brass casing, then returned her eye to the scope. A prolonged thirty seconds later, the crusher with the telescope spoke again, tone clipped but not so much that Layla couldn't hear the bitter note of failure: "Crosser down."

A ripple of curses ran through the crowd, loudest from those who had hedged their bets. Only one name could now claim the win, and even that wasn't guaranteed.

"It's Slatt," Pinstripe said. He pressed himself against the balustrade, near manic energy lighting his creased features as he scoured the wasteland with hungry eyes. "Has to be."

"Crosser in the open!" the crusher called out, even though Layla still couldn't discern any change in the view beyond a deepening hue to the gathering clouds. Then she saw it, a faint flicker of movement near the edge of the ruins.

"Who is it?" someone demanded, the question heralding an upsurge in excited babble.

"It's a woman," another voice called out, Layla glancing back to see a tall man rising from the benches, a monocular pressed to his eye. Others with various ancient viewing devices confirmed his judgement, Layla hearing the name "Slatt" repeated most often.

"Knew it!" Pinstripe enthused. He clutched his chits to his chest, as if cradling a precious, fragile creature. "Knew it! Knew it!" From the pitch of his glee, Layla guessed this might be one of the few moments in his life he had been proven right about something.

"She's not running," the man with the monocular said. "Why's she not running?"

Layla could discern the figure now, though it was still faint. Straining for a clearer view, she saw that monocular man was right. The figure moved at a faltering, slumped walk. The minutes stretched as it drew nearer to the wall, falling at one point, but then slowly regaining its feet to stumble on.

"Blood," monocular man said, not so loud this time. "I see blood. She's hurt." A pause, his face crinkling around the optic. "I see her face. It's Slatt."

"Fucking feeders!" Pinstripe snarled, hands now pressing the chits hard against his chest. "Fuckers . . ."

Watching the stricken woman stagger an erratic course through puddle and ditch, Layla was keenly reminded of why she hated return days. This, in turn, stirred the guilty urge to ponder why she could never resist coming to watch.

This is the last time, she told herself, knowing it to be a lie. *Strang never came to these, even before he got sick. I shouldn't either.*

Slatt, veteran crosser of six trips through Old City and whatever lay beyond, halted fifty yards short of the wall. By now Layla could see the dark stains on her clothing, and the way her limbs shook with pain as she tried to stay upright. She lost the battle after a few tottering backward steps and sank to her knees. Layla suffered a jolt of shame for being more interested in Slatt's pack than her suffering. It definitely held something, but didn't seem overly heavy.

"Retrieval team!" the crusher with the walkie

shouted. "Deploy the retrieval team!" His face darkened when the walkie squawked something back at him. "No feeders in sight! Deploy the fucking team!"

Rain began to fall as ropes were cast out from the wall alongside. The shower was heavy, partially obscuring the quartet of crushers, each with a rifle strapped across their back, abseiling down the wall. Layla had seen this play out before, but not for a while. She noted that the last time the crushers on the team had all been equipped with at least four magazines apiece. Now each bore only one. She blinked rainwater and watched them hurry towards Slatt, now slumped and immobile. Three pointed their rifles in the direction of Old City while a fourth crouched at the fallen woman's side.

"It's dark enough now," a thin, female voice murmured close by. Layla didn't turn to view the speaker, but could hear the weight of memory in those words. "Feeders always liked the rain . . ."

The rain cast a grey veil over what came next, but not thick enough to fully conceal it. The crusher crouched at Slatt's side hunched lower, Layla assumed in an effort to conceal the act of putting a pistol to the stricken crosser's head. If so, it was wasted. The echoing gunshot made the outcome plain. "Bastard crushers!" someone hissed, answered quickly by a grim retort. "They have to. Can't bring her in if she's going to turn."

The crowd began to thin as the crushers scaled the wall. Layla saw that the man in the pinstriped suit had already left, leaving a scattering of chits behind. The non-gamblers stayed, rising from their seats to stare at the Retrieval Team being hauled over the balustrade, all eyes fixed on the pack they bore.

"Any meds?" called a woman in a ripped rain jacket. Of course, she received no answer as the pack was swiftly ported into the guard post. After that, the crowd drifted away, although Layla saw a few continuing to sit on the benches, uncaring of the rain. Most were crying.

"At least they got her stuff," Dresh said as they descended the stairwell. "Bound to be meds in it. They carry mixed loads."

"I know," Layla said. She knew he was trying to be kind, but the knot of worry in her gut made her tone harsher than she liked. "You'd best get home," she told him. "I'll go to Velna's. We'll divvy up tomorrow. Anything in particular you want?"

"The usual," he said with a shrug, a forced smile on his narrow face. Washed of grime by the rain, she had to admit there was an attractiveness to that angular concoction of bone and muscle, especially when his innate compassion showed through. "She must have had meds," he added, before turning and jogging away into the rain.

Sighing as she started towards the Arts, Layla conceded that he was probably right. Slatt had brought

A. J. Ryan

meds, but with only one pack the chances Strang would get his share, even if she'd brought the right kind, were close to zero.

Chapter Two

Velna always made the same noise when she surveyed the stuff Layla brought her. Something that mixed a musing hum with a grind of her discoloured dentures. Layla had learned that the tone of the noise itself meant little, but the duration could reveal a lot. Today, as Velna raised one of the many pairs of spectacles dangling from her neck to peruse the wares set out on the counter, it was short. Knowing her reward would be meagre today, Layla smothered a sigh.

"Only one quarter full," Velna said, shaking the bottle of bleach Layla had risked her arm to retrieve from under a precariously balanced concrete slab. "And these——" liver-spotted hands played over the various wires and insulated leads "——I can get anywhere."

"Not the audio jacks, you can't," Layla said. She was careful to strip any heat from her voice. Curiously, for a shopkeeper, Velna detested bargaining and had little tolerance for argument. Her lack of toleration was enforced by the ever silent but substantial person of Leron, the huge man who always sat by the iron-braced door to Velna's shop. It was locked even during opening hours, and tales abounded regarding the fate of those foolish enough to test its security.

Velna made the noise again and resumed her scrutiny, taking longer this time. As she did so, Layla scanned the trove of riches arrayed on the shelves at the old woman's back. A good portion of the most valuable stock was hidden from view, but Velna had a liking for displaying things most of her customers could never afford. Among the eclectic collection of typewriters, glass globes, watches, porcelain crockery and books, one item always captured Layla's full attention. Positioned in a glass case on the top shelf, the pair of running shoes, black with a white curved stripe on the side, drew her gaze like a magnet. Her own shoes were as well made as any in the Redoubt, an amalgam of tyre rubber and rabbit skin stitched together with care and artistry. But they needed repair every few weeks and, fast as she was, Layla knew if she could get the shoes in the case on her feet, she would run so much faster. They were, Velna had assured her with evident malice, Layla's size. *Never been worn. What they called a limited edition, see? Even during the Peace they were worth more than you'll ever be, my love.*

"Told you last time I need circuits more than anything," Velna said, recapturing Layla's attention. "Processors and such."

"If it's not there, I can't bring it." A carefully phrased piece of obfuscation since Layla had, in fact, unscrewed a circuit board complete with processor from a smashed laptop Dresh spotted lying under a crushed office desk. Before coming here, she had consigned it to one of her carefully hidden stashes near the market. Velna had a habit of randomly ordering Leron to check her pack for anything she might be holding back.

"One ration pack," Velna pronounced. "And one issue for whatsisname."

"His name's Dresh," Layla said. "And I need meds, not food." She paused, disliking the necessity of sharing valuable information but seeing no option. "Anti-bios. You know that's what I need. I can pay. I found copper today. I'll get it tomorrow."

This earned an arched eyebrow as Velna jerked her head to free the spectacles from her nose. "And, if you'd brought it to me, I still couldn't sell you anti-bios, my love. Fact is, there are none. My contact at the hospital hasn't been able to lay their hands on any for weeks now."

"There was a return today. The crossers didn't make it, but Slatt got close to the walls. They brought in her pack . . ."

"I know. But, you can bet whatever was in it has already gone to those who can pay a damn sight more than you. Reckon we both know there's only one way you're getting your hands on any meds." The statement contained a suggestion, one Velna had made before, but Layla chose to ignore. Today, she felt it tug more than she liked.

"I'm not that dumb," she said, hating the suppressed quaver in her voice because she knew Velna would hear it. *Probably thinks she'll make a packet betting on me. Greedy old bitch.* She had one more gambit in reserve, something she rarely used because Velna's reaction to this subject could be unpredictable. "You know Strang," Layla said. "You owe him. For the old days—"

"Anything I owed him got paid back years ago," Velna cut in, a worrying edge to her voice. "With interest, my love. Don't try to pluck my strings. I don't like it. And I told you: there's no fucking meds."

Her stare was hard, but Layla matched it, resisting the urge to check if Leron had risen from his chair. As with any predator, it wasn't a good idea to show weakness in Velna's presence.

It was a rare thing for this woman to exhibit respect, but Layla saw a measure of it now as the old woman made the noise again, her pink painted lips curling just a little. "Two ration packs," she said. "Two issues, and I'll throw in some aspirin." Her lips snapped back into a hard, flat line. "Don't test me further."

She chose a circuitous route home, since predictability was an unwise habit in the Arts. It wasn't the worst neighbourhood in the Redoubt, but neither was it the best. True gangs, like those in the Garrison or the

Riverbank, were rare here but basic thievery remained a threat. Layla's knife usually sufficed to see off anyone keen for an uninvited look at her scavengings. When the more desperate or shine-addled pushed their luck, she was forced to do more than just twirl the blade. Luckily, thanks to the unabated rain, she enjoyed an uninterrupted passage through the various walkways and underpasses that formed this old complex of theatres and conference halls.

Sitting alongside the entrance to the central complex was a row of shiny chrome letters spelling out the words "Municipal Arts and Performance Centre". Unlike much of the infrastructure beyond, the letters had proven resistant to degradation and defacement over the years, the chrome shiny as ever, even in the rain. Entering the gloomy interior, she scaled the spiral concrete steps to the upper levels. The people she encountered in the maze of corridors and vestibules were content with a cordial nod by way of greeting, since they knew her well enough not to attempt conversation. Most were old with a growing list of infirmities, meaning they no longer troubled themselves with the stairs and relied on the Ration Distribution Team. Some had been here since the Peace. The Arts had been a place where people gathered rather than lived then, but a few musicians and sundry performers had found themselves caught in its precincts when the Feeding began in earnest.

As was customary come evening, Cuhla sat playing

her cello on the open walkway connecting the main Arts building with the smaller structure Layla called home. Cuhla did this regardless of the weather, erecting a large, extensively patched umbrella to ward off the rain when need arose. Layla could never resist lingering a while to listen. When she was younger, Cuhla had taken her fascination as a desire to learn the instrument and attempted a few lessons. However, Layla could never quite get her fingers to form the chords in the right sequence and quickly grew bored. Her younger self had always found the Redoubt's abandoned and often unexplored corners far more appealing than structured education. When City Admin closed the schools, a twelve-year-old Layla had rejoiced in her liberation.

Cuhla smiled at Layla, but didn't stop playing. She recognised the tune as Pachelbel's Canon in D – not all her lessons had been forgotten. Cuhla only played this one when she felt down. From the strained smile she offered, and the glance at the far end of the walkway, Layla concluded Cuhla had paid Strang a visit today. Feeling the knot tighten in her gut, Layla forced a smile of her own and moved on.

The sign above the entrance flickered as she approached. It tended to do that when it rained, regardless of how much time Taxo spent taping the wires. The words "Electric Palace Theatre" strobed above a chalkboard announcing the evening showing in variably coloured chalk:

Classics Thursdays Return for an
Exciting Double Bill
Roddy McDowall in *Lassie Come Home*
&
Humphrey Bogart in *The Treasure of the Sierra Madre*
One ticket per entry – Refreshments Extra –
No refunds.

Silently thanking her luck for having missed the first half of the showing, Layla entered the foyer to be swamped by the booming soundtrack of a key scene from *Sierra Madre*, the moment where they turn the rock over to reveal the Gila monster. Layla resisted the impulse to linger at the entrance to the auditorium and watch it play out. She had seen it countless times and could mouth along to the dialogue. Yet, it never got old. A glance at the audience filling the seats – they almost always had a full house regardless of the movie on offer – revealed the rapt faces of a mostly older audience who felt the same way.

Climbing the ramp into the projection booth, she found Taxo hunched at his workbench, soldering iron leaking vapour as he worked his magic on some ancient piece of tech. A tray laden with punnets of mostly untouched roasted chestnuts lay nearby.

"Told you they wouldn't sell," Layla said. She unhitched her pack, dumped it on the bench next to him and sank into an old armchair that was more duct tape than leather. "Old folks' teeth don't appreciate nuts."

Taxo didn't look up from his work, broad shoulders flexing a shrug. "Worth a try. Gotta do something since the ice cream machine died its final death."

"Cake," Layla said. "Everyone likes cake."

"Baker charges too much." Taxo set aside his soldering iron and straightened his back with a groan before turning his attention to Layla's pack. "Nice," he said, extracting the circuit board complete with processor. "She'll need a new one soon."

He cast a brief, worried glance at the projector. Once a compact piece of technology housed in durable plastic, thanks to endless modification, it now resembled some kind of mutated creature. Myriad wires sprouted from its revealed innards, connecting to various drives and power banks. The only part that remained original, and irreplaceable, was the lens. It had been casting its blue-white stream of magic onto the screen since they first took over this place when work on the wall came to an end. Where Taxo found the projector remained a mystery. Layla discerned a flicker of shame in his face whenever the question came up, indicating some dark, best undiscussed deed. Dark or not, she was grateful for it. The lure of the projector and the old discs it played kept them well fed over the years, comparatively speaking.

A bout of coughing came from the adjoining room, the wet hacking audible even above the sound of gunshots and swelling music from the auditorium. She and Taxo exchanged glances, his heavy-jawed, perpetually stubbled face forming a grimace before he swivelled his wheelchair and resumed his work. "Word came round about a Mayor's Assembly tomorrow," he said. "We should go."

"It'll just be Flak telling everybody there's nothing to worry about and we should just forget the last crossing. That's all it ever is. And I have work."

"Grubbing around in the Undercut is work, is it?"

"Didn't you just get your hands on a new processor? And maybe my maths is off, but I count two extra ration packs in there we didn't have yesterday."

She saw the heavy muscles of his back tense and knew he was steeling himself for a repeat of their favourite argument. Taxo hated what she did, regardless of how much tech she brought him. But she knew his anger was mostly self-directed, since he had no good rationale for why she should stop. A fresh upsurge of coughing from the other room forestalled the inevitable escalation into a shouting match, stirring a guilty pang of gratitude as Layla rose from the armchair. "I'd best check on him."

These days Strang was mostly confined to the large, many-shelved space that had been the theatre's film library. He had once explained that, instead of discs, projectors were fed by strips of transparent stuff called celluloid imprinted with thousands of individual still pictures. Consequently, places like the Electric Palace, "arthouse cinemas" he called them, had needed copious storage space. What became of all the celluloid remained a mystery, since the room had been just empty, dust-covered shelves when they moved in. Instead of flat steel cans, the shelves now held books. Strang had been collecting them ever since she had known him. Some he traded for, others he had rummaged out of houses in Old City back in the days when it was still relatively safe to venture there in daylight. City Admin maintained a library, of sorts, but it was mostly technical manuals plus a lot of history and medical textbooks. Strang's collection was almost all fiction, and he had read every word of it at least twice.

She was ashamed of lingering in the shelves until his cough subsided. Sitting helplessly and watching him convulse, occasionally spitting pink phlegm into a rag, was her most detested chore. *At least he's sitting up*, she thought. Always a big man, bigger even than Taxo, he appeared increasingly shrunken with each passing day. The once impressive, densely tattooed muscles of his arms and shoulders were wasted down to the bone in places. Still, a measure of the old vitality shone in the gaze he settled on her when she stepped from the shadowed shelves into the multihued light cast by the stained glass lamp on his bedside table.

"Heard the sirens," he said, the grating sigh of his voice holding only a mild note of rebuke when he added, "You went, didn't you?"

"I always do. You know that." She sat in the office chair beside his bed, shaking the box Velna had given her before placing it on his table. "Aspirin. Velna sends her regards."

"Bullshit." The word was accompanied by a worrying guttural rasp which, to her relief, failed to blossom into another bout of hacking. "How is the old demon, anyway?"

"Still doesn't like to be reminded of her debts."

They shared a short smile. He had told her many tales about the early days of the Redoubt, back when they built the wall. Even then, Velna had been the one you went to when you wanted something you couldn't get elsewhere. Some oldsters spoke of that time in nostalgic, even fond terms, but Strang made it clear that the Redoubt had been birthed in as much blood as it had tireless labour. In Layla's dim infant memories it was all a vague melange of rowed tents, electrified fences, and a nightly chorus of gunfire. She knew Strang had taken her there, having found her somewhere in Old City, a solitary, tottering four-year-old. She had memories of a woman's face she now saw in the mirror with increasing clarity, of a nightmare of running and screaming, but her first encounter with the man who saved her life remained infuriatingly absent.

"I'd rather have that copy of *Bleak House* she's been keeping from me for years," Strang said, glancing at the aspirin.

"And I'd rather have the meds she says can't be had." Layla regretted the words instantly. They usually hedged around his illness. He would talk to Taxo about it in simple and honest terms, repeating what Doc Piller said about progressive infection rates and the importance of regular expectoration. But he never did with her. Even so, she knew what he had. She knew the nature of the sickness that was eating away at his lungs. She even knew the names of the drugs that would stop it. *Amoxicillin, clarithromycin, doxycycline.* Broad-spectrum antibiotics, Doc Piller called them. All now more rare and precious than anything she might dig out of the Undercut.

"I found copper today," she said. "Couldn't get it out, though. Should be able to tomorrow. Then we'll see how dry of meds the old demon really is. Bet she'll even throw in *Bleak House*." She didn't mention the dogs. As far as Strang knew, the Undercut was free of predators. Still, the slump of his already haggard face told of both disapproval and guilt. He wasn't as vocal as Taxo when it came to her scavenging, but she knew he hated it even more.

He began to say something, but she forestalled him by reaching for the book on the table, opening it at the marked page. He still read, when the cough allowed, but had to hold the books close to his eyes. They had yet to find a pair of glasses that didn't give him a migraine. "Ready?" she asked.

He met her eyes, and she saw both gratitude and

shame before he blinked and settled back onto the bed. The cushions were arranged so that his upper half was always elevated, otherwise the fluid in his lungs would choke him when he slept. "Sure," he said, closing his eyes. "Where were we?"

Layla swallowed a catch from her voice, blinking so the words on the page didn't blur. "'Chapter Six: Baskerville Hall. Sir Henry Baskerville and Dr Mortimer were ready upon the appointed day, and we started as arranged for Devonshire. Mr Sherlock Holmes drove with me to the station and gave me his last parting injunctions . . .'"

Chapter Three

The Stadium was one of the oldest buildings in New City Redoubt, a faux classical brick and marble monument to a time when architects didn't care much about wheelchair access. Consequently, Layla and Taxo were obliged to get there early to avoid the crush in the tunnel leading to the playing field. Even so, it was already busy. People were filling the oval of tiered seating enclosing the field and a solid line of crushers had taken up position in front of the stage. The field itself was sparse of grass and paved in places, enabling Taxo to navigate around the mud and puddles left by the rain. They found Dresh at the wooden barriers set out to the front of the crushers' line, engaged in some good-natured bartering with a pair of green-capped Agris.

"Two ration chits each?" Dresh scoffed at a cheerfully unimpressed man holding a box of apples. "You could just pull a knife on me. It'd be more honest."

The woman standing at the apple vendor's side was

of a far less amiable disposition, scowling and flicking her hand in weary dismissal. "Two chits is the price, laddo. Pay up or piss off." This clearly wasn't her first complaint of the day.

"How about one chit per apple?" Taxo suggested, bringing his chair to a halt. As the woman began to voice another profane response, Taxo reached into his saddlebag and flourished a pair of wooden pegs bearing the neatly painted words "Electric Palace Theatre". "And two tickets to tonight's showing of *Bad Day at Black Rock*."

"Seen that one six times," the woman said. "When're you fuckers gonna get something new?" Nevertheless, she took the pegs and jerked her head at the man with the box to hand over the goods.

"They used to do candy apples," Dresh complained once the Agri couple moved on. He rubbed the fruit on his sleeve before taking a bite. "Not bad though."

"Sugar beet harvest failed this year," Taxo said. "Some kind of blight, I heard. How you doing, young-ster?"

"Still breathing so can't complain, oldster." Dresh exchanged a fist bump with Taxo before turning an expectant gaze on Layla. "Got something for me?"

"Oh, yeah." Layla watched his face brighten as she extracted the two issues from her pack. They were old, with curled edges and faded colours, but Dresh didn't care.

"A *Daredevil* and a *Judge Dredd*," he said, tracing his

fingers over the improbably muscled figures on the covers. "Last time I was in there, Velna said she didn't have any. I always knew she liked you better than me."

"The only thing she likes is a good deal." Layla cast a nervous glance around the rapidly filling seats and thickening crowd. A big audience for an assembly portended trouble, especially if their esteemed mayor had bad news to impart. "Maybe we should move to the side," she suggested to Taxo.

"Screw that. I want to see his face when he talks. Makes it easier to tell when he's lying. If it all kicks off, just hold tight to my chair and keep your heads down."

Layla's nerves grew more taut as the numbers continued to swell, making her shift her pack to her front. She put a hand inside so the weapons could be easily grabbed. In addition to her knife, she had lead-weighted sap and a spray bottle filled with a potent mix of ammonia and pepper. She heard plentiful anger in the accumulated voices and saw a twitchy discontent on many faces. The perennial subjects of maintenance and meds were the most common points of grievance. Agris and Cons complained of worn-out tools and busted engines, while other, more strained voices spoke of older relatives with untreated arthritis and children with croup. Somewhere, the apple vendors were engaged in an increasingly voluble dispute regarding their prices.

"You Agri bastards are just parasites. Stuffing your faces and robbing us blind . . ."

The argument was abruptly drowned by a vast squeal from the stadium tannoy as a white-capped tech appeared to check the microphone. He departed the stage after a few adjustments, whereupon they were treated to a rendition of the city anthem. It had been composed during the Raising and, according to Strang, originally featured several verses of inspiring verse to go with the bombastic melody. During the succeeding years, the lyrics had gradually faded from public performance. People just found them embarrassing.

Confounding expectations, Mayor Flak didn't appear immediately. Instead, he was preceded by a group of six people, all wearing the black caps that made their role clear even if they hadn't been instantly recognisable. They lined out to assume a semblance of military rigidity that Layla felt to be almost comically at odds with their appearance. Apart from the caps, their garb was non-uniform, even dishevelled in places. However, the presence of the city's most celebrated crossers provided a significant clue to the nature of today's announcement, provoking a shift in the crowd's mood. Layla wouldn't have described the sound that rippled through the stadium as optimistic, but it lacked the undercurrent of anger from seconds before. The aggrieved apple buyer had even stopped arguing with the Agris.

The simmering malcontent resumed when the

stocky figure of Mayor Flak strode onto the stage. His role made him the single most important person in the Redoubt, but also the most hated. Consequently, Layla could never bring herself to fully share her fellow citizens' detestation. No amount of rations could ever persuade her, or anyone with a brain, to take his job. Still, he was hard to like, partially thanks to his permanent expression of grim resolve whenever he appeared in public. He had the blunt, coarse features of a man who suffered such a continual weight of opprobrium that it had come to represent just the baying of a mob too ignorant to comprehend his responsibilities.

"Citizens of New City Redoubt," Flak began in his gruff, uncompromising tones. "I will not waste your time with empty platitudes, nor, as I'm sure many of you will be relieved to hear, relate the quarterly results of the Production and Maintenance Survey." He paused for the subsequent laugh, which amounted to no more than a scattering of groans and a few grudging chuckles. "The bald facts are that the last crossing did not go well. Nor, as you all know, did the one before that. Twice now, all Special Retrieval Team members have perished in the attempt to bring the most vital supplies to this city. Stand now with me and honour their sacrifice with your silence."

He stood back from the microphone and lowered his head, eyes closed. The silence for fallen crossers was supposed to last for two full minutes, but this time Layla counted only sixty seconds before it ended.

"Their names will be engraved upon the wall," Flak said. "Alongside the many who gave all for our future. May they never be forgotten." He paused again, casting an expectant glare across the crowd. The response was slow in coming but loud enough to indicate most present had consented to join their voices to the ritual echo.

"May they never be forgotten."

"Right, then." Flak coughed before continuing in clipped, businesslike tones, all surety and composure. However, Layla suspected there was a reason why he kept his hands clasped behind his back. "For obvious reasons, the Special Retrieval Team now finds itself in need of recruits. Accordingly, this morning I authorised a new Selection to commence three days from today."

An excited thrum of expectation ran through the crowd. There hadn't been a Selection for over a year. Rumours abounded as to why, with most agreeing that Flak took a dim view of the gambling and general disruption generated by such occasions. Public entertainment was rare in the Redoubt, so any form of spectacle invariably attracted considerable crowds. This created a headache for the crushers as well as raising the ugly spectre of potential riot. The last Selection had seen a massive brawl erupt between the Agris and the Cons. Several deaths occurred when the crushers waded in with their typically unrestrained approach to crowd control. That Flak was willing to risk another such calamity said much for the current state of the Special Retrieval Team, as he and the City Admin bureaucrats described them. Everyone else just called them crossers.

There was another potential, and more worrying, reason for the failure to run a recent Selection. When Layla was young, City Admin would conduct a census every year, posting the results for all to see. "Hundred and twenty-nine thousand," she remembered Strang saying when he squinted at the public noticeboard. "More than I thought." The population had risen over the next few years, but not by much. Then, three or four years ago, City Admin ended the census. These days, no one was sure just how many people lived in the Redoubt but it didn't require a genius to conclude that the recruitment pool wasn't what it used to be.

"The standard rules apply," Flak went on, cutting through the hum of excited voices. "Candidates must be fully able and aged between eighteen and thirty. Candidates from Construction, Maintenance and Agriculture must obtain the permission of their Team Supervisor before applying. Also . . ." Flak's heavy brows formed a squint as his gaze roamed the stadium. "Any form of gambling during the Selection is strictly prohibited, as is consumption of alcohol at public trials. These strictures will be rigorously enforced. Persistent transgressors will be subject to Ultimate Sanction."

This heralded an abrupt silence in the stadium.

Ultimate Sanction was typically reserved for the worst offenders. Sending murderers, rapists and the like over the wall to fend for themselves was a rarely imposed punishment, but aroused scant sympathy among the citizenry. Applying this most severe penalty to gamblers and shiners was something new.

"Must be getting desperate," she heard Taxo grunt before the mayor's voice flooded the stadium once more.

"I think it appropriate at this point," Flak said, "to join in showing our appreciation to the Special Retrieval Team for their courageous and selfless efforts." Unclasping his hands from his back, he turned to the line of crossers and began to clap. It required a pause of several seconds and repeated hard glares from the mayor before people in the crowd began to join in. Some did so with mounting enthusiasm, embellishing their acclaim with whistles or calling the name of their favourite crosser.

"You'll always make it, Stave!" a woman nearby cried out, both arms raised and straining against the barrier. The target of her adoration barely reacted. The oldest of the crossers, Stave was of average height but muscular build. His face might have been carved from granite in the way it failed to exhibit any emotion beyond what Layla thought might be a twitch of irritation. The reaction of his fellow crossers was mixed. Eylsa, the trim woman at Stave's side, rolled her eyes in patent disdain while a couple of the others evidently enjoyed the attention, smiling and waving at the crowd. Layla noticed that these were the youngest of the group. Some might not even have made a crossing yet. Stave and Eylsa had made many, and lost comrades in the process. Stave, in particular, had lost more than most. Out of the last three crossings, only he had come back alive. Three returns back he had appeared alone at the wall, all his team lost, including Rehsa, his wife, who had been just as celebrated a navigator of the Outside.

Flak made some efforts to prolong the applause, but people had already begun to drift away by the time he started speaking again. He voiced a variety of platitudes regarding the dangers of listening to false rumours and reminded people of the strictures against unlicensed public meetings and "the selfish, criminal practice of unsanctioned commerce". When he sounded off, voice strained with forced bombast as he proclaimed, "Together we strive for the future of the Redoubt!", the field was already a quarter empty.

Dresh took his leave when Flak and the crossers departed the stage, keen to dive into his comics, while Layla and Taxo were obliged to wait until the stadium cleared. She didn't look at him, but felt the weight of his eyes. She had made the mistake of looking thoughtful.

"You can't," Taxo stated. "It'll kill him."

She didn't say anything, falling in alongside when he started to wheel himself towards the tunnel. Still, the answer rang loud in her head: *It'll kill him if I don't.*

They found Cuhla waiting at the entrance to the Electric Palace, pacing with her arms folded tight across her chest. She greeted them with a strained grimace. "I fetched the doc," she said. "I had to."

Strang's coughs sounded more like shouts. The depth of pain evident in the barrage of hard, grating hacks froze Layla at the door to his room. As ever, when it got bad, she had to fight the urge to flee. *Go to the roof and wait it out. Let Taxo deal with it.* She never succumbed to it, always compelled by shame to step through the door. Tonight, for the first time, she wished she hadn't.

"Concentrate," Doc Piller repeated, crouched in front of Strang's hunched form as he continued to unleash his tirade of coughs. "Remember the rhythm. Breathe in for three counts. Out for four."

Much as Layla could never quite hate Mayor Flak, she could never quite like Doc Piller. A thin man of middling years, he possessed an aura of imperturbability she found irritating at best and callous to the point of cruelty at worst. She tried to remind herself that, as clinic doctor for the Arts, his role required emotional armour far beyond the norm. But still, the essential hardness of the man rankled.

She came to Taxo's side, watching Strang attempt to comply, but the ragged, saw-like inhalation quickly degenerated into another bout of coughing. His chest convulsed and a spasm of agony made a rictus of his face before his mouth opened to let loose a thick wad of blood.

"It's OK," Doc Piller said, catching the blood in a bowl held under Strang's chin. "Let's try again. In for three counts . . ."

Layla couldn't look away from the bowl. It was already half full, the contents dark and viscous.

"Out!" The word was accompanied by a sputtering of red spittle from Strang's lips, his gaze fixed on Layla. She saw a plea among the anger in his brimming eyes.

"You better go," Taxo said, clasping her hand. "It's all right. I'll be here."

Again the welling shame stirred by a shudder of relief. She didn't have to stay. She didn't have to watch him die. "I should . . ." she began, but another blood-flecked grunt from Strang cut her off.

"Go!"

Dragging her hand free of Taxo's grip, she fled.

For a while, she sat on her bed, arms wrapped around her drawn-up knees and resisting the urge to put a pillow over her head to blot out the dim but persistent sound of Strang coughing. The rooftop shed where she slept was small but sturdy, always equal to the rain and wind. A legacy of her early adolescence, Strang had built it for her from materials pilfered during the Raising. It had been a fraught time of near constant arguing and hormone-fuelled rebellion that had seen her threaten to leave several times a week. She had initially begun building the thing herself, only for Strang, without asking permission, to take over the project when her nailed together abomination fell apart. Over the years, what had been the refuge of a truculent teenager became her primary living space, and a welcome den of privacy when things with Thorn turned intimate. The walls were decorated with photographs cut from Strang's least favourite books, the landscapes of Ansel Adams being the most prominent. As a child, those vistas of mountains and forests had seemed an invitation to endless adventure, and still exerted a considerable pull even now. She was staring into the Yellowstone valleys when she realised Strang had stopped coughing. A short while later, she heard the quiet murmur of voices outside.

Rising from the bed, Layla exited the shed and went to the edge of the roof, looking down to see Taxo, Cuhla and Doc Piller on the walkway.

"You must know people," Taxo was saying. "People with meds. We can pay."

"So can everyone else who asks me, my dear old friend," Doc Piller replied. A tendency towards patronising endearments was another reason she didn't like him. "At least so they claim. And I have the same answer for them as I do you – I have nothing that can properly treat his condition. Nor do I know anyone who does. Complex, hard-to-manufacture drugs were a product of the Peace. No one makes them any more. Not here, and not anywhere else, so far as we know. We are told some can still be found at Harbour Point, but with the recent crossings going so badly . . ." He trailed off to offer an apologetic shrug.

"They retrieved Slatt's pack," Cuhla said. "We thought maybe . . ."

Doc Piller forestalled her with a shake of his head. "I have a friend at the central clinic. The pack contained mostly batteries, wiring and a few bottles of OxyContin." He gave a short, bitter laugh, then sobered at Cuhla's baffled anger. "A highly addictive pain medication," he explained. "Vile stuff. Stands to reason there'd still be some hanging around after the world went to hell. In any case, it's no use to him either."

Layla's mind churned over the doc's every word, fixating on two in particular: *Harbour Point*. The crossers visited various places to garner supplies, but she knew most came from Harbour Point.

"I'm sorry, my dear," the doc went on. "But I believe things have reached a stage where the most we can do is see to his comfort."

Layla found she didn't want either of them to ask the obvious question, but Taxo did anyway. "How long?"

"There's no way to tell for sure. Given the state of his lungs, perhaps a month. Though you should prepare yourselves for a sudden deterioration." He handed Taxo a small bottle. "Concentrated diamorphine courtesy of an Agri friend who works the poppy field. It'll help with the pain and . . ." He paused, features forming a muted grimace. "For when things get worse."

She wanted to punch him then. Leap from the roof and land a solid blow right in the centre of his face. Not because of his callousness, but because he was there. Hitting someone offered the chance to release the pressure building in her chest, and she couldn't hurt Taxo or Cuhla. Instead, she turned around, hugging herself tight, staring out at the dim lights of the Arts and the city beyond.

After a half-hearted refusal, Doc Piller accepted payment for the diamorphine in the form of six ration chits and took his leave. Layla didn't watch him go, knowing the temptation to go after him would be hard to resist.

"I'll come by tomorrow," she heard Cuhla say. "With soup."

Layla turned to watch her go, the fading sound of her footsteps followed by Taxo's raised voice. "You coming down?" he called. "Or do you really want me to climb up there?"

Together on the walkway, she gripped the balustrade, veins standing out on her forearms, before she forced them to relax. Taxo didn't ask how she was feeling, or any of that shit, which birthed a pang of gratitude, but not enough to smother the uncomfortable mix of anger and helplessness roiling in her gut.

"You heard what he said." Her voice sounded strange to her ears, far calmer and more controlled than it should. "Harbour Point. They'll have what he needs. Crossers get to choose one thing of their own to bring back. It's worth the risk."

"Is that what Thorn said?"

Layla's grip tightened on the balustrade to vent the resulting pulse of anger. Taxo hadn't liked Thorn. Strang had, but Taxo never warmed to him and she knew he hadn't shed many tears when he went over the wall. Until now, however, he had always done her the courtesy of avoiding the subject. Now, it seemed restraint didn't matter in the face of her determined stupidity.

"You saw what Selection did to him," he said with merciless persistence. "And he didn't even make it through—"

"Strang is fucking dying!" she cut in, deciding she could also be merciless. She turned to confront the pale resentment on Taxo's face, refusing to shrink from it. "He'll die if I can't get him the meds he needs. It's as simple as that."

She expected more anger, so the subsequent silence served only to further stoke the tension. "Do you remember the Outside?" Taxo asked finally. There was a steadiness to his voice that compelled a reply, an inescapable awareness that she had better listen to what he had to say.

"Not much," she said, calming a little. "Small things mainly. Toys I used to play with. Other kids in the nursery. And smoke. When the Feeding began, I remember there was a lot of smoke."

"And the feeders? Do you remember them?"

This time she said nothing, since it was clear where he was going.

"No," Taxo went on. "You don't, because you've never seen one. If you had, you wouldn't be here now. They're not just diseased people turned savage. They're not even people at all. All you know is the stories you've been hearing since you were a kid and even I don't know if they're true. The Feeding was a mad scramble to get to the Redoubt. A nightmare I do my best to forget. Back then, if you saw a feeder chances were you'd be dead a split second later. But I saw them, Layla, with these two eyes. I saw enough to know that once I got behind a wall tall enough to hide behind, I was never going Outside again. Mean as you can be, Layla, they're meaner. Fast as you are, they're faster. And there's more of them than there are of us. Why'd you think so few crossers are making it back these days? The Outside doesn't belong to us. It hasn't since the Feeding."

"If you could walk, wouldn't you go?"

The question heralded a silence that pained her more than if he had exploded in anger. It persisted until, after a long shuddering breath, Layla whispered, "Sorry." More silence until she consented to turn and face him. "I'm sorry."

His face was hard but lacking the rage she expected. Mostly she saw just a very worried man. "What do you think it'll do to him?" he asked. "Knowing you're out there?"

"Don't tell him. Say I ran off. Couldn't face watching him . . . watching it happen. Tell him I got a job in Agri or something."

"He always knows when I'm lying, whatever I say. He'll hate you for going and hate me for letting you."

"As long as he's still breathing, I'll take all the hate he has to give. And you're not letting me. I'm just doing it."

She moved past him, determined to grab as much sleep as possible. The crusher patrol was due to check the entrance to the Undercut in the early morning, and she wanted to be through it as soon as they left.

The call of his voice stalled her at the door to the theatre. "You won't make it through Selection."

She didn't shout back, her reply a tired but utterly certain mutter as she climbed the ramp to her room. "Yes. I will."

Chapter Four

"**B**astards." Layla kicked a rusted can in frustration as she regarded the door to the Undercut, more particularly the padlock securing the chains in place. Today of all days, the crushers had chosen to be scrupulous in their duties. Instead of the weathered and pitted old friend so easily opened by her key, she looked upon a completely unfamiliar lock. It was annoyingly solid in appearance, and a good deal heavier than its predecessor. Probably the product of some Con in the workshops who had found a store of corrosion-free metal. Smashing it was out of the question, which left only one option.

Sighing, Layla crouched at the lock and unslung her pack to extract the plastic bag containing her pick kit. She had inherited the tools from Strang, her tutor in this particular art. Where he had learned it remained a vaguely alluded to mystery, but she knew that some of the tattoos adorning his skin contained oblique references to prisons and criminal affiliations. *The Peace*, he was fond of telling her, *was anything but. It was just better than this.* Taxo was similarly adorned in places, but not to the same extent. Before Strang got sick, the two of them would occasionally get drunk and raise a toast to "Wheeler and the Cracksman". When she asked about its meaning, Strang claimed it was an old movie. She knew he was lying, because she'd never seen it in their collection of discs.

Picking the lock required nearly two hours of work. The mechanism was unfamiliar and the inner workings featured several burrs from inexpert welding that would often impede her instruments. She was forced to probe the insides and build up a mental picture of the arrangement of lever and pin. After a few unsuccessful attempts, she finally succeeded in applying pressure in the right places, the lock snapping open as she sagged in relieved satisfaction.

"Now for the easy bit," she said, a ritual she shared with Dresh every time they levered the door open. But Dresh wasn't here today, by her deliberate choice. He would probably turn up at the theatre come noon, only to find her gone. She hoped to be done by the time he inevitably tried to follow her, an outcome made less likely by the need to pick this new lock.

With the door heaved aside, she wound the lever to charge her headlamp and switched it on. Once inside and fully swallowed by the gloom, she would normally pause. It was smart to spend time listening for the dogs or a change in the grind and hiss of the

Undercut that might indicate an imminent, crushing slide to the rubble. But she couldn't afford the luxury of caution today, starting her descent immediately and following the memorised route to the copper pipe.

As was typical, the strata of the Undercut had shifted in her absence, her way partially or fully obstructed by fallen chunks of concrete or a grate of overlapping rebars. Fortunately, some parts of this subterranean maze retained a semi-permanence, enabling her to detour while she chafed at the inevitable delay. She sighed in relief at finding the copper pipe where she left it, still gleaming its bright invitation despite a fresh pall of dust. It was, however, as stubbornly resistant as before. There was no option but to find another route and work it free with the tools in her pack.

Her nose picked up the sting of dog piss as she explored the tunnel, judging it not recent enough to be worth worrying over. Also, she heard nothing to indicate the Underdogs were on the move. They tended to grow more active as the day wore on, emerging from whatever den they called home to predate on any mice or rats lured out by warming air. Reaching the far end of the tunnel, she glimpsed the worm-like whip of a rodent disappearing into a shadowy nook and hoped it was just an early-riser.

Finding no obvious path to the pipe, she headed towards what she and Dresh had dubbed the Funnel. Beginning some twenty feet below the surface, the vertical channel provided uninterrupted access to the deepest regions of the Undercut. It went so deep, in fact, that neither of them had ever ventured all the way to the bottom. She had once descended low enough for her headlamp to play upon a pool of water, the uninviting glisten of inky blackness persuading her to turn back. Before starting her downward climb, she positioned herself so that the location of the copper pipe was directly to her front. Maintaining a straight line course would be difficult given the erratic nature of the Funnel's walls, but she had no choice if she wanted to find it again. Getting turned around down here was perilously easy.

She was aided by a large concrete slab, cracked in two decades ago. Exposed steel rebars provided excellent hand and foot holds. Just a few feet down, she saw the gleam of copper again, maybe twenty feet away. Layla swallowed an expletive at the sight of the thick steel cable between her and the prize. The passage to either side was too narrow for her to squeeze through. Unless she was willing to go deeper and seek out another route, she would have to shift it.

Crawling into the restricted channel, she gripped the cable to test it, finding it immovable. Somewhere, this thing was fixed tight to an ancient chunk of fallen machinery. Unhooking one strap of her pack, she squirmed until she could access the contents, extracting a small recoilless hammer and an eight-inch iron chisel. A year ago, she had traded Velna a nearly intact flatscreen monitor for these tools and never regretted

the expense. She forced herself to work with method-
ical slowness, tapping the hammer to the chisel rather
than pounding it. The concrete surrounding the upper
end of the cable fell away with welcome swiftness,
but the rope of corded steel let out a high-pitched
thrum at the disturbance.

"Quiet," she scolded in a whisper, gripping the
cable to quell the noise, then resuming her work when
it faded. Another few minutes' labour and she saw the
obstruction begin to shift. "That's it," she murmured
as it scraped powder from the surrounding material.
"Nice and slow . . ."

Somewhere far above, an echoing thud told of
something big dislodging itself from the strata. The
cable's steady grind instantly became squeal, dust
exploding as it cut through concrete and loose detritus,
carving a path a yard long. It came to a halt after only
a second, shuddering and emitting a constant, rhythmic
tick while whatever it was attached to birthed a series
of booming crunches above.

"Shit," Layla huffed, grimacing in self-reproach as
the treacherous noise continued. At least her path to
the pipe was now clear. Scrambling deeper into the
channel, she gave the pipe an experimental heave,
finding it still unwilling to shift. Closer examination
revealed one end to be free, the other buried in an
overlapping wall of rubble. Simply pulling it clear was
impossible. She would have to cut it. As she pulled
the hacksaw from her pack, she detected a change in

the echoing noise. The tricky soundscape of the Undercut made it hard to gauge the distance, but she was sure she heard the yapping of dogs among the general cacophony. During any previous scavenge, she would have left, knowing she had pushed her luck way too far. This time, she fixed her eyes on the pipe, gripping it tight with one hand as she sawed with the other.

The grate of the hacksaw's blade clearly marked her location, but there was no way to muffle it. Heart pumping, Layla barely registered the strain of her muscles as she worked. It was probably the fastest she had ever cut anything down here, perhaps four minutes of toil, but it felt like an hour. Finally, blinking sweat, a yard of copper piping came free in her hand. Too long for the pack, she had to carry it as she made her way back to the Funnel. The ever louder tick of the straining cable added urgency to her movements, not that she needed further encouragement.

She had no prior warning of the dog's attack, the beast cunning enough to still its yapping in the seconds before launching itself through the fissure carved by the cable. Snapping jaws missed Layla's ankle as she jerked it clear, teeth catching the edge of her shoe's rubber sole, tearing away a chunk. The dog thrashed as she back-pedalled, its pale, mostly hairless body still caught in the fissure, resembling a maggot wriggling in an infected wound. Hampered by the pipe and her pack, Layla's progress became a grinding, scraping exercise in frustration and rising panic. The dog freed itself, letting out a growl shot through with a chillingly recognisable note of triumph. How much these things could see after generations in the dark remained a mystery, but Layla saw the gleam of her headlamp on the black orbs of its eyes and knew it had no difficulty identifying its prey.

As the dog tensed for a lunge, the cable emitted a vast twang as it lost a decades-long contest with its unseen burden and snapped. The channel instantly filled with dust, Layla flinching from the sting of tiny pieces of shredded steel upon her hands as she shielded her face. The dog's growl transformed into a short whimper of surprise. When the dust cleared, she saw two chunks of bloody, twitching meat, white ribs jutting from exposed red flesh. It was a dangerously transfixing sight. "Move!" she grunted, knowing hesitation to be fatal now. Tearing her gaze from the bisected dog, she dragged herself the last few yards to the Funnel.

Upon reaching it, a quick upward glance revealed several sets of gleaming eyes and snarling maws. Her only direction now was down. Pausing to manoeuvre her pack onto her back, she drew the straps as tight as possible and slid the pipe between her shoulder blades. With both hands free, she began the descent. Unwilling to give up their hunt, the dogs scattered dust and debris in an unsuccessful effort to follow her down. Layla had never been this close to the entire pack before, and the hunger-filled clamour of their rage was deafening.

Amoxicillin, clarithromycin, doxycycline, she recited to herself like a mantra, navigating from one rebar to another, constantly dipping her head to illuminate footholds. *Amoxicillin, clarithromycin, doxycycline* . . .

The dogs' collective yammering seemed to rile them even more, as if psyching themselves up for the coming frenzy. Soon, the pack's combined hunger eroded their caution until one lost all reason and launched itself at Layla. The headlamp illuminated the animal in free fall, drool trailing from its gaping mouth, rear legs flailing. With nowhere to go, Layla could only jerk her head aside as the dog collided with her. The snap of its closing jaws sent a jolting pain into her ear, the impact of its bulk dislodging both feet and hands from their holds. The Funnel became a confusion of flickering chaos as she and the dog fell, plunging into the freezing embrace of the water seconds later.

The shock of the cold spread instantly to every extremity, banishing all sensation apart from a searing stab of agony through her brain. She sank several feet before returning coherence caused her to spasm. She blinked, seeing only a hazy, dirty flecked fog illuminated by the waterproof headlamp. The beam flickered. *Needs winding.* The realisation finally summoned action. Kicking for the surface, she dragged in the musty air of the Undercut as if it were the sweetest thing and cast the headlamp's dimming light around. Spying a slope of cracked concrete, she thrashed a clumsy passage towards it. There were no pools in the Redoubt where children could be taught to swim. The Agris had the benefit of the river that irrigated their fields, but for most youngsters, it was a lost art. Fortunately, the distance was small and Layla slapped a hand to the damp roughness of the slope after a short but frenzied interval of splashing.

Dragging herself from the water, she slumped onto her side, exhausted but elated by the feel of the copper pipe still wedged between pack and spine. The sputtering headlamp forced her to sit up, unhooking the strap from her head to work the lever. The resultant steady glow revealed the sight of another inexpert swimmer making its way towards her across the pool. The dog had been injured in the fall, its front paws twitching as they latched onto the slope to drag it halfway from the water, revealing the ragged scar on its side. It let out a series of piteous whines as Layla rose to her haunches, its wide black eyes imploring. She drew her knife from the sheath at the small of her back and stabbed it in the neck. *Always go for the neck*, Strang had told her once. *If you have to fight, finish it quickly. The neck is where you'll find the densest collection of veins. And don't stop until you're sure it's done.* By the time she sat back, chest heaving from the effort, her arm was red and sticky to the elbow, and the dog had long stopped its whining.

Getting to her feet, she heard a chorus of howls

from above. It held a plaintive, almost sorrowful note, making her wonder if the pack had somehow sensed the passing of their brother. If so, their grief failed to arouse any sympathy.

"FUCK! YOU!" she shouted into the dark reaches of the Funnel, brandishing the knife for emphasis. Incredibly, the howling slowed, then stopped altogether. She stood in the silent gloom until the heat faded from her strained muscles and she began to shiver. It was time to find a way out.

The rats were more plentiful in this deepest recess of the Undercut. They also weren't as skittish in the presence of humans. Each time she paused to rest, Layla had to kick away rodents darting from the shadows to sniff at her feet. She worried that the more she wandered this unfamiliar maze, the bolder the rats would become. Fortunately, this basement level of the Undercut was far less constricting than its upper reaches. The rubble was piled thick in places but constrained by a series of mostly intact concrete pillars. She could actually walk upright most of the time, and periodically emerged into spaces that were room-sized or even bigger. Although she welcomed the sense of liberation from the cramped passages above, unfamiliarity with a previously unexplored corner of the Undercut also summoned nervous caution.

She noticed the light when she entered the largest chamber so far, a cavern formed around a tall pillar ascending to a darkened summit outside the reach of her headlamp. The pillar's base was adorned with some kind of writing, the letters a mishmash of garishly coloured shapes and black scrawls. Thanks to Strang and his books, Layla read with a fluency far beyond most who had grown up in the Redoubt. She recognised some words among the melange of abstracted scrawls, but others were too distorted to discern any meaning. Still, they fascinated her in much the same way as the cable mangled dog. This was another remnant of something dead.

As she played the beam over the curious find, the headlamp dimmed again. Taking it off to wind it, she realised she could still make out the writing on the pillar. Switching off the headlamp, she looked around for the source of the illumination, seeing a dim glow a dozen feet off. Moving closer, she found that it came from a narrow arch formed by the conjunction of two ancient sections of fallen roadway. She had to adopt an increasingly pronounced stoop to make her way towards the light, blinking away a blur as it grew in brightness. When her vision cleared, she saw a semi-circular opening she recognised as the upper half of a drain outlet. It was barred by a rusted iron grate, but beyond lay a patch of sun-kissed grass.

Layla came to a halt as realisation dawned: she was beyond the wall. This was the Outside. Crouching for a better view, she saw more grass covering an undulating plain dotted with the red and black mounds she recognised as the rotted corpses of cars. When she was small, the mayor at the time used to drive around in a car. Long, shiny and black, it was the only working example of a motor vehicle Layla could remember seeing since the Feeding. The mayor in those days was a steel-haired woman who always wore a white suit and never stopped smiling. She possessed a fondness for driving through various neighbourhoods, waving at the residents and throwing candy at gaggles of pursuing kids. The white-suited mayor and her long black car had disappeared about the same time the schools were closed. Reputedly, Mayor Flak took a dim view of anyone who raised the subject of his predecessor, and no one seemed to miss her.

A decade and a half of complete neglect had long since denuded these wrecks of all but the smallest flecks of paint. Some lay on their sides revealing complex mechanical innards while most were just slumped in mangled degradation. Hearing a skittering behind her, Layla turned, switching the headlamp back on to illuminate a cluster of rats. They kept to the edge of the light cast by the opening, noses twitching as they displayed a clear aversion to coming any closer. *Something out there?* Layla wondered, turning back to the Outside. Her gaze settled on the closest wreck. It was bigger than most of the others, its rear end larger and box-like. One of the doors was partially open, the others closed. The car lay at an angle that afforded a partial view of its interior, but concealed by shadow.

Still, something held her attention. Years of scavenging had instilled a keen sense for things that weren't quite right. Also, this confluence of instinct and awareness told her when she was being observed. But, after a full minute of staring, the shadow remained just a shadow.

"Wasting time," she murmured, shuffling back. As she did so, the car's door slammed open. Layla jerked in fright, her eyes detecting a movement in the shadow. Something long and pale lashed out into daylight. Before it drew back into cover, she saw the faded ink on the lashing arm, a tattoo.

Various thoughts flicked through Layla's head as she scrambled away from the opening, two rising from the torrent of panic with singular importance: *Feeder. It heard me.* The wreck was a dozen feet away, and she had spoken barely above a whisper. But whatever lurked in that wreck had heard her.

Heart thumping, she regained her feet and fled back to the cavern, the rats scattering before her. *Have you ever seen a feeder?* Taxo had asked her. *Now I have.* The thought provoked a laugh, short and shrill, until she clamped her teeth against it. She looked back at the archway and the dim light within, watching for any change. The sight of the tattoo on the thing's skin loomed large, demanding more notice than she wanted to give it. *They don't move in daylight*, she reminded herself. But still, the sense of being observed lingered.

"Enough," she breathed, walking in a circle until

her heart calmed and hands stopped shaking enough for her to don the headlamp.

Further exploration of the concrete pillar revealed the fact that someone had carved a series of handholds into its side. They ascended in a reasonable straight line to disappear into the gloom twenty feet up. Wherever they led, Layla felt sure it had to be better than here. Sending unspoken gratitude to whichever long vanished soul had seen fit to craft her this escape route, she settled one hand into a hold, her foot into another and began to climb.

The man emerging from Velna's shop wore a hooded waterproof smock, pulled low to conceal his face. The sight of him brought Layla to a halt. The journey here had been trouble-free. Looking like she did was enough to discourage unwelcome attention. She also didn't want to gain the notice of anyone else who did business with Velna. Stepping into the narrow alley opposite the shop, she watched the man make his way through the market square. It wasn't raining, but he kept his hood in place. Before he turned a corner, he cast a careful glance to his rear. Layla frowned in recognition. *Stave.*

He rounded the corner and disappeared from view, leaving her to ponder the question of why the city's most celebrated crosser would have needed to visit one of its least reputable citizens. Whatever the reason, she knew Velna would probably have Leron snap her neck if she dared ask. *Probably won't like the fact that I saw him, either.* She forced herself to wait, counting off five minutes before approaching the door.

Inside, Velna arched an eyebrow as she looked at the pipe Layla placed on the counter. She had wordlessly noted Layla's besmirched appearance, from her irregular step, thanks to the dog taking a chunk out of her shoe, to the mingled grime and blood covering her arms and face. The pack had left her alone during her protracted egress from the Undercut, kept at bay through fear, or perhaps even grief for their lost sibling. Once out, she found the sky tinged red with the onset of evening. She had secured the lock and spent a moment regarding the chained barrier with the knowledge that this might well be the last time she ever ventured through it.

"I wasn't lying, my love," Velna said. "I don't have any meds."

"Not meds." Layla pointed a finger at the glass case above the shelves. "Those."

Chapter Five

"Before we start, understand one thing: this is not training."

The tall woman standing atop the platform at one end of the stadium's playing field spoke without benefit of a microphone. Nevertheless, her voice carried easily across the untidy ranks of the candidates assembled before her. Layla knew her name, of course; they all did. Nehna was another veteran crosser with almost as many successful returns as Stave. Her hair was shaved down to the scalp apart from a narrow strip along one side that swept red tresses over the ragged scar where her left ear had been. She was flanked by four other crossers, all clad in the same utilitarian garb of grey or brown overalls. Layla found it curious that none of those who had been on stage with the mayor were present this morning.

"This," Nehna went on, "is Selection. We test you. If you fail, you leave. That's it. No amount of griping, excuses, or begging will change our minds. We've heard it all before, so don't bother trying. After two days, the few of you who are left will become crossers."

Keen to be noticed, Layla had placed herself in the first rank of candidates, so she was close enough to see the tic of discomfort on Nehna's face when she paused. "There is no more important role in this city than that of a crosser," she continued after a small cough. "There is also no other role more likely to get you killed. You know what's out there. So, before you start down this road, you better be sure you're willing to face it. The first test starts in fifteen minutes. I suggest you use them to think hard about the choice you made today."

She stepped down from the platform without further preamble, leaving the assembled candidates to mill about as they digested her words. Layla reckoned the full number must be close to six hundred, mostly her age or a little older. It was a bump up from the last Selection, and a measure of how desperate so many people had gotten in the interim. Some of these hopefuls had been lured by the heightened status, improved rations and better living quarters afforded to crossers. But most, she knew, had reasons that mirrored her own. *Meds*, Layla sighed inwardly as she surveyed her competition. *They all want meds.*

There were some plainly at the cusp of thirty, possibly older. Documentation was rare in the Redoubt. Ration cards were the principal form of identification, but they were easily forged. She saw one man who must have been at least forty, a stocky figure wearing the red cap of a Con. He stood with his head downcast, presumably hoping the brim of his cap would conceal lined and weathered features. Even if the crossers didn't send him away, she found it hard to believe he would make it through a single test.

Some candidates had evidently come in a group, youthful Agris and a few Cons and Techs clustering together to buttress their resolve with ribald banter. Nehna's warning had more of an effect on those who had come alone. Layla spotted a dozen or so heading for the tunnel, despite the taunts of the audience. They had been arriving in a steady trickle all morning, filling the lower tiers of seating and adding a constant background hum of conversation to the proceedings. Regardless of Flak's injunctions, Layla knew the first bets were already being made. She had briefly entertained the thought of asking Cuhla to make a wager on her behalf. As an unknown quantity, unaffiliated with any group, she was bound to attract long odds, meaning a big pay day when she made the grade. But Cuhla would no doubt take an even dimmer view of this decision than Taxo. That morning, Layla had risen at dawn and departed the theatre without a word. She was willing to face Selection but not the argument that would erupt when Strang learned of her decision. She worried over how Taxo would explain her absence, but refused to dwell on it.

Amoxicillin. Clarithromycin. Doxycycline.

As she repeated the inner mantra, letting her gaze rove her competitors, she saw him. Like the old Con, he wore a cap pulled down low to conceal his face, but she would have known the slouch of his shoulders anywhere. Advancing towards him, drawing a few protests from those she collided with, she resisted the urge to deliver an instant, and hard, punch to his wincing face.

"What," she grated, "the fuck are you doing here?"

Dresh's wince became a tremulous grin, though the evident scale of her anger caused him to retreat a step. "Same as you," he said with a shrug that only added fuel to her fury. "Hey!" he exclaimed, noticing her shoes. "You got them. How do they feel?"

The urge to punch him rose again, but she steeled herself against it, not knowing what the crossers would make of a brawl breaking out among the candidates. Closing her eyes, she took in a series of steady breaths before fixing him with a glare of implacable command. "Go home, Dresh."

His grin slipped away, but so did his wince. Straightening, he replied with a simple shake of his head.

"There's no fucking way you make it—" she began, only for him to interrupt, something she couldn't remember him doing before.

"Got just as good a chance as you, I reckon. Even with those on your feet. Besides, won't it be an advantage to have at least one friend during this thing?"

"You're not my friend. You're my dead boyfriend's kid brother." She watched the words sting him and clamped down on the impulse to take it back. She had spoken in haste, but also with calculation. She had to make him leave and if he hated her for it, then so be it.

But, though the hurt lingered on his face, all he did was shrug again and say, "Bet on myself, too. Ten chits. The odds were *long*."

"Dresh . . ."

"If you're here, so am I." He was all seriousness now, his eyes steady on hers. "Unless you want to quit. Then we can both go home."

Amoxicillin. Clarithromycin. Doxycycline . . . "You know I can't."

"Then neither can I. Look lively." He turned, nodding to the crossers rolling oil drums into place on the playing field. "I think they're about to start."

Crossers with clipboards began harassing the candidates into a semblance of order. "Form lines, ten across," a wiry man with a permanent scowl instructed. Layla recognised him as Olver, another veteran who had been absent from the stage two days ago. "The rest of you line up behind. No talking. It's not just failing a test that gets you eliminated. Any back talk or chatter and you can fuck off right now."

Evidence that he wasn't bluffing came swiftly when two Techs in the second row insisted on exchanging jokes. Their voices were muffled and laughter confined to smirks, but it didn't save them from Olver's wrath. "You two. You're deaf or stupid. Either way, we can't use you." He gestured towards the tunnel with his clipboard. "Leave."

The duo's protestations were cut short when two other crossers moved through the crowd to encourage their departure.

"Right," Olver said, eyeing the now utterly silent ranks. "The first test is a sixty-metre sprint. Crossers need to be fast." He flapped his clipboard. "Before each heat you'll give your details and be allocated a number. There will be three heats. To proceed to the next round you have to place in the first five in all heats. The rest will be eliminated. Remember what you were told about griping."

Layla and Dresh stood ten ranks deep so had a clear view of the preceding heats. The candidates would answer Olver's clipped questions as he scribbled on his clipboard before marking the backs of their hands with a pen. They would then proceed to the ad hoc running track. It had been created by placing two pairs of oil drums sixty yards apart. Watching her competitors' attempt to sprint buttressed Layla's confidence considerably. The number who could manage little more than a laboured run was surprising, as was the number of fallers. Before she reached the first rank, however, she did see one standout, a young Agri of willowy appearance belying an impressive turn of speed. She finished well ahead of the others in her heat, long blonde hair trailing from her cap as she crossed the line with a practised, loping stride.

"Name?" Olver snapped when Layla stepped into the front rank.

"Layla."

"Age?"

"Nineteen."

"Place of residence?"

"The Electric Palace Theatre, Arts Centre."

A small crease to his brow at that. Layla assumed he must have been a customer at some point, but couldn't recall seeing him in the audience. "State any current illnesses. Lying will result in elimination."

"None."

"Number sixty-four." He clamped his clipboard under his arm and took hold of her wrist. The pen he used to inscribe the number on her skin had a thick, uncomfortably hard nib. The ink it left dried quickly, and she knew it wouldn't fade for some time.

Olver moved onto Dresh. "Name?"

"Dresh."

"Age?"

"Eighteen."

"Place of residence."

"Belvedere Heights, in the Arts."

"State any current illnesses. Lying will result in elimination."

Layla sensed a fierce temptation to make a joke in

the pause that followed, but Dresh, for once, disappointed her by showing restraint. "None."

"Number sixty-five."

With the formalities complete, they were told to go and line up between the oil drums. "Standing starts only," an impressively muscled crosser told them at the start line. "Wait for the handclap. Any false starts will be eliminated."

Layla crouched, grinding her shoes into the dry earth of the playing field. *Time to see what you can do*, she thought, centring her focus on the space between the two oil drums sixty metres away. Although new to her feet, the shoes felt comfortable enough. She had experimented with a few short runs upon leaving the theatre, impressed by the way they gripped the ground. Whether they would give her the edge she craved was a still unanswered question.

Amoxicillin. Clarithromycin. Doxycycline.

She was gone the instant the crosser clapped her hands, arms and legs pumping. Catching a glimpse of blurring limbs in her periphery, she pushed herself harder until they disappeared. From behind came the scrape and curse of someone falling, raising the guilty hope that it was Dresh. Crossing the line first, she immediately relaxed, knowing she would need all reserves of strength today. Turning, she let out a sigh at the sight of Dresh's broad smile.

"Just a little further and I'd have caught you."

Behind him, a woman kneeled where she had fallen,

head bowed and sobbing. Layla watched tears and snot drip from her reddened face until the muscular crosser came to harry her from the field. The failed candidate wept all the way to the tunnel, desolate grief still echoing as the next heat started.

"Guess you're not the only one with a lot riding on this," Dresh commented, making her want to punch him again. She had only a marginal hope that the sprints would see him sent home. He had always been only a little slower than her. She was also aware that other tests would favour him more, given how strong he was.

"You're trying to take my place," she said in realisation.

"Only needs one of us to fetch the meds." He grinned again. "And if two of us make it through to the end, that doubles our chances. I can be smart too, Layla."

It turned out that her initial estimate of the numbers had been off by a considerable margin. By the time the first heats were done, about two hundred remained out of the over eight hundred hopefuls. The crossers mixed up the numbers for the next round, meaning she no longer ran against Dresh. He won his heat with relative ease, as did she, although the blur of competitors to either side was more noticeable this time. Watching the other heats play out, she experienced scant surprise at seeing the long-limbed Agri woman coast through, and more at the sight of the stocky, too-old Con powering his way to victory. Like the Agri, he ran with a practised stride, but much more controlled. His head barely moved as his arms and legs described measured arcs. This, Layla felt sure, was the kind of muscle memory that could only be a product of the Peace. Back then, according to Strang's books, there were people who got rich doing nothing but running or playing games. The Con's ability confirmed her suspicions regarding his age but confounded her expectations of his performance. It was something the crossers must also have noticed. She assumed they were happy to stretch the rules because he ran so well.

There were a few other standouts she marked as potential competition. Another Agri, a large man who placed second in his heat, would surely do well in later stages. There was also a skinny, lank-haired youth with densely tattooed arms. He won both his heats despite an inefficient running style that was all flailing arms and corded neck muscles. His tats were rich in the signature swirls of the Riverbank. Layla hoped he would fall in the final heat. Despite a lack of expertise, his obvious determination made her nervous.

The final heats saw her matched against both the old Con and the Riverbanker. The latter afforded her a disparaging glance of dismissal that was way too mannered to be genuine. The Con, however, exhibited only shrewd appraisal as he looked her over. She was tempted to voice an insult. *Just stick your hand down your pants and start jerking, you old fuck. It'll be quicker.* But the swift ejection of the two gossiping Techs stalled her tongue. It would have been a dishonest jibe, anyway. There was nothing carnal in the way he studied her and she knew her resentment was in fact pragmatic in nature: he was a possible barrier to what she needed, like a dog in the Undercut, and you didn't survive an encounter with a dog by liking them.

Her heat began with a false start, the first of the day. A youth Layla recognised from the Arts market, jerky with restrained energy, tried to beat the handclap by a half-second. To his credit, he accepted the muscular crosser's curt dismissal with a chastened smile and a lack of argument. Instead of heading for the tunnel, he slouched off towards the seats. Layla wondered who he would bet on.

As they crouched at the line, the Riverbanker, positioned to her left, kept jerking his arms. She assumed it to be an attempt to lure her into a false start. She tried to ignore it, but the notion that he might beat her off the line vied with the need to avoid elimination. So, when the handclap came, she was a fraction too slow. The Riverbanker instantly gained half a yard on her, while the Con was two strides ahead already. With the rest of the field already crowding her vision, Layla concentrated on chasing the Con, trying to match his pounding stride. She knew he was too fast to catch, but if she could get within reaching distance she might finish second. Her efforts quickly bore fruit, the Riverbanker letting out a snarl as she drew ahead of him. His sprint grew more ragged as he tried to keep up, one of his wildly flapping arms catching her shoulder, but not enough to distract her. He stumbled when they were only a few feet from the finish, tumbling into an untidy sprawl. Sadly, his foot had been over the line when he fell, so he wouldn't be eliminated.

Layla wasn't especially out of breath. Sprinting, she had come to understand, was all about reflex and nerves rather than stamina. However, the victor of this race seemed to have felt the strain. Layla saw sweat shining on his forehead and a certain hollowness to his eyes. She took comfort from the knowledge that, although possibly the fastest sprinter here, he was also old. There was a reason why there were no crossers his age.

To her dismay, Dresh made it through the final heat, coming second. She couldn't bring herself to offer any congratulations, but did consent to accept his hug. "Piece of piss, that was," he said. Despite his good humour, Layla saw a tight apprehension in his face as they watched the crossers remove the oil drums. Others were setting out wooden pegs along the outer edges of the field to delineate a new, much longer track. Having spectated at previous Selections, they knew what came next.

"As well as speed, crossers need stamina," Nehna told the remaining candidates. There were about fifty left. Getting the losers to leave had been more protracted and difficult this time, a few scuffles breaking out as some protested the unfairness of their exit. These were short-lived affairs, since only an idiot would start throwing hands at a crosser. The miscreants, sporting bruises and bloodied noses, soon departed.

Extending a hand, Nehna swept it around the newly created track. "You will run and keep running until twenty are left." She raised a hefty pack in her other hand. "Each of you will carry one of these. Take it off and you're out. Slow to a walk for more than ten seconds and you're out. If you stop or fall, you have five seconds to resume running or you're out. Walk, stop, or fall twice and you're out. Any interference with another candidate, in word or deed, will be punished with immediate elimination. Water has been provided." She pointed to a table in the centre of the field laden with cups. "Drink plenty. You'll need it. We start in fifteen minutes."

"Wasn't it an hour last time?" Dresh grumbled as they crowded around the table with the others.

"It was," the tall Agri woman said. She had won her final heat, despite being pushed the last few feet by her fellow Agri, the tall, well-built man Layla had noted earlier. "I get the feeling they're going to be harder on us this time. I'm Luce." She offered Dresh her hand, smile warm and eyes lingering on his face.

"Dresh. This is Layla."

"You're both really fast," Luce said. Layla noted she clasped her hand only briefly before taking Dresh's again. Keeping hold of it, she added, "Glad I didn't have to race you."

"You'd still have won," Dresh assured her, which annoyed Layla even though it was probably true. "What about this?" He inclined his head at the track. "You just as good over distance?"

"Pretty much. More worried about lugging one of those, if I'm honest." Her gaze soured as it shifted to the packs the crossers were setting out nearby. They tested the weight of each one, adding or removing rocks to ensure they carried an equal burden. "I bet Brann won't have any trouble, though." Gulping water, she nodded at the tall Agri man. "Seen him throw potato sacks around like they were nothing."

"You know him?" Layla asked.

"Only a little. His folks are in Distribution while mine are in Irrigation. He's always been strong, even when we were kids at the annual fair."

"Starting to wish I'd been smarter in my bets," Dresh said, watching Brann go through a series of stretches.

"Don't." Luce leaned closer, voice dropping to a conspiratorial whisper. "There's no way he'll get selected in the end. He's just too nice." She released his hand and moved back, offering Dresh a wince of sympathy. "And so are you, my pretty friend. Which is a shame. *Her*, on the other hand . . ." Luce turned to Layla and winked before picking up a cup and walking away. "I think we'll both be seeing the other side of the wall pretty soon."

Chapter Six

The first few laps weren't so bad, but Layla knew the various aches she accrued would only worsen as the test wore on. So far, her shoulders hurt the most, being continually assailed by the thump of the pack's straps as it bounced. She had tightened them as much as she could, but still the rise and fall of the burden she carried felt more and more like twin punches with every stride. She made no effort at speed, happily allowing herself to be overtaken by a dozen candidates opting for a full run rather than her steady jog. None of those she had identified as her principal competition were among the leading group. The foolishness of their tactic became clear a lap later when one dropped out. He didn't fall or slow to a walk, just moved to the outer edge of the track and stopped. Dumping his pack, he then walked off towards the tunnel without a backward glance or a word to the crossers. The leaders slowed, perhaps finally understanding that this was not a race but an endurance test. Still, the initial expenditure of energy cost them. A Tech woman faltered to a walk half a lap later, drawing an instant call from the crosser overseeing this stretch of track.

"Number three-eighty-two walking! Ten. Nine. Eight. Seven . . ."

The Tech resumed her run, limping now, but managed only a few steps before stumbling to a halt.

"Number three-eighty-two stopped! Four. Three. Two . . ."

This time the Tech threw up her hands and staggered away from the track. Layla heard her voice a harsh, angry sob as she shrugged off her pack.

After that, the number of dropouts escalated with every lap. All the leading group either gave up or suffered elimination as exhaustion took its toll. With the candidates so widely spread out, it was easy to gauge the numbers. Layla reckoned at least half had already gone, but all of her competitors remained. Brann plodded along with an inelegant gait, but showed no signs of tiring. Luce loped with an equal resolve, though Layla felt the inexpressiveness of her face indicated some measure of suppressed pain. Dresh didn't bother to hide his discomfort, intermittently gritting his teeth as his feet met the track. His shoes were old, after all. The status of the Riverbanker was harder to discern since he had decided to keep pace with Layla. A few backward glances revealed sweaty but determined features behind a swaying veil of unwashed hair. She assumed his proximity to be another ploy, intended to provoke her to a faster pace. Instead, she slowed as much as she dared. Of all the principal competition, the old Con was the slowest. Plainly built more for speed than endurance, his plodding jog was a muted echo of his sprinting style. Despite the fatigue adding more lines to his face, his stride never faltered, and he showed no indication he might drop out.

"Number twelve fallen!"

Layla ran past a hefty man who had collapsed to his hands and knees. He kept crawling forward even after the crosser had counted him out.

"That'll be you soon." A hissed comment from the Riverbanker, just loud enough for her to hear. "Best give up now, bitch."

Layla felt only a vague urge to retort with a suitable insult. *Fuck off, grease boy.* But she didn't. It was another trap. Plainly, he had fixated on her as an obstacle that needed to be removed to win his place. She could also hear the harsh grating pant in his voice. She might be a threat to him, but she was increasingly sure he was no threat to her.

She deliberately chose not to count off the laps, deciding it would only add to the sense of mounting strain. There was no overtaking now, consistent gaps emerging between the surviving candidates. Layla and her would-be tormentor remained an exception until his harsh gasps began to fade and she realised he was falling behind. The crosser's call came a few seconds later.

"Number one-twenty-six walking! Ten. Nine. Eight . . ." The countdown continued until it reached two, then stopped. Layla muttered an obscenity. The grease-haired little shit was still in the fight.

Although the ache in her shoulders had now grown to a constant flare of agony, she became distracted by a new pain. It began after what she estimated to be the second hour of running, a familiar build-up of pressure in her lower abdomen. *The water*, she groaned inwardly. *Shouldn't have taken on so much*. She had assumed she would sweat it out, but her bladder had other ideas.

She took only marginal comfort from the fact that the rest shared her plight. On the other side of the track, a woman wearing a Con cap came to an abrupt halt and stepped to the side, dropped her leggings and let loose with a stream of piss that would have matched a hosepipe. From the blissful sag of her features, Layla concluded she was beyond caring when the crosser dismissed her for a second stop. To her surprise, Brann went next. Letting out a rueful laugh, he stopped, whipped his cock out and unleashed a copious flow before putting it away and resuming his run, all before the crosser reached the count of three.

Deciding embarrassment was a shitty reason to lose, but unwilling to risk a stop, Layla resolved to do the deed on the run. Initially unsure if it was even possible, she was surprised at the fulsomeness of the stream leaking down her legs and staining her sweatpants. Dimly heard jeers and taunts from the crowd, grown considerably in size throughout the day, failed to quell the wonderful sensation of relief that spread from her groin to her chest. It was enough to banish the pain in her shoulders, but only for a moment.

Up ahead she saw the Riverbanker and blinked in surprise upon realising she was close to lapping him. His stride had degenerated into something between a stagger and a jog. He trailed liquid and, as she drew closer, exuded a stink that made it plain he had let loose with more than just piss. *Give it up, bitch.* She clenched her teeth against the temptation to return the favour as she closed on his shambling form, contenting herself with slowing a little to enjoy his inevitable fall.

"Number two-seventy walking! Ten. Nine . . ."

The call came from the other side of the track, Layla seeing an Agri about her own age staggering on legs that appeared to have lost the ability to bend at the knee. He wept as his body jerked and spasmed, refusing to spur into the run it was no longer capable of.

"Seven. Six . . ."

Her gaze snapped back to the Riverbanker, feeling a feral sense of anticipation at the state of him. He maintained the semblance of a run, but the nearest crosser had drawn closer in expectation of an imminent fall. A quick count of the remaining field told Layla that only one more dropout was needed to end the test.

"Fall!" the word emerged from her gritted teeth in a garble whisper, eyes fixed on the tottering youth and willing him to stumble. "Fall, you bastard!"

"Three. Two. One. Number two-seventy dismissed!"

Layla didn't bother to conceal her groan of dismay at seeing the sobbing Agri stumble face down to the hard ground. He lay there, his wails of despair competing with Nehna's loud pronouncement that the test was over.

Stopping, she lost no time dumping the pack before sinking onto her backside. Her arms and legs twitched with uncomfortable violence and a vein throbbed in her head with such aching force that she thought it might burst. However, she took cheerful satisfaction from watching the Riverbanker. He lay flat on the track in a spreading pool of piss, convulsing as repeated gouts of vomit flowed from his slackened mouth. Layla hoped he was dying. Sadly, he wasn't.

With the endurance test complete, the stadium slowly emptied of spectators. Only the first day of Selection was open to public view. As they left, some called out encouragement to the surviving candidates, waving the chits they had won. Others, presumably those who had gambled and lost, were even more verbose in expressing the hope that they all ended up as feeder bait.

With the seats vacated and the sky beginning to
dim, Layla and the others were ordered to line up in
the tunnel.

"Strip," Nehna told them as a pair of crossers
unwound a fire hose from a circular bracket on the
wall. "Don't want you lot stinking up the place."

With the last dregs of embarrassment extinguished
during the run, Layla complied without demur. The
smell of her own piss was bad, but the Riverbanker
was worse.

"You stinky fuck," a Tech woman told him. She
had the leanness of a regularly exercised body and a
pinched face that appeared to be set in a permanent
scowl, made more acute when tensed in disgust.
"Should've been you instead of Brock." Layla recalled
the loudly weeping Tech who had been counted out
last and saw an echo of his features in the woman's
tightened face. *Brother*, Layla decided. *Got sent home,
leaving her all alone.*

The Riverbanker barely spared the Tech a glance
as he pulled off his clothes, expression bland with
indifference. Once naked, and moving with careful
deliberation, he scraped a fleck of dried shit from his
skin and flicked it at her.

"You fucking animal!" the Tech woman erupted,
lurching towards the Riverbanker, clawed hands
reaching.

"Careful now," Brann said, moving into her path.
He wore an easy smile, though his voice held a note

of accustomed authority. "They can still kick you out, remember?" He shot a meaningful glance at the crossers readying the hose.

"If you children are done playing," Nehna said. She moved along the line, reaching into a sack to hand them each a bar of soap. "Crossers need to be clean. Feeders prefer us unwashed. You may have heard they can scent human sweat from one mile away, and blood from five. It's not just a story."

"How do we stay clean when we're Outside?" Layla asked. Asking a question seemed reasonable now the crosser was actually imparting information.

Nehna afforded her a short, hard glare of reproach before consenting to grunt an answer. "You don't. But being clean when you go over the wall might buy a few miles. Better to get into the habit now." She stepped back, nodding to the crossers with the hose. "Lather up."

After a quick, breath-stealing blast of freezing water, they worked the soap over their bodies. It was coarse stuff, the kind they dished out in ration packs from time to time. Velna had a whole range of sweet-smelling cleansers and shampoos, illicit products from enterprising artisans in the Agri-zone. Layla had occasionally been tempted to expend some scavenged items on these luxuries, but not since Thorn went over the wall. Mostly, her daily ablutions consisted of a dousing from the rain bucket on the roof, and a more extensive wash with boiled water once a week. The Cons among them reacted the worst to the hose. Layla had heard they usually ended their shifts with a hot shower. Consequently, she viewed their chorus of protesting profanity with both amusement and contempt.

Once scrubbed and rinsed, Nehna handed each of them a set of plain grey overalls and a pair of well-made shoes with thick rubber soles. "Take them," she said when Layla pointed to her own Peace-made wonders. "Always good to have a spare. The Outside can shred the best shoes in a matter of days."

The crossers' barracks were a legacy of a major sporting contest once hosted by the stadium during the Peace, proclaimed by an old, partially destroyed sign as the ATHLETES' VILLAGE – WORLD STUDENT GAMES with an accompanying date long lost to weathering or vandalism. The crossers all lived in the small, two-storey houses arranged in a series of cul-de-sacs, but Selection candidates were obliged to bunk down in the cafeteria. They were each given a bedroll and pointed to a cleared section near the far wall.

"Second tier testing starts tomorrow," Nehna said. "I suggest you grab as much rest as you can. Leave the hall without permission and you're eliminated."

She walked off before anyone thought to ask any questions, principally: what about food?

Apart from yesterday's tests, the rest of the Selection process remained the mysterious subject of many lurid rumours. Layla remembered how Thorn, having made it through the first day, returned the following evening, sternly unwilling to discuss anything that had happened. She counted several fresh bruises on his body that night, and a few scratches. When she touched them, Thorn turned on his side, offering only silence to her whispered questions. It was the last time they shared a bed. Although a few months passed before he took his own trip over the wall, Layla was sure the second day of Selection had pushed an already frayed mind to the point of breaking.

"They're not going to feed us," Luce said, unfurling her bedroll on the cracked tile floor. "That's the third test for today: see how long we can go hungry. Makes sense when you think about it. Not much to eat in the Outside."

Her words stirred an unwelcome churn in Layla's belly. Her last meal had consisted of a single ration pack oat bar consumed on the way to the Stadium.

"Seems to me we should introduce ourselves," Brann said. Moving to the Tech woman, he offered his hand. "I'm Brann. Agricultural Specialist Grade Two."

"Don't recall anyone putting you in charge," the woman muttered.

"They didn't." Brann laughed, continuing to hold out his hand until she took it.

"Meena, Technical Engineer." She didn't offer her grade, which Layla assumed meant Brann outranked her.

"Good to meet you, Meena." Brann clapped her on the shoulder and proceeded to introduce himself to everyone else, making Layla wonder if she might end up hating him more than she already hated the Riverbanker. Still, she watched each interaction carefully, keen to learn what she could about her competition.

Most were cordial if cautious in the greetings they exchanged, apart from Luce, who cheerfully told Brann to go stick that hand up his rectum. Layla detected both familiarity and insincerity in their subsequent shared laughter. The old Con was the most taciturn, accepting Brann's hand but offering only a curt statement of his name: "Lenox."

When it came to Layla's turn, she decided to adopt the same demeanour. Brann evidently saw an advantage in making friends, but she didn't.

"Layla," Brann repeated, his large hand engulfing hers. "You work at the Electric Palace, right?"

She shrugged. "Yeah."

"She probably sold you an ice cream once," Dresh said. "Her dads run the place. I'm Dresh."

"Ice cream." Brann gave a nostalgic chuckle as they shook. "It's been a while since I had any of that."

"The machine broke," Layla said, instantly berating herself for being lured into the conversation.

"With any luck, we'll bring back the parts to fix it." Brann gave her a reassuring grin and moved on to shake more hands. He even approached the

Riverbanker, the skinny youth exhibiting only faint interest as he regarded the outstretched hand. "Pitt," he said, not taking it. "Now piss off, eh?"

Instead of anger, Brann's expression shifted into puzzled amusement. "Good to meet you, Pitt," he said before retreating to his bedroll.

"Bastards."

Layla turned to find Meena staring at the crossers now filing in to sit at the tables. Her scowl lingered, but her mouth hung open in naked longing. Layla's belly lurched as a new scent reached her nostrils. Doors opened and two large steel urns were wheeled out. A wonderfully enticing pall of onion-scented steam leaked from the lids to fill the cafeteria.

"Don't look," Dresh said, lying down on his bedroll with his forearm over his eyes. "It'll make it harder."

It was good advice, but Layla kept watching. The sight and smell of the soup being ladled into the crossers' bowls were distracting, but she watched them rather than their meal. She saw Stave silently spooning soup into his mouth alongside Nehna. Conversation was muted and brief. It seemed they found little worthy of discussion in their pool of candidates. Counting them, Layla was surprised by the number: just thirty-two in total. Once, the Special Retrieval Unit had numbered over two hundred, but that had been years ago. *The Outside doesn't belong to us*, Taxo had said, and here was inarguable evidence he was right.

Once the soup course was over, the doors at the

rear of the cafeteria opened again to flood the place with the gut-roiling smell of roast chicken.

"Fuck this," one of the candidates said, getting to his feet. "Do I get to keep the clothes and shoes?" he called to the crossers. Receiving a dismissive wave from Nehna, he cast a pitying glance at Layla and the others before making for the exit with a purposeful stride.

The sight of the chickens, accompanied by bowls of roast potatoes and steamed carrots, was enough for Layla to follow Dresh's example. She lay on her bedroll, facing the wall, taking only small comfort from the fact that the rumble of Brann's belly was even louder than hers. For a time, the big Agri maintained a steady stream of conversation, assailing them with various questions. Mostly they consented to answer, but, as time passed and Brann's questions diminished into short, distracted mutterings, they stopped bothering. By the time the crossers' feast ended, he was completely silent. When the scrape of chairs and clatter of cleared plates faded, Layla opened her eyes to see him hurrying to scour the tables for scraps. He came back disappointed, as their tormentors had been scrupulous about cleaning up.

"They could've at least given us water," he grumbled, sinking down onto his bedroll.

"Water would be good now," Luce agreed. "Nice big plate of goat curry would be better, though." She rolled onto her front, facing Brann with her head propped on her hands, crossed ankles swaying. "You ever have Misha's curry? Things that woman can do with just a few spices . . ."

"Shut up, Luce." The flash of anger in the big man's eyes made Layla wonder if he was as nice as she claimed.

"And the flatbreads." Luce sighed. "Seasoned with coriander and garlic. That elderflower wine, too. Just as good as anything from the Peace, my mother said . . ."

"Shut up!" Veins stood out in Brann's neck as he ground his jaw, voice pitched to a dangerously low note.

"That didn't take much, did it?" Luce let out a small laugh, shifting onto her back. "Sleep light, everyone. Otherwise, you might wake up with this one trying to chew your arm off."

Chapter Seven

Sleep came with surprising swiftness, despite the recurrent spasms of hunger-induced pain. Layla assumed it was the combination of an empty belly and the previous day's events that summoned the dream. It hadn't tormented her for months, but now arrived with a fresh clarity. Thorn on the wall, just before he jumped. The most curious thing about the dream was the fact that Layla hadn't actually been there when it happened. She had only heard about it from the crushers. Still, whatever sadist lurked in the recesses of her imagination was skilled in crafting convincing detail.

Thorn wore his favourite jacket of black and white leather, the one she had pulled an Undercut skeleton apart to retrieve. The sleeves had been rat chewed, so he cut them off, which served to reveal the wiry, tattooed muscle of his arm. His hair, short at the back and sides but long on top, trailed in the stiff breeze. The hour was late and the sky moonless, Old City rendered into abstract jaggedness by the dark. Thorn had always been fascinated by the degraded cityscape, often coming here to stare at it for hours until the crushers shooed him away.

"Come home," Layla said, like she always did.

"I can't," he replied, same as ever. "Can't you hear them, Layla?"

"Hear who?"

He turned to her, his part-shadowed face a more angular version of his brother's, but with eyes that were so much older. "You know who. They're calling to me. To all of us. I don't know why we try so hard not to answer."

"Thorn . . ."

Then he jumped, like he always did. No preamble. No parting words. He just put a hand on the top of the balustrade and vaulted over. Gone in an instant. It never ended here. Her inner sadist wouldn't let it. A heartbeat later came screams and inhuman growling, followed by the sound of ripping flesh and breaking bones. This was another cruel invention. The crushers had seen him twitch for a while before lying still. It was tradition that anyone who chose to go over the wall was not retrieved, alive or dead. So they just left him there. In the morning, his body was gone.

"Feeders come up to the wall at night sometimes," one of the crushers explained. "Used to shoot 'em, but we can't spare the ammo these days."

As usual, the sound of Thorn's death drew her with

irresistible force. Moving to the balustrade, she leaned over. A face stared up at her from the blackness, slicked in red, the surprised, antagonised visage of a predator interrupted in its gorging. Two pale eyes fixed upon her with a mix of depthless malice and hunger . . .

"GET UP!"

Layla hunched in her bedroll, hand instinctively covering her ear against the shout that invaded it.

"Up, candidate!"

She felt an ungentle tug to her arm dragging her from the last vestiges of sleep.

"On your feet!"

Blinking grit, she winced at the flare of a flashlight aimed directly into her eyes. It flicked away, revealing the vague smear of Nehna's features. "Stand up, Sixty-four," she instructed, not shouting now but with a note of harsh impatience.

Layla reached for her shoes, pulled them on and managed to fumble the laces into knots. A loud groan escaped her as she got to her feet. It felt like every muscle she possessed had acquired its own unique ache. Looking around, she saw the other candidates being roused by the same group of crossers that had overseen the first day's tests. Beyond the mostly cracked and boarded-up windows, the sky was still dark. How long had they been allowed to sleep? The powerful desire to collapse back onto her bedroll made her think it couldn't have been more than a couple of hours.

Of the whole group, only one candidate refused to

rise. Flapping a listless hand in response to being told that he would be eliminated if he didn't stand up right now, he pulled his bedroll over his head with a muttered, "OK."

"Be out of here by first light," Nehna instructed before ordering the rest of them to line up. "Good news," she informed them with a bland grin, "it's time for breakfast."

Despite the nausea induced by interrupted sleep, mention of food birthed an instant, savage hunger in Layla's core. From the abrupt attentiveness of the others, the feeling was shared by all.

"But before you eat," Nehna went on, "you will commit the following to memory. Listen close: this won't be repeated and you will be expected to recite it on command." Her grin gone, she scanned their faces with a stern, unblinking intensity before continuing: "This is the Crossers' Creed. One: Stay in the light. Two: Run before you fight. Three: If you fight, kill. Wounding is not enough. Four: If caught, end yourself or they will know what you know."

Nehna paused, her flashlight flicking from one face to another until she barked: "Say it back!"

The recitation was a collection of faltering mumbles, far too inaccurate for Nehna's liking. "Again!" she commanded, voice echoing loud. "No one eats until you get it right."

"One: Stay in the light. Two: Run before you fight . . ."

The flashlight beam snapped from one face to the other as they went through the recitation. They were more unified and accurate this time, but still unequal to Nehna's standards. "Again. Anyone who fucks it up this time will be eliminated."

Shutting her eyes against the distracting flare of the wayward flashlight, Layla focused all the resources of her still partially befuddled mind to the task of precisely reciting every word of the creed. ". . . If caught, end yourself or they will know what you know."

Silence descended, the beam halting its random course. Layla knew the threat of elimination was no bluff, and fully expected at least one dismissal. However, Nehna clicked off the flashlight without calling any numbers. "Right. Time to get you little piggies to the trough."

Harried into a run by the crossers, they were led from the cafeteria and ordered to circuit the building. Layla worried they were going to be run to exhaustion again, so sagged in relief when Nehna called a halt at the rear entrance. Two crossers went to a large steel hopper resting against the wall, raising the lid and tipping it over. A thick odour of rotting food wafted over them as the contents spread out on the gravel track. But for the dominating grip of her hunger, the stench would have made Layla gag. Instead, it brought a small trickle of drool to her parched mouth.

"Three days' worth of yummy goodness," Nehna

said, gesturing to the spilled garbage. "Plenty to go around. You have ten minutes. Try not to overindulge."

Brann was the first to plunge into the pile, scattering bones and other inedible detritus in a frenzied search for sustenance. The rest of them were close on his heels, Layla suffering visions of her childhood days rooting through the Tip. Old habits proved to be useful, though, and she quickly plucked out a partially consumed chicken wing. Wiping off as much gravel as she could, she bit into it, mouth flooding with saliva at the first taste of meat. She tore every scrap of sinew and flesh from the bones and then licked them clean before tossing the remains aside and looking for more. She munched down the stub of a carrot next, followed by the brown remnants of a half-eaten apple, body thrumming with joy and disgust.

Unearthing a root-sprouting potato, she paused in the act of bringing it to her mouth. *How long until they feed us next?* Her hunger still exerted its bestial hold and she couldn't resist taking a couple of bites before forcing herself to stop. *Save it.* Consigning the potato to the pocket of her overalls, she saw Dresh busily gnawing a mouldy turnip.

"Don't," she told him. "Keep some for later." She regretted the words the moment they were out of her mouth. *Do you want him to stay?* It was too late. Dresh, ever heedful of her guidance, stuffed the half-consumed vegetable into his overalls.

"Fuck off!" A harsh feral snarl snapped Layla's gaze

to Brann, seeing him shove Pitt away from a chicken carcass. It retained nearly a third of its meat, a prize regardless of the maggots squirming over it. "Get your own, you Riverbank shit . . ."

"Number one-eight-three!" Nehna's strident call brought a sudden halt to their foraging. "Eliminated."

Brann rose slowly from the piled refuse, his face set in the forlorn blankness of a caught child. "I . . . I was just hungry."

"Any aggression towards a fellow candidate results in immediate elimination," Nehna said. "You can't cross if you fight with your teammates." She jerked her head. "On your way."

"I can't." The big Agri cast a beseeching, demanding gaze around the onlooking crossers. "My gramps . . ."

"Time to go, big fella," the muscular crosser said, coming forward to take Brann's arm. He was gentle but firm as he led him from the pile. "Try again next time, eh? Probably won't be too long, way things are going."

"My gramps," Brann said again, sobbing now. He tottered off into the gloom, still clutching the chicken carcass to his chest, his large, stumbling form soon lost to the dark.

"Four minutes left," Nehna told the rest of them. "Unless you've lost your appetite."

After breakfast, they were each given a small leather flask of water. Most of the others gulped the entire contents down immediately. Layla fought the urge to do the same, limiting herself to just one-third. She sighed in annoyance at seeing Dresh follow her example. As did Luce, Lenox and, to Layla's considerable disappointment, Pitt. Their pockets also bulged with half-eaten morsels from the pile.

"Time for some fun in the woods," Nehna told them before she and the other crossers hounded them into a run. The Athletes' Village was fringed on one side by a thick band of trees. The city park had some copses of ash and birch, but this was the closest thing the Redoubt had to an actual forest. Dense with bush and ferns, it put Layla in mind of the photographs on the walls of her shed, and the promise of discovery they held. But, with the dawn light crafting deep, formless shadows, this reduced echo of such wonder felt no more inviting than the Undercut.

Lining them up at the edge of the woodland, Nehna barked: "Crossers' Creed. Let's hear it."

"Stay in the light," they intoned in ragged unison. "Run before you fight . . ."

Once again, she made them repeat it until it had become a strident chorus of conjoined voices, the tenets echoing through the trees.

"Let's play another little game," she said when finally satisfied. "See that?" She pointed to an oil drum rising from a patch of ferns, its upper side painted a shade of white. "That's your first marker. There are another two in the woods painted blue and red. You will each be given a colour sequence. Each drum must be touched in the correct sequence. There will be five runs in all and the sequence will be longer each time. After each run, the candidate with the slowest time will be eliminated. Mess up the sequence and you're also out."

As was typical, she didn't pause to ask if anyone had any questions before turning to Layla. "Sixty-four, you're up first. The sequence is white, blue, red, white." She reached into the collar of her overalls, pulled out a stopwatch and thumbed the start button. "Time starts now."

Layla ran to the white-painted drum and slapped a hand to it. Scanning the enclosing foliage, she grunted in frustration. *Green, green, nothing but fucking green . . . Wait. There.* A flicker of blue about fifty feet away. She covered the distance in a sprint, coming close to falling when her toe found an inconvenient tree root. She kept her feet by virtue of colliding with the drum, nearly tipping it over. Looking around again, she searched in vain for any scrap of red, frowning at the absence of any crossers to confirm her progress. Still, that old familiar itch from the Undercut told her she was being observed.

With no visual cues to follow, she settled for pushing deeper into the woods, keeping to a steady jog, gaze tracking back and forth. For the space of a full minute, she saw nothing. Coming to a small stream, she took the opportunity to crouch and refill her flask and saw a wavering patch of red reflected in the water's surface.

"Tricky," she murmured, looking up to see the drum suspended from the branches of a tree. The drum hung a few feet above eye level, obliging her to take a run up. It emitted a dull, echoing boom as she slapped her hand to it. As soon as her feet touched the ground, she pivoted and sprinted back the way she came.

Nehna thumbed the stopwatch's button when Layla thumped a hand to the white drum. As the crosser wordlessly scribbled something on her clipboard, Layla searched her face for some indication of approval, but saw only faint amusement before she turned to Lenox.

"Number two-twenty-three, you're up."

Layla judged Lenox's run to be just as fast as hers, maybe even beating her by a second or two. Number eighty-two went next, a heavyset Agri man who disappeared into the trees for so long Layla wondered if he had chosen to give up and go home. Eventually, he plodded back into sight, shoulders sagging with the knowledge of defeat as he put his hand to the drum. When all the first runs had been completed, a number of crossers emerged from the woods to confer with Nehna.

"Didn't see them," Dresh said. "Did you?"

Layla shook her head.

"Think they'll teach us how to do that?"

"You heard what she told us yesterday," Luce put in. "This isn't training. You saw how few of them were left last night. Starting to get the feeling we'll be lucky if they teach us anything. We're here to fill the ranks, that's all."

"Eighty-two!" Nehna called out after a short discussion with the other crossers. "Eliminated."

The heavy set Agri's shoulders slumped even lower as he walked away. It had quickly become custom that no one said anything in these moments, either out of respect or basic embarrassment.

For the next run, Nehna turned her back on the candidates, keeping her voice low when she called Layla forward to relate the sequence. "White, red, white, blue, red, white."

Layla half-expected the crossers to have moved the drums, but found both the blue and the red in the same place. This was as much a test of memory as it was speed and stamina. She was sure her time for the second run was even faster than the first, but as before, Nehna betrayed nothing as she noted the time and called out Lenox's number.

Two candidates were eliminated in the second run, one for being slowest, the other for forgetting the sequence. During her third and fourth runs, Layla realised that remembering was the hardest part of the test.

"White, red, blue, white, blue, red, white."

She repeated the sequence out loud during her final two runs, experiencing a moment of panic during the fifth when she became sure she had mixed up white with blue. Several more repetitions, her voice increasing in volume with each one, cemented it in her head, but she endured Nehna's subsequent murmured discussion with the crossers in fretful expectation that she had got it wrong.

"Four-oh-six and two-seventeen!" Nehna called. "Eliminated."

Looking around, Layla found that their number had been reduced to twelve. All her principal competition remained, though she had been fastest overall. Dresh also made it through, thanks mainly to his aggravating refusal to forget the sequence. Like Layla, he repeated it out loud as he ran. To her surprise, Lenox performed the worst out of those who survived the test. Judging by the tense frown of his creased features whenever he returned to the white drum, she knew it was recalling the sequence that slowed him down.

"Time for lunch," Nehna told them once the two eliminated candidates had slouched away. Fortunately, neither of them cried this time. "*Our* lunch, that is," Nehna added as she and the crossers started towards the cafeteria. "You lot stay here until we get back."

"You'd think she'd try to make us like her more," Luce observed, resting her back against a tree and sinking to the ground. "Since we'll be going Outside together."

"We won't be going with her," Layla said. "It's Stave's turn to lead the next crossing."

"Then why isn't he running this?" Dresh asked.

"I don't know." She sat on a comfortable-looking

patch of grass and took the half-eaten potato from her pocket. Her hunger was still fierce enough to overcome any repugnance at the taste. Those who hadn't taken the opportunity to fill their pockets with scraps stared in unabashed envy as the rest of them ate. Finding the weighty gaze of a nearby Con oppressive, Layla tossed her the quarter apple. "Here."

The Con, who had named herself Gella during the unfortunate Brann's round of introductions, hastily put the morsel to her lips, then paused. "Thanks," she said, before cramming it into her mouth. She chewed and swallowed it down quickly, sitting back on her haunches, face tensing with the onset of tears. "I hate this, you know. If it wasn't for my boys—"

"I don't want to know about your boys," Layla cut in, turning her back.

She felt more eyes on her as she chomped through a carrot stub, catching a grimace of reproach from Dresh, which earned him a glower in response. She turned it on the rest of them, face hard in rejection of their judgement. This was not a game and none of them were here to make friends. They all wanted what a crossing would give them, and for her to get it, most of them would have to fail. She noticed how Lenox alone deliberately avoided her eye. Although, just for a second, she saw him dart a glance in her direction, short but narrow in its focused appraisal.

Your shitty memory will see you gone soon enough, she answered silently. *Bye, bye, you old fuck.*

Chapter Eight

Nehna and the other crossers returned from lunch an hour later, all of them carrying packs. Dumping them on the ground, they disappeared into the forest. Layla heard a muted exchange before Nehna came back alone.

"Put them on," she said, pointing to the packs. "It might appear that they all contain rocks, but that's wrong. Each one holds supplies vital for the continued wellbeing of New City Redoubt. Your task this fine afternoon is to get them to where they need to be. You'll be separated into teams of four for this test. Each team will be given a different destination and must stay together for the duration of the test. Teams must stay together unless one or more chooses to self-eliminate. My colleagues will be playing the role of feeders and will seek to capture you along the way. Any candidate they capture will be eliminated. You have three hours to deliver your payloads. Maps are in the packs. The choice of route is left to each team."

She then called out the sets of numbers that comprised each team. To Layla's relief, Dresh was allocated to a different group that included Luce, and Pitt another. She found herself standing alongside Lenox, Gella and a wiry Tech named Delph.

"The river," Delph said, face bunching in disdain as he surveyed one of the maps they had been given. "Then the Boneyard. That'll be fun."

Layla was familiar with the Boneyard thanks to her early scavenging career, although most of anything worth having had been picked clean by now. Looking over her own map, she saw no obviously safe route. It was hand drawn on coarse paper with an X marking their destination on the northern side of the Boneyard. She remembered it as a place rich in hiding places for roleplaying crossers.

"The shortest distance between two points is a straight line," Lenox said, the most words she had heard him speak so far.

"Sounds good to me," Delph said. "I say we run all the way. Less chance of being caught if we move fast."

Layla doubted the test would turn out to be so straightforward, but couldn't see any reason to argue. Also, from the fatigue evident in Gella's sagging features, running the whole route would probably see her drop out. *One less to worry about.*

Nehna's voice cut through the murmured discussions of the other teams, stopwatch raised above her head for emphasis. "Test starts in three, two, one."

"This way," Lenox said, shouldering his pack and setting off into the woods at a steady run. "It's about a mile to the river."

As they ran, Layla had to fight the temptation to push ahead. *Teams must stay together.* Delph was only just capable of maintaining a decent pace, and despite taking the lead, she knew Lenox was no good over distance. As for Gella, she trailed behind from the start, constantly forcing them to slow. Upon clearing the woods, they entered a series of sparsely grassed fields. The ground bore the faded furrows of land once given over to farming, but the Agris had abandoned it years ago.

"They used to irrigate it with water from the river," Delph explained in a strained pant. "My pa worked on the pumping stations. That was back before they built the dam and the reservoir. The soil dried out after that."

"That who you're doing this for?" Gella panted back. "Your pa?"

"Nah. The old shit died years back. I'm doing this for me. Always wanted to see the Outside, y'see."

Gella let out a gasp in an attempt at a disparaging laugh. "Then your head must be cracked."

They reached the river after a ten-mile run. Layla found it punishing, thanks mainly to the pack. It wasn't as heavy as the one she had borne through the stamina test, but she knew it would take an increasing toll as the day wore on. She took comfort from the state of her teammates, all staggering to a halt at the edge of the slope of cracked concrete. Gella was the worst, falling to her knees and heaving as if about to throw up. However, her body refused to surrender what meagre sustenance it held.

"We should follow it that way," Lenox said, nodding to the left where the artificial canyon stretched away in a wide curve. It was dry except for a narrow channel of grey water tracking through its centre. "It leads to the Boneyard, and it's flat. Makes for easier running."

"Why not straight across?" Delph said, face dripping sweat as he nodded to the opposite bank. Unlike the fields they had traversed, it was all overgrown buildings, remnants of storehouses and living quarters abandoned when the Agris moved out.

"Feeders," Layla said. "Lot of places to hide in there. He's right. We follow the river." Tightening the straps on her pack, she started down the slope.

"I need a moment longer," Gella called after her.

"Then self-eliminate and stop slowing us down," Layla snapped back. She descended the slope at a run, refusing to slow this time. Soon, she heard the scuff and strained breathing of the three of them labouring to catch up.

They followed the river for about a mile before Delph called a halt. "Wait up!"

"We can rest when we reach the Boneyard," Layla said, resenting the immediate flood of relief as she slowed to a walk. It would make it harder to resume running.

"Look," the Tech said, pointing to a large oval opening in the angled concrete of the Riverbank. "Noticed these earlier. See?" They crowded round as he unfurled his map, tracing a finger along the river. At various points a number of straight lines led away from the curving track. "Sluice tunnels, from back when the sewers were still working," Delph explained. "Unless I've got it wrong, this one comes out at the Boneyard. It'll cut at least two miles off the journey."

"Sounds good to me," Gella said.

"No." Layla shook her head.

"Why not?" There was a clear gleam of desperation in Gella's hollowed eyes, also in the thinned pitch of her voice. She knew she wasn't going to make it without a short cut.

Stay in the light, Layla thought. But voiced no other objections as the other woman moved closer to the tunnel. Delph, it turned out, had less calculating instincts.

"We need to be careful about this," he said, edging forward to peer into the dark recess. "They're out here waiting for us, remember?"

"We've passed loads of these already." Gella continued to edge towards the opening. "What are the chances they chose this one?"

She was less than five feet from the tunnel when the rope whipped out from its black depths. It looped over her head and tightened around her torso before she had time to even flinch. She did summon a plaintive shriek as she was dragged into the gloom, the sound quickly trailing off into pitiable sobs. Layla was sure she heard the words "my boys" among the despairing echoes.

"Number one-nine-four," a voice called from the darkness. "Eliminated."

Layla exchanged brief glances with Delph and Lenox before they all resumed running. "Yeah," the Tech said. "Best if we just stick to the river."

Delph collapsed when they ascended the bank bordering the Boneyard. Halfway up the slope, he let out a sharp, agonised grunt, hissing in pain and clutching his lower leg. "Fucking hamstring!"

"Can you move it?" Lenox asked, crouching at Delph's side. The Tech clenched his teeth to smother a shout as the Con gently touched his leg.

"Shit! Shit! Shit!" Delph pounded a fist on the concrete, voice thick with frustration.

"Can't leave him," Lenox said, glancing up at Layla. "Teams are supposed to stay together, and she didn't say anything about injuries."

"If we were Outside he'd be good as dead," Layla pointed out, drawing a grating laugh from Delph.

"You're a nasty little cunt, you know that?"

The thought of crossers lurking nearby forestalled Layla's instant desire to stamp on his ankle. Instead, she joined Lenox in taking hold of Delph's arms and dragging him up the slope. Their first glance at the Boneyard brought them to an abrupt halt. The hulks of vehicles, large and small, spread out before them in a jungle of rusted scrap and tall weeds. Trucks, cars, vans and every variation in between left to rot here after the Raising. The fuel they ran on was needed for generators and dozers to build the wall, all long since consumed anyway. Engines, wires and anything else of use had been mostly stripped away by the time Layla made her early forays here and she played no small part in scavenging the rest. Consequently, this lingering monument to the machines of the Peace was rarely visited but for the rats and sundry vermin that made their homes among the wrecks. It was more overgrown than she remembered, concealing many of the larger hulks that would have provided useful landmarks. However, three hundred metres off, an old radio tower rose above the jagged redness of the Boneyard.

"There's no way we're making it through that with him," Layla said, shrugging Delph's arm from her shoulder. "There's bound to be at least one crosser waiting for us." She cast a glance at the fast dimming sky. "And it'll be dark soon. We'll have to sprint it." Meeting Lenox's eye, she added, "The priority for any crossing is the delivery of supplies. Making hard choices is just another part of the test."

"She's right," Lenox said, Delph collapsing into an untidy heap as the Con stepped away. "Sorry."

"I'm not," Layla said, still angry. "Just so you know."

"Oh, get fucked." Fixing them both with a harsh glare, he added, "I hope you get eaten."

"Wasting time." Layla turned her back on him, unfolding her map. She pointed to the X, then the radio tower: an obvious destination. "Shortest route is a straight line," she reminded Lenox.

He grunted agreement, shrugging his broad shoulders to settle his pack before adopting the crouch of a sprinter at the start line. "No stopping."

"I hope you get eaten!" Delph called after them as they pelted away, more in despair than anger. "I hope you both get fucking eaten!"

Layla did her best to skirt the larger wrecks as she sped through the maze of dead machinery. The smaller cars were mostly hollowed out, making for poor hiding spaces. The trucks and vans, however, retained enough of their form to host deep, threatening shadows lengthened by the fading sun. Once again, Lenox was content for her to take the lead, even though she was sure he could outpace her over so short a distance. As she ran, a semblance of her familiarity with the place returned. The sight of a digger, tracks fallen away from its wheels, the crane arm collapsed into segments like the neck of some fossilised beast, reminded her that they would soon come to a line of trucks. Placed end to end, they formed a near impassible barrier through the centre of the Boneyard. It was also the perfect site for an ambush.

"We have to veer left," she told Lenox, slowing a little. "It's too tight up ahead."

He didn't argue, replying with a stiff nod and once again following her lead. The bus was where she remembered it. It had diminished in height, paint and faded advertising panels stripped from its flanks. Either by accident or design, the bus had been jammed at a right angle into the line of trucks, creating a useful pathway. Hopping onto the bonnet of the tow-truck nestled alongside, Layla leaped to clamp her hands to the edge of the bus's roof, hauling herself up.

"Seems sound," she told Lenox, testing the surface with a tentative prod of her shoe. She kept her voice to a low murmur. The sense of being watched was much less acute now, but that might mean the crossers were just really good at concealment. "Best keep to the edge," she advised, putting one foot in front of the other as she moved to the rear of the bus. She crouched before jumping down, eyes scanning the sparsely grassed field beyond the wall of trucks. There were fewer wrecks here, leaving a relatively clear run to the tower.

"Looks OK," she whispered, leaping nimbly to the ground. "Straight li—"

Air exploded from her lungs as he landed on her back, knees pressing her into the hard-packed soil, both hands clamped onto her head so tight she thought her skull would crack. "Prednisolone!" She felt spittle on her brow as the word hissed between clenched teeth. His voice was shot through with the suppressed sob of a man performing a hated task, but the increasing pressure on her head made it clear he wasn't about to shirk it. "She needs prednisolone."

This, Layla realised as her vision turned an increasingly deep shade of red, was Lenox's mantra. She had her anti-bios. He had whatever this stuff was. She didn't care if it was for his wife, daughter or lover. In that moment, like Delph, she wished him and whoever he was doing this for the ugliest death. The wave of hate pulsing through her provoked a snarl, jaw opening as she jerked beneath him, forcing him to adjust his grip. As he did so, his index finger invaded her mouth. She bit as hard as she could, not stopping when the invasion of blood flooded her throat, continuing to grind her teeth through skin, muscle and sinew until they met bone. She dimly heard Lenox swallow a scream, his hands still exerting their crushing grip.

He'll tell them I fell, she concluded. *Cracked her head. Pity. I liked her.*

The thought summoned a fresh tide of hate, fuelling a last, spasmodic effort to force her teeth together. Lenox's grip finally slackened as the two inches of bone and flesh separated from his hand. She thrashed herself free, kicking and scratching. Shouting in rage, he came for her again, reaching for her throat. Layla spat the finger into his face in a cloud of blood, following it up with a hard kick to his nose. It bought her enough time to roll away and shrug the pack from her shoulders. Roaring now, Lenox charged, letting out a grunt as the rock-filled pack collided with his head. Although stunned, he remained a strong man and successfully dodged her next blow.

Retreating from each other, they both crouched, eyes blazing with mutual hatred. Layla knew she should run, but the need to kill this man was all-consuming.

"She needs prednisolone," Lenox repeated through mangled lips, crouching lower.

"Amoxicillin," Layla spat back, tightening her grip on the pack. "Clarithromycin. Doxycycline."

Something shifted in the melange of shadow behind Lenox, a small flicker of metal slicing the gloom. He shuddered as if beset by a sudden chill. Clamping his undamaged hand to his neck, his features spasmed between puzzlement and terrible disappointment. As he staggered, Layla saw the blood jetting between his fingers. Lenox tried to say something, but it emerged as a brief stream of wet nonsense before he collapsed face first to the ground, twitched for a few seconds, then lay still.

"Number two-twenty-three," Nehna said, stepping from the shadows to crouch beside Lenox's unmoving form. "Eliminated for aggression towards a fellow candidate." She wiped her knife blade on the Con's overalls, then glanced up at Layla with a frown of disapproval. "Right now, a feeder would be distracted by gorging on the carcass."

Layla blinked, then tore her gaze away. Hauling the

pack straps over her shoulders, she turned and ran full pelt for the tower.

"It happens sometimes." Nehna said. "More often the last few years. People are getting desperate, I guess."

Layla had reached the tower a half-hour before. Finding no crosser with a clipboard to greet her, she worried she had identified the wrong end point despite repeated, squinting scrutiny of her map in the fast fading light. Knowing it was too late to do anything about it now, she resolved to sit and wait. She washed her mouth out with gulps from her flask, but the taste of blood still lingered. Nehna appeared when the sky turned a pale shade of red, striding from the darkness to sink down beside her with a tired groan.

"If he'd killed me, would you still have killed him?" Layla's question lacked any note of deference. She felt a cold certainty Nehna had waited before intervening. "Let him stay, even?"

"Of course not." Nehna huffed a laugh. "A candidate willing to do murder to improve his chances is of no use. If he'd killed you, we'd have turned him over to the crushers for Ultimate Sanction. Wasn't my idea to let him enter Selection, anyway. Too old. But one of my colleagues remembered him from the Peace. He won bronze in the hundred metres at some games or other."

She sniffed and peered closer at Layla. "How's your head?"

The question surprised her, but didn't wipe the scowl from her face. "It fucking hurts."

"Yeah, well, if you get dizzy or start throwing up, let us know. Here." She took something from her pocket and dropped it in Layla's lap. "It'll come in handy out there." She got to her feet, brushing dust from her overalls. "Congratulations, you're a crosser now. Be back at the village by morning."

She started to walk away, then paused. "Believe it or not, but Selection used to be much harder." Before she strode off, Layla perceived a genuine sympathy in her face, even a sense of apology.

Alone again, Layla looked at Nehna's gift: a five-inch-long piece of heavy-duty plastic with a button on one side. Pressing it, Layla started in surprise when a blade shot from one end. It was shorter than her own knife, but, she saw as she peered closer, the steel was free of scratches and the edge much keener.

Be back by morning, Nehna had said. So Layla had enough time to go home and say the goodbyes she had avoided. But she wouldn't. If she went back to the theatre now, she knew she would never leave. *Was this what happened to you?* she asked Thorn's memory, remembering his bruises. *Did you kill someone? Did you pass Selection but couldn't face the Outside when the time came?*

Thumbing the button to retract the blade, she stood up and started the trek back towards the river, nurturing the fervent hope Dresh wouldn't be there when she reached the village.

Chapter Nine

Upon returning to the village, Layla's relief swelled at finding Dresh absent. The sensation dwindled into bitter disappointment when Luce told her she and Dresh had completed their test. "He said he needed to go home. Be back in the morning." She frowned in a manner that reminded Layla she hadn't yet washed the blood from her face. "You cut yourself?"

She shook her head, moving past Luce to slump onto her bed. The successful candidates, six in all, had been allocated the same house in the village. Furnishings were sparse but the clean, freshly painted walls, laundered sheets, and the fact that water actually came out of the taps and the shower heads, instilled a palpable sense of unfamiliar luxury.

"Took the one by the window," Luce said, guiding her to a room with two beds. "Hope you don't mind."

Layla's eye was immediately drawn to the image painted on the wall beside her bed. A black and white depiction of a rose bush. The style was loose but still convincing, conjuring the colours of the flowers despite its monochrome nature. Below it, a large letter R had been inscribed with a flourish.

"Rehsa," Luce said. "This was her bunk before she hooked up with Stave. Quite the artist, wasn't she?"

Luce wittered on some more, but Layla barely heard her, curling up on the bed and marvelling at the softness of the mattress. She slept for a time, showered, then slept again, waking the next morning to find Dresh sitting on the neighbouring bed. His usual affability was gone, as was any sense of triumph or satisfaction she might have expected. Instead, he regarded her with a steady, serious gaze, conveying the impression of having aged years in the space of a day.

"Taxo thought you might want these," Dresh said, handing her the leather wallet containing her lock picks. "He said to tell you Strang's stabilised. Doc Piller came up with some better pain meds. Cost a bit, though."

Layla knew she should thank him, but couldn't.

"Lenox?" Dresh asked. She assumed Luce must have told him about her coming back covered in blood.

"If you bet on him, you lost," she said. After she took the lock picks from him, they both sat in silence, either because there was too much to say or any words exchanged now would be pointless. Finally, she forced herself to look him squarely in the eyes and say, "I won't be able to protect you out there, Dresh. Got a sense of what it's going to be like now, and I just . . . can't."

A vestige of his old rueful grin returned, but the edge to his voice told her how deep she had cut. "Maybe you won't have to," he said. "Get dressed. They're choosing teams this morning."

"In light of the urgent requirement for specialist supplies, the Mayor's Office has decreed there will be two back-to-back crossings."

Nehna's announcement heralded an anticipatory murmur from the crossers assembled in the cafeteria. They seemed mostly indifferent to the newcomers in their midst. Some offered short, expressionless nods of greeting, but most didn't. Layla didn't have to think too hard to reason out the lack of overt welcome. Why make friends with people you expect to die soon?

She had wolfed down an impressively hearty breakfast, not attempting to hide her disappointment at finding Pitt at the table. He matched her resentful glares with his own, but was otherwise as taciturn as ever. His lank, unwashed hair was now mostly gone, trimmed close to the scalp to reveal a face that might have been called delicately handsome but for the old scars on his forehead and cheeks. He also sported a livid bruise on his jaw, which Layla took as evidence that his last test, like hers, had been eventful.

With the meal done, they gathered around while Nehna climbed up onto a table to address them. Stave stood at her side, arms crossed and face like stone.

"Team One will be led by Stave and Team Two by me," Nehna went on, pausing to quell the twitch to her lips before adding, "Each team will feature three crossers from the recent intake."

Among the subsequent muttering of discontent, Layla heard some sighs of relief, even a few gasps of laughter. It was a commonly held belief that these people lived for the crossings, an elite band of adventurers addicted to the thrill of traversing the Outside. Stories abounded of the endless, deadly game of evasion and pursuit they played with the feeders. Surveying the faces around her, Layla saw hope on some, for the rewards of a successful crossing were famously substantial. In addition to the personal items they were allowed to bring back, they would also receive extra rations and basic medicines. These were supposed to be passed on to family and dependants, but a good portion inevitably found its way to the likes of Velna. Layla assumed that explained Stave's presence at her shop the other day. She tried not to feel overly disappointed. Her brief exposure to this select group had made it clear that, for all their undoubted skills, they were just people.

"All right, shut your yap," Nehna instructed, raising a clipboard. "Team allocation is as follows. Team One: Stave. Eylsa. Romer." Her eyes flicked towards Layla and her fellow selectees. "Luce. Pitt. Layla. Team Two: Me, obviously. Ellin. Lumin. Smitt. Linkin. Dresh." Lowering the clipboard, she continued. "You all know the rules. No bitching, no moaning and no trying to persuade us different. These are the teams and the choices stand. Team One sets off in two days. Team Two the moment they return. That's it." Nehna waved the clipboard in dismissal. "Team members stay; everyone else leave. Remember, there's a fitness test in one week, so make sure you're ready."

While the cafeteria emptied out, she and Stave climbed down from the table to approach their teams. "You lot with me," Nehna said, gesturing for her teammates to follow as she made for the exit. Layla tried to catch Dresh's eye, exchange some kind of acknowledgement before they were separated, but he made no effort to look in her direction as he followed Nehna from the building.

Stave stood regarding them all, arms crossed once again and face as unreadable as before. He greeted Eylsa and Romer, the two veteran crossers, with a short raise of his eyebrows before concentrating his full attention on the trio of novices.

"Something you need to understand before we begin," he said, voice a soft rasp, "I don't care why you're here. We all have a why, but why doesn't keep you alive in the Outside. Only listening to what I tell you will do that." He turned and started walking away, Layla and the selectees following the veterans' lead by hurrying to catch up. "Lesson number one," Stave said. "Feeders."

It turned out the crossers had their own projector. It was smaller than the one Taxo continually nursed into workability, but with an even more extensive and untidy collection of wires and scavenged circuits. Stave had led them to a large chamber in one of the buildings near the cafeteria. The sign above the door, dusty but intact, read: Humanities Faculty Lecture Theatre. They all sat in the front row while he dimmed the lights before switching on the projector and the attached, also extensively modified, laptop. The still image that appeared on the screen was mostly bleached of colour and too blurred to discern much detail. Squinting, Layla thought it might show a portion of a tall building and a patch of darkened sky.

"There are three feeder types," Stave began. "Alpha, beta and gamma. These—" he tapped a button on the laptop "—are gammas."

The image unfroze into a jerky view of a city from ground level. Unlike many images of Peace-era cities at night, the surrounding buildings lacked the myriad lights Layla's childhood eyes had marvelled over. The camera tracked across a disordered group of people wearing crusher-type gear, all carrying rifles. Unlike the crushers, their armour had a mottled appearance, and the weapons were all the same type. Also, given the amount of bullets they were firing, they had a lot more ammunition.

At first, the camera kept swivelling about too much to make out what they were shooting at. Whoever was carrying it moved around some kind of vehicle, crouching to offer a glimpse of tarmac littered with spent shell casings. It then swung up to reveal a barrier of some kind bisecting a broad avenue. The barrier was about twelve feet high and seemed to have been formed of cars piled on top of each other. There was no sound but Layla saw the camera snap towards a panicked, blood-spattered face below a helmet. It looked like he was pleading with the camera operator, Layla seeing his lips form the words "gotta fucking go", before the view snapped back to the barrier.

She saw them then, dozens of pale figures cresting the barrier, moving with animalistic swiftness. They were met by a hail of tracer bullets, the barrier shuddering as it suffered a series of small explosions. Some of the pale figures fell, blown to pieces or blasted by gunfire, but more kept boiling over the wall of piled cars. The screen flooded with a yellow, strobing light Layla realised was the flash of the camera operator's rifle, meaning he must have the optic strapped to his helmet. She had unearthed a few such cameras from the Undercut over the years, GoPros Velna called them, always encouraging her to find more. Layla understood now that the value didn't lie in the devices themselves, but in the images they contained.

When the gun flash faded, the image shifted again, becoming a collage of panicked faces and running feet interrupted by the flare of explosions. For an instant, it was chaos, a swirl of confused light and dark before coming to an abrupt halt. The camera was almost level with the tarmac, unmoving except for a small, rhythmic jerk every couple of seconds. The jerks became more pronounced as a shape crept closer. One of the pale figures came to a halt a few feet away, at which point Stave hit pause.

"This is a gamma," he said. "Take a good look. See one this close in the Outside and it'll probably be your last look at anything."

Looking at the feeder, Layla was struck not by its differences, but its similarities to a human form. It was undeniably deformed, the face stretched, eyes sunken into dark holes, and the skin an unnatural shade somewhere between white and grey. But still, two arms, two legs, and, she saw with surprise, clothing. She guessed it had been male, recognising the torn remnants of a suit partially covering its emaciated frame. It even wore a tie. The least human aspects were the hands and feet, elongated into claws, nails enlarged into talon-like barbs. She couldn't see its teeth, but had heard enough about feeders to know they would be similarly altered. This was a thing dedicated to one task: sating a hunger that would never die.

"Some refer to gammas as ferals," Stave went on. "And it's a fair description. They display minimal intelligence, attack on sight, and have no apparent fear of danger. This vid is from the Capital Delaying Action, where a group of gammas estimated at two thousand strong was completely wiped out in the first fifteen minutes. But, as you saw, that didn't stop the next four thousand. Luckily, for us, they're pretty dumb, easily distracted and can be evaded if you know what you're doing. They also die more easily than the others. Their advantage is their dormancy. All feeders are capable of adopting a dormant state, but only gammas can do so for years. Alphas and betas are a lot more restless. Speaking of."

He tapped the laptop again, clearing the screen and calling up another vid. This one showed a sprawl of ground rendered in a green, glowing light. "Nightvision footage from a recon drone early in the Feeding," Stave explained. "When the outbreak, as they called it then, was still confined to rural areas."

The camera continued to track along the ground until it encountered a cluster of bright specks. Slowing, it zoomed in, revealing six figures loping through the grass. They were slower than the gammas but moved with an economy of movement that Layla could only describe as elegant. Their limbs appeared longer, as did their heads, though that may have been a distortion of the image.

"Note the triangular formation," Stave said. "Pack behaviour. Gammas will attack in groups but without coordination. And they fight each other for prey. Betas don't. They also display sophisticated hunting strategies, as you see."

On the screen the pack split apart, four maintaining the same course, while two split off in opposite directions. The camera kept tracking the main group, following it to a grassy verge alongside a single-lane road. A van sat on the verge, blazing bright as someone inside cast a flashlight beam over the surrounding grass. There was a frantic quality to the beam's movement, indicating the occupant had sensed the approaching danger.

As they came within range of the beam, the four betas began speeding back and forth, criss-crossing through the undergrowth. Layla knew it all as a deliberate distraction, and it worked. The brief flare of a shotgun blast sparked from the van's window, followed by two more. Undaunted, the betas continued their dance until the two that had split off crept from the opposite verge and launched themselves at the van. The rest closed in with blurring speed, ripping it, and presumably its owner, apart in seconds.

"Here's one that got taken alive in the early days," Stave said, calling up a still image of a pale, snarling shape viewed through a grate of steel bars. "Unfortunately, the autopsy report got lost along with the video, so all we have is a series of stills."

He called up another image. The cage's occupant had moved closer to the bars, the camera angle confirming the deformation of its head. The cranium was shaped like a stunted crescent, the creature's jaw pushed forward and the nose receded. The sharpness of it put Layla in mind of the Undercut dogs, as did the evident hunger in its eyes. They seemed less shrunken than the gamma, bigger with dark orbs catching a gleam. Stave called up the next image, blurred with motion. More bars were visible now, indicating the camera operator had made a speedy retreat. But, probably by accident, the beta remained in focus. Frozen in the act of lunging at the bars, its mouth was opened to an impossible angle, revealing rows of barbed teeth. They were irregularly spaced along the jawline, misaligned and some larger than others.

"Feeders never stop growing their teeth," Stave explained. "One gets damaged or falls out, they grow another. Remember, one bite from any type is enough to turn you. It doesn't always happen, since a single bite from a beta or a gamma can often be instantly fatal. Sometimes betas don't bite cornered prey. Instead, they'll inflict an injury with their claws so they can play with you a while. No one knows why, but it seems to happen when they've been active for a time. When freshly roused from dormancy, all they want to do is kill and feed."

This time, there was a longer pause before Stave cleared the screen. Layla heard a small cough before he spoke again. "All right, concerning alphas."

The vid he called up was preceded by a title card, white letters on black:

Northern District Hospital
Trauma Centre Entrance – Security Cam
Footage
Outbreak Day 63 – Time period:
02.32 – 04.46
Classification: Emergency Response Command
Level One Clearance Only – Not for public
distribution

The screen flickered and the card was replaced by another vid, a monotone shot of double doors and a lobby. It was a busy place, the doors repeatedly sliding open to permit a steady stream of people pushing wheeled stretchers. Those on the stretchers were mostly still, faces covered in oxygen masks and limbs encased in bandages, although some jerked or flailed about. Fortunately, they passed through the eye of the camera too fast to make out any injuries in detail. The footage sped up after that, the flow of injured becoming a blur until it resumed the standard frame rate. A man and a woman wandered into shot. They both wore loose-fitting clothing and had respirator masks dangling about their necks. Their shoulders had the bowed look of people emerging from an exhausting bout of labour. The woman was the more tired of the two, also emotional, palming tears from her eyes and forcing a laugh when the man said something. It was clear he was trying to cheer her up, delivering a playful punch to her shoulder before producing a pack of cigarettes.

At her nod, they both started towards the doors, then stopped when they opened to admit a third figure.

The new arrival appeared to be a young man, but it was hard to tell due to the hood pulled over his face. He moved on unsteady legs, hunched over with his hands clutching his belly. Once through the doors, he collapsed to his knees, the man and the woman rushing to his side. What came next happened so fast Layla thought the vid had skipped several frames. One second the man with the cigarettes was crouched close to the apparently injured youth, the next he was jerking on the floor, his head twisted at a sharp, patently fatal angle. The woman, mouth gaping in an unheard scream, was on her back, scrambling away. The hooded youth, now standing tall with no sign of injury, watched her, head tilted. Then he moved. Once again, it was so fast the camera failed to capture it. Neither youth nor woman was fully in view now, but Layla could see her plimsole-covered feet flailing. Her struggles slowed, then stopped as a pool of dark liquid spread across the floor tiles.

After a long pause, the youth stepped into view again. He had lowered his hood, revealing dark hair and pale skin stained dark below the nose. Thanks to the monochrome footage, Layla couldn't tell if his complexion matched that of a gamma or beta, but the tone was similar. She watched him step over the woman's legs and approach the man with the twisted neck. Crouched down next to him, the youth paused, then raised his bloodied mask of a face to stare directly into the camera. And he smiled.

Among Strang's library were a number of magazines. He called them "gossip rags", claiming they were cultural artefacts. *One day these'll be behind glass in a museum*. But Layla knew he liked to flip through them just to indulge his nostalgia for the lost world of the Peace. The magazines were full of improbably good-looking people, often walking into or out of places while dressed in absurdly impractical clothing and bedecked with all manner of shiny trinkets. "Paparazzi shots", Strang called them. Some of the subjects of these photos were plainly angry at the intrusion, but others reacted with smiles. It was these that came to mind as she stared back at the smiling youth on screen. This was someone enjoying the act of being observed.

"Fuck me," Luce breathed. "It's true. Always thought it was a myth."

"No myth," Stave said. "Alphas look like us. Some can also talk like us, but not always. What is clear is that they can think in a way the others can't." He gestured to the screen. "Subterfuge. Ability to infiltrate. All signs of reasoning consciousness. The Feeding was over too fast to allow for any in-depth studies, so everything we know now has been pieced together from what fragments we've been able to scrape up in the Outside. However, from what we can gather, there are indications that alphas may have been around long before the other types. Living among us, you could say. Unlike the other types, they appear to be able to turn people at will. Get bitten by a gamma or a beta and you might turn or you might just die. With alphas it's different and no one's quite sure why or how. One study theorised that gammas and betas are recent mutations. It posited that the alpha is the purest form of feeder and the others some kind of genetic accident. If they hadn't appeared, the Feeding would never have happened. Might explain why alphas are known to shun the other types, even attack them if they get too close."

A silence followed, Layla's mind churning over all she had heard about feeders and realising much of it was fragmentary and wrong. *Not just diseased people turned savage*, Taxo had said. *They're not even people at all.*

To her surprise, it was Pitt who broke the silence. "They're faster than us," he said to Stave. "Stronger too. And smart. Some of them, anyway. So, how do we kill them? The Creed says we can, right?"

The line of Stave's lips briefly formed a curve. "Then I guess it's time for Lesson Two."

Stave took them back to the woods. A fenced-off section further away from the village. The fence formed a U-shaped enclosure, one end of which was stacked high with oil drums and sandbags. To the front of these stood a row of three wooden targets. They were shaped and painted in an approximate rendering of the three feeder types.

"Forget what you've heard about sunlight turning

them to dust," Stave told them. "It doesn't. They don't like it, but they can survive it. We're not sure why they're mostly active at night, probably something to do with an inherently nocturnal physiology. Nor do they run away from religious iconography and don't need an invite to come into your house."

"What's iconography mean?" Pitt whispered to Layla.

She didn't like the assumption in his question. *Thinks I have to help him now we're on the same team.* A short bout of annoyed reflection, however, forced her to conclude that he was right. Unwilling to draw Stave's ire by speaking aloud, she drew a cruciform shape in the dirt with the heel of her shoe.

"Oh," Pitt muttered. "Right."

"Garlic doesn't do anything either," Stave went on. "Or holy water or sticking a length of wood through their heart. They bleed like we do. Do enough damage, and they die. Just like us." He paused to raise the items he held in each hand. In his right was something that resembled either an enlarged pistol or a miniature shotgun. In the other, a small cylindrical object Layla assumed to be some kind of bullet.

"There is one thing the old stories are right about," Stave said. "They really don't like silver. Or, more accurately, quicksilver, better known as mercury. For humans, it's toxic in liquid form in sufficient quantities. For feeders, just a pinch is enough to kill them. In here—" he tossed the bullet into the air and caught it

"—is a mix of standard black powder, steel pellets and fulminate of mercury. One shot is enough to bring down any feeder, which is fortunate because this—" he thumbed a catch on the stock of the pistol-like weapon, opening its breach, then slotting in the shell "—only takes one round at a time. We call it a blaster, because that's what it does." He snapped the breach closed and pointed to Pitt. "You first, since you're so keen."

He had Pitt stand with his feet in line with his shoulders, both hands gripping the curved grip of the blaster as he pointed it at the target representing a gamma. "Lock your elbows," Stave told him. "It's got a fierce kick. Aim for the central mass of the target. The trigger is heavy by design, so the weapon won't go off when you drop it, so give it a hard pull." He stood back, putting his fingers in his ears. Seeing Eylsa and Romer do the same, Layla quickly followed suit.

"Fire when ready," Stave said.

Pitt's wiry arms tensed as he exerted enough pressure to pull the trigger. The recoil forced him to take a backward step, the weapon almost jarred from his grasp. The blaster coughed out a substantial plume of smoke, emitting a flat boom that still hurt Layla's ears despite her fingers. His shot was on target, though. Splinters flew from the wooden feeder as pellets obliterated much of its crouching, snarling form. The sparkle of flame and black charring appeared a half-second later. It quickly caught fully alight, burning bright until Eylsa quenched it with a bucket of water.

"The only thing that draws feeders more than the scent of blood is a gunshot," Stave continued, taking the weapon from Pitt. "Animals retreat from loud noises. Feeders don't because they know we probably made it. The blaster has an effective range of thirty feet. Anything beyond that is a waste of ammo. So, the rules of engagement are: only fire if you have to, don't miss, and don't hang around afterwards. Two things get you killed in the Outside: curiosity and hesitation. We're not going out there to sightsee. Nor are we engaged in a cull. That's been tried and it didn't work. This—" he opened the blaster's breach again "—is only a last resort. In the Creed, run before you fight is second only to stay in the light. That's not accidental. All right." He turned, eyes fixing on Layla. "You're up next."

"Don't I get to practise more?" Pitt asked. The question drew a laugh from the two veterans and a reproachful frown from Stave.

"These don't grow on trees, young man." He slotted another shell into the blaster. "One shot is all you get. Just like in the Outside."

Chapter Ten

The crowd that gathered atop the wall to see them off was large, but muted. Stave had them out of bed and geared up well before dawn. After the firing range, they had spent the day under intensive instruction from him and the pair of veterans. The information was copious, and Layla knew she would be lucky to remember half of it. "Move in the day. Sleep at night. Don't be tempted to set off before it's fully light. Avoid cars: feeders nest in them. Never venture underground unless you absolutely have to, and always change the batteries in your flashlight before you do. Don't trust street signs or road signs. Alphas have been known to change them . . ."

In addition to the cautionary diatribe, there were lessons in the hand signals used by crossers when they needed to stay silent. There were only six, and Layla found them easy to memorise. Finger to the lips meant quiet. Raised fist meant stop. Splayed fingers meant feeders in sight. Raised thumb meant all clear. Wave meant run. Thumb across the neck meant kill.

Upon examining the pack she had been given back at the village, Layla found three one-litre flasks of water and four days' worth of ration packs, along with a filter mask and thick rubber gloves. The gloves felt overly large on her hands and she couldn't imagine wearing them to accomplish any task requiring even basic dexterity. There was also a steel box lined with cotton wool containing another five shells for her blaster, which was worn in a holster under the arm. Medical supplies consisted of a rolled bandage and a bottle of what Eylsa described as "Go Bads".

"Best not to ask what's in them," she said. "But they'll get you through that last mile to Harbour Point when all you'd rather do is lie down and die. Save them for when you need to *go bad*. Get it?" She punctuated this with a laugh. Of all the crossers Layla had met so far, Eylsa was by far the most upbeat. Her round, freckled face was rarely without a smile and she exhibited none of the cryptic cynicism common to the other veterans. Although her penchant for cheerful honesty could be unnerving at times.

"Just this?" Layla asked, holding up the rolled bandage. "No splints or stitching kits?"

Eylsa laughed again. "You get a cut needs stitching out there, girl, feeders'll be on you before you even get a needle to it."

"Then what happens if we get wounded?" Luce

asked. Her usual demeanour had dimmed considerably this morning, her eyes sunken as a result of lack of sleep. Last night, Layla had been woken by the sound of weeping. It was soft and controlled, but just loud enough to invade her brain and pull her from sleep. Blinking, she made out Luce's slender form in the gloom, sitting on her bed, knees drawn up so she could rest her head on them. Layla didn't ask her what was wrong, it being so obvious. All their recent lessons had left no illusions what awaited them in the Outside. Luce was weeping for herself.

Some of the faint light from the window must have caught a gleam on Layla's opened eyes, making Luce straighten up. "Just tension." She sniffed, hands wiping at her eyes. She forced a laugh. "Pre-match nerves, they used to call it." She forced a laugh. Feeling a tug towards conversation she didn't want to engage in, Layla turned away and went back to sleep.

A grin lingered on Eylsa's lips as she shrugged in response to Luce's question. "What d'you think happens? Right, kiddos." She clapped her hands together and reached for her own pack. "Wall's a-waiting. Don't wanna disappoint the audience now, do we?"

Of them all, only Stave carried a rifle. It was an extensively taped-up and battered-looking AK-74 with an eight-inch suppressor attached to the muzzle and two spare magazines. Eylsa had a small semi-automatic pistol at her hip and Romer a stainless steel revolver under his arm. Layla and the other novices had been given a short demonstration of how to use each weapon, but no opportunity to fire them.

"Ammo's too precious," Romer explained. A stocky man of blunt features, he was the oldest crosser she had encountered. Although he exhibited little of Eylsa's humour, Layla was grateful for his gruff but straight-forward approach to questions. He opened the cylinder of his revolver and extracted a bullet, holding it up for her to see. It had a hollow point filled with what appeared to be melted wax. "Steel slug filled with liquid mercury," Romer said. "Hard to come by, and the propellant is a bitch to manufacture. The Cons are doing well if they can put out a hundred useable rounds a year."

Before leaving the village, Layla had taped Nehna's gifted knife to her ankle, concealing it beneath the leg of her overalls. She had also added her lock picks to her pack. They didn't weigh much and she found their presence reassuring, albeit tinged with regret over her last words to Dresh. It was strange to consider that the most precious cargo they carried was also the lightest. Each of them had been given ten small packets of waxed paper weighing a couple of ounces. They were labelled in neatly inscribed ink. Layla's consisted of two marked "Garlic", three "Radish" and five "Rapeseed".

"Seeds," Eylsa said, consigning her own supply to her pack. "That's the only valuable commodity this shit-hole city produces any more. That and ammo, of course, but that's far too scarce to trade. Remember, you only get half the packets for yourself. The rest you give to Stave when we reach Harbour Point. My advice, choose the rapeseed. Other settlements grow it for fuel."

Neither Dresh nor any of the other crossers had been there to see them off that morning. Apparently, it was custom not to.

"When you go out, you're considered dead until you come back," Eylsa said as they set off for the wall. "Apparently they used to make an occasion of it in the early days, lotta backslapping and well-wishing. I guess it got old pretty quick."

Casting a glance at the village, Layla searched the windows for some sign Dresh might be watching. He wasn't, or was too well hidden to see. She suspected the former. *Didn't know they were going to put us in different teams*, she thought, suffering a sharp pang of regret at the hurt she had seen on Dresh's face when they'd last spoken. She had told her sole remaining childhood friend she would let him die in order to save Strang. No wonder he wasn't there to see her off.

Upon arriving at the wall, it transpired that Mayor Flak had come to see them off. "Oh fuck," Eylsa muttered with a weary roll of her eyes as they ascended the stairs to the parapet. It was the only overt expression of negativity Layla had seen from her. "He's gonna make a speech, isn't he?"

The Mayor was quick to fulfil her prediction,

although his oratory was mercifully brief. "Here we stand at the dawn of a new day." He stood atop the guardhouse, microphone in hand and amplified voice echoing across the crowd. "Our hopes rise with the sun, bright with trust in these six people, the finest our city has to offer." Flak extended a hand to the team lined up along the edge of the parapet. "Carry with you our gratitude and our love, for you risk all so that we may live."

He put a fair amount of gusto into the last few words, hoping, no doubt, to rouse a cheer from the onlookers. Their response was certainly loud, but directed entirely at the crossers. Stave's name was the most shouted, although Romer and Eylsa got some adulation too. As the crushers stepped forward to cast the ropes over the wall, Layla straightened in amazement at hearing her own name. Turning, she saw them in the front row: Cuhla, staring with tears streaming down her face, Dresh, with tired eyes and a forced smile, and Taxo, both arms raised in a frantic wave. Dresh and Cuhla must have carried him up the stairs. She wanted to shout back, ask who was watching Strang. But she couldn't push words past the sudden tightness in her throat, not that they could have heard her above the crowd's baying.

Next to her, Luce let out a laughing sob as she waved at a group of green-capped Agris. Romer and Eylsa responded to those calling their names with affable nods, while Stave stood in inexpressive silence, ignoring the many waving the chits they bet on him. Pitt, it seemed, had neither friends nor family in the crowd and endured it all with his head bowed, tendons standing out in his tensed jaw.

The crowd fell to an abrupt silence when Stave held up a hand. "Time to go," he told the team before casting an enquiring glance at the crushers atop the guardhouse. When the woman with the long scope rifle raised a thumb, he stooped to take up his rope.

"We run as soon as we hit the ground," he said, hopping up onto the balustrade, the rope drawing tight as he leaned out. "No stopping until we're out of sight."

Layla resisted the temptation to indulge in a final look at her family, fearful it might provoke a last second bout of cowardice. *Amoxicillin. Clarithromycin. Doxycycline.* She joined Stave and the others atop the balustrade, the rope tight about her hands and looped around her upper thighs. Tutelage in this part of the Crossing had been sparse, Romer showing the novices the basics of descending the wall with a terse: "Most important thing: don't fall."

She started down the instant Stave did, clumsy and untidy compared to him. Yet, despite her collisions with the wall and some painful rope scrapes to her palms, it seemed to take no more than thirty seconds for her feet to touch the ground. True to his word, Stave set off at a steady run towards the Old City the moment they were all down.

"Don't look back," Eylsa said, running at her side

as the crowd's cheers faded behind them. "It's bad for the brain. When you're out, you're out. All that matters is the Crossing."

They slowed to a walk upon entering the sprawl of ruined tenements. Having viewed this most evident remnant of the Peace since childhood, actually being among it felt strange, like walking into one of the pictures in Strang's books. She quickly recognised the surrounding structures as little more than shells, hollowed out and degraded to the point that it was a wonder any remained standing. Vanished walls revealed rooms and stairwells where ancient pipes leaked grey water onto rotted furniture. Birds roosted and wheeled around the roofs and upper floors, letting out loud alarm calls at the sight of humans. They were the only source of sound beyond the occasional clatter or hiss of collapsing concrete.

Scaling a mound of rubble, Layla's gaze caught something under a bed in one of the lower-floor rooms. The mattress had sunken into mouldy fabric and rusted springs, but still retained enough substance to cast a shadow over the skull that grinned at her from the gloom. Pausing to return the stare of those empty eye sockets, she wondered if they had preferred to remain there under that bed, starving, rather than come out and face the world remade.

Although the veterans had clearly been here before, Layla noticed that they traversed the tenements with a vigilant caution, lacking any impression of bored routine. They skirted every wrecked car by a wide margin and kept to the centre of the thoroughfares, eyes flicking from one shadowed doorway to another. They also maintain a rigid silence, communicating only with exchanged glances and infrequent hand signals. When Luce made the mistake of voicing an "Aww" at the sight of a discarded doll lying beneath a set of playground swings, she instantly suffered a hard jab to the shoulder from Eylsa.

"Shut the fuck up!" the veteran whispered into Luce's ear, speaking with precise vehemence. For once, she wasn't smiling.

It took about an hour to clear the tenements, Stave leading them across a stretch of tall grass towards what Layla recognised as a collapsed road junction. The disordered mass of tumbled concrete and tarmac covered a wide area, an uninviting landscape rich in shadowed fissures and hollows. Raising her gaze from the mess, Layla saw a domed building rising through the haze about a mile away. It was the tallest and most impressive structure they had seen so far, making her wonder about its purpose. But, watching Stave hold up a fist to bring them to a halt, she knew it wasn't a good time to ask.

Stave beckoned to Romer and Eylsa, the three of them sinking into a crouched huddle. "Had to fall sometime," Eylsa said, voice low as she jerked her head at the collapsed junction.

"It's recent," Romer said. "Might not have attracted

any nesters yet. Skirting it means another day out here."

Layla watched Stave direct a long, appraising look at the junction. "We'll take a closer look," he decided. Pausing, he turned to the three novices and put a finger to his lips before starting forward.

Their pace slowed considerably as they approached the junction, Stave and the veterans moving with increased caution. Layla mimicked them, peering hard into every shadowed nook and rusted wreck. She wondered if it was significant that the birds were silent now. Their passage through the tenements had been marked by a continual alarmed cawing. Now there was nothing. Nor did she catch sight of any rats or other creatures among the rubble.

Feeders prey on anything that bleeds, Eylsa had told them back at the village. *If they can catch it. My first trip, there were still a few feral dogs and cats around, rats too. These days, not so much.*

The Outside belongs to them, Layla reminded herself in a silent whisper. She resisted the urge to draw the blaster. Stave kept his rifle pointed down while neither Romer nor Eylsa had drawn their handguns.

Stave came to a halt again at the base of a supporting pillar. It was similar in form to the one she had discovered in the Undercut, but far larger, ascending to eighty feet or more. The rectangular slab forked halfway up its length, two mighty fingers reaching up to buttress a vanished stretch of road. Like the one in the Undercut, its base was covered in a melange of painted symbols, but far more dense and confusing. The garish shapes and scrawls overlapped each other to create an indecipherable mural, apart from a proclamation emblazoned in fuzzy red letters: FEEDER FREE ZONE. Hearing Eylsa smother a laugh, Layla sensed a ritual in the sound. The red letters represented a bad joke made funnier by repeated visits.

Stave had crouched beside what appeared to be a six-foot-long patch of scorched tarmac. Looking closer, Layla made out blackened bones among the charring.

"One less to worry about," Romer murmured, sparing the patch a glance before resuming his tense vigil of their surroundings.

"That was one of them?" Luce blurted. She spoke in a rapid whisper, but still drew an admonishing glare from Eylsa. Stave, however, showed no annoyance as he poked a toe to the largest piece of blackened bone.

"Gamma, I'd guess. Taken down by a blaster shell."

"Another over there," Eylsa said, pointing to a black stain beyond the pillar. It sat close to a deep shadow cast by a mass of tumbled road slabs. They had come to rest in a vaguely pyramidal arrangement, creating a narrow tunnel.

"Chalk them up to Slatt's team," Romer concluded. "Guess they must've found the junction fallen on the way back." He nodded to the accidental tunnel. "Decided to come through there rather than skirt it."

"Why the fuck would they do that?" Eylsa squinted in puzzlement. "Slatt knew better."

"Cloud was thick that day. Could be they had no choice. Low on water, maybe? Getting chased?"

"OK," Stave said, voice firm to forestall further discussion. "Route change."

"Railyards?" Eylsa suggested.

He shook his head. "Too long. Airport."

Layla saw the other two veterans exchange glances, reading mutual concern on their faces. Yet they said nothing when Stave resumed walking, turning left and tracing a path through the rubble towards the distant edge of the junction.

At first, Layla wondered why they couldn't just edge around the destruction and follow the road beyond. The explanation became obvious when they crested the rise to the left of the junction, affording her a view of their original route. The road itself was mostly clear of obstructions, albeit cracked and pitted at every yard. But to either side lay a veritable jungle of dense vegetation. Reaching the road would require cutting their way through it. *Feeders love wild places more than they love ruins*, Eylsa had cautioned back in the village. *Some claim that's because they were bred for the forest. But who knows? Either way, if you've got a choice between streets or trees, always take the streets.*

Stave led them along a narrow side road leading away from the junction. They kept to the centre line, moving in single file, eyes always tracking the overgrown build-ings to either side. Layla understood this to be a place in the process of being re-conquered by nature. Tree branches jutted through windows and masses of roots displaced foundations amid an abundance of bushes and saplings. Birds continued to screech from above, but once again she glimpsed no sign of any other form of life, save the occasional cloud of bugs.

With the trek wearing on past noon without any stops for rest, Layla found it hard to remain vigilant. Occasional relief from the monotony was provided by spectacular examples of destroyed infrastructure, like the pine tree that had grown tall through the centre of an apartment block. Its conical crest jutted from the roof, branches poking from every window. She also saw some remnants of the Feeding, the rusted hulks of tanks and military trucks slumped in green shrouds of vegetation.

To her surprise, Stave called another halt well short of evening, pointing to a two-storey building set apart from the overgrown mass fringing the road. Alongside it, a large sign with some kind of red and white logo rested atop a pillar, and the blackened remains of a tracked vehicle sat in its forecourt alongside a row of fuel pumps. Layla recognised these from infrequent visits to Con districts when she decided to try her luck trading scavenge beyond Velna's reach. They were always guarded, and the amount dispensed strictly controlled.

"You three wait here," Stave told the novices before nodding to Romer and Eylsa. This time they all readied their weapons before moving off, Stave jacking a round into the rifle's breach while the two veterans drew their pistols. They approached the building in a tight group, Stave in the lead and the others watching the flanks and rear. Rounding a corner, they disappeared from view.

"They didn't tell us to do that," Luce said.

Turning, Layla saw Pitt drawing his blaster. "So what?" he replied, scanning the overlooking buildings, eyes bright and unblinking.

You shouldn't be here, Layla decided. It was clear in the sweat on his forehead and upper lip, beading despite the slight chill to the air. Catching her studious glance, he rounded on her. "Fuck you looking at?"

Layla flicked her eyes upward at the empty windows of the building to his rear. "Something moving in there."

Whirling, Pitt gripped his blaster in both hands, fanning it across the face of the building. His hands shook so much it would be a miracle if he hit anything.

"My mistake," Layla said. "Must've been the wind."

The murderous glare he turned on her made her acutely aware of the gun he held. Scared shitless he might be, but he was still a ganged-up Riverbanker who had almost certainly taken at least one life in his time. *No*, Layla admonished herself, pushing her fear away and returning Pitt's glare in full. *Just another dog in need of putting down.*

"They're back," Luce said. Layla broke the stare to see Romer beckoning to them from the building.

"Put that away," he hissed at Pitt as they hurried to his side. The Riverbanker, abruptly drained of defiance, re-holstered his blaster and Romer led them around the front of the building. Its once broad windows were boarded up, the wood gouged with claw marks and the surrounding brickwork pocked by bullet impacts. Glancing at the charred hulk of military hardware on the forecourt, Layla saw another skull beneath its mass. It was scorched black, but she recognised it thanks to the gold teeth shining along the jawline. Another hider, this one preferring to burn than face the Feeding.

"Layla." Turning, she found Romer gesturing to a rope ladder dangling from one of the building's upper windows. "You first."

The ladder was a rudimentary contrivance of wooden pegs wedged into knots that creaked in protest as she scaled it. Reaching the window, she hauled herself into a room so dark she had to blink several times to make out Eylsa and Stave. They were both crouched at a small pile of flasks and jars in the far corner. Looking around, she saw that the other windows, and the walls, were covered in some kind of rough material. The only seating was a stool positioned alongside the front-facing wall.

Hearing Luce huff her way to the top of the ladder, Layla turned and helped her through. Apparently unable to forgo a question, she immediately asked, "What is this?" Fortunately, this time she kept her voice low and drew no punishment from Eylsa.

"Safe house," she said. Rising from the pile, she tossed each of them a jar. "Apple and peach preserve. Enjoy."

"There's still plenty of daylight left," Layla said.

"Not to reach the airport, there isn't. Be dark before we got there. Sit, eat, sleep, and be glad you can."

After Pitt and Romer joined them, the veteran dragged up the rope ladder and hefted a large rectangular panel into the window frame. Taking a closer look at the material covering it, Layla found it to be soft to the touch and formed of small pyramid-shaped protrusions.

"Soundproofing," Romer explained. "Rare stuff these days. The Techs haven't come up with a decent substitute yet. It works well enough, but it's still best if you keep your voice down. Feeder ears are a lot keener than ours." He moved towards the piled goods in the corner. "Any crackers?"

"Not many," Eylsa said, chewing on a pickle. "Slatt's lot must've been awful hungry."

With her eyes fully adjusted to the gloom, Layla saw that she was sitting on a quilted bedroll. Spying several more lying about the place, she claimed one and sat down to shrug off her pack. The strain of the day immediately began to tell in the ache across the top of her shoulders. Her legs and back didn't feel too bad, though.

"First watch at ten p.m.," Stave said, checking his wristwatch. "Two-hour shifts. Eylsa first, then Pitt, Luce, Romer, Layla and me." Producing something from his pack, he tossed it to Eylsa. "Standard rules. Don't be shy about waking us, even if you're unsure." Layla guessed this was for the benefit of the novices.

"What's that?" she asked, nodding to the object in Eylsa's hands. It resembled an old pair of binoculars Taxo owned, but with smaller lenses and a mask-like attachment covering the eyepieces.

"Night-vision goggles," Eylsa said. "One of only two pairs left. I'll show you young 'uns how to use them later. For now." She gestured to the jar in Layla's lap. "Eat. Never know when you'll get another chance out here."

It had been a while since Layla had tasted any fruit preserve. It turned up at the market from time to time, but the cost had become prohibitive these last few months. She ate it with the aid of some crackers Romer handed out, the first sweet and crunchy bite causing her to wolf down the rest. She had more questions, mainly about their route and what they might expect at the airport, but the abrupt quietude of the veterans silenced her. Stave sat cleaning his rifle while Eylsa and Romer had already settled onto their bedrolls, eyes closed. Of her fellow novices, Pitt was the most restive. Sitting with his back to the wall, he kept his gaze down, forearms atop his knees. Layla noted how his hands clenched repeatedly into fists, even though he clearly tried to stop it, face tensing in frustration every time it happened. By contrast, Luce had followed the veterans' example and turned onto her side, body relaxed in apparent slumber.

Settling down, Layla fully expected a lengthy period of restlessness. Yet, with her head rested on her pack and arm thrown across her eyes, the strain of her body overrode all distractions and sleep came quickly. Sadly, so did the dreams.

Chapter Eleven

*S*he stood in the doorway to the film library, frozen once again in the act of watching Strang cough blood into a bowl. For some reason, his lamp was off, leaving him a dim, heaving outline in the dark. Curiously, the blood in the bowl was bright, glowing a vibrant shade of crimson.

"Come here, Layla," Strang said. He spoke in his old voice, soft but assured, and lacking the grating rasp that had become the norm. "See what I made for you."

She didn't want to. She wanted to flee like she had before. Yet, at his word, she strode into the library, moving with a confident poise that seemed outrageously out of place. Her body felt strong, free of the aches and pains of a day spent in adrenalised exertion. Also, she found the gloom concealed nothing. Her eyes registered the shadows but pierced them with ease, the sight of the books and film posters stirring a warm familiarity. Any comfort aroused by this faded when her gaze fixed upon the bowl in Strang's hands. The shining blood swirling with a silky, inviting slowness.

"For you," he said, holding it out to her. "Drink, daughter. Are you not thirsty?"

The scent of it invaded her nostrils, reaching deep to inflame a savage hunger. It hurt, but there was a joy to that pain, an exhilaration that came from surrendering to something primal. Yet, instead of lowering her face to the bowl and drinking, she let out a snarl, casting it aside and lunging forward to sink her many teeth into the soft flesh of Strang's neck . . .

She managed to cage the shout before it escaped her lips, clamping a hand over her mouth as she jerked upright. Hunched on the bedroll, she kept her hands in place, dragging air through her nostrils. Sweat stuck her shirt to her skin, summoning a shameful reminder of the judgemental taunts she had cast at Pitt. *Maybe he's not the only one who shouldn't be out here.*

"Bad dreams, huh?"

Her eyes snapped to Romer. He sat on the stool, the night-vision goggles perched on his head. To his front she saw that a small circular patch of the sound-proofing material had been removed to afford a view through the covered window. "They happen out here," Romer added, voice scarcely above a whisper. "More than seems natural, I always think."

Layla dropped her hands from her mouth and swallowed, finding her throat scratchy and dry. "Is it my shift yet?" she whispered back, reaching for her water flask.

"Nah. You got a half-hour or so." He paused, glancing at the viewport. "Wanna see something?"

Layla nodded, gulping water before moving to his side. He passed her the goggles, getting them to fit after some fumbling. They had been made for heads bigger than hers.

"It's a little confusing at first," he cautioned. "Just keep blinking until the image settles."

He clicked a switch and a green light flooded her eyes. Some rapid blinking revealed the hazy circle of the viewport and the garage forecourt beyond.

"Look past the APC," Romer said. "Just beyond that tree."

It took her a few seconds to find it: a bright shape, low to the ground, partially obscured by the trunk of a pine that had sprouted from the cracked road. The shape's edges were rendered fuzzy by the goggles, but she gained a definite impression of a living thing. It was mostly still, but she could detect the slow rise and fall of its breathing.

"Is that . . . ?"

"A gamma. Yeah. Looks like he's got the scent of something. A rat, probably. There's still a good many about, even though we can't see them."

The shape moved then, just a small jerk of its bright body. As it did, its head came fully into view. It appeared to be hairless, like the rest of it, but she found a disconcerting humanity in the features. The nose was stunted and the lips made prominent by the many teeth crowding its mouth. But the way its brows furrowed, and the glitter of its receded eyes, conveyed the impression of a being engaged in thought rather than pure instinct.

"Any chance he's smelled us?" she asked. "Heard us?"

"Nah. He'd be sniffing around the building already if he had."

She started as the image blurred and the gamma disappeared. She thought at first the goggles had malfunctioned, but the tree was still there. The feeder wasn't.

"It's gone," she said, removing the goggles.

"Hold on to them," he said. "There's a good chance he'll circle back around. Best to save the battery in the meantime." His stubby finger flicked a switch on the side of the device and the green glow faded from the eyepieces. "Check every fifteen minutes. No more than thirty seconds at a time. You see nothing, shut it down."

He stood, gesturing for her to take the stool. "Shit," he groaned, rubbing at the base of his spine. "This isn't getting any easier."

"How many crossings for you?"

He didn't have to think about it. Every crosser knew their number. "Eighteen, including this one. Only Stave and Nehna have done more. Not that I'm jealous. Told 'em before we set off that this is my last. I'm just too fucking old now. Most of us are, though we don't like to admit it. That's why we need young-sters like you."

"What made you start?"

"Same reason you did, I'd guess: had people that

needed things. Not actual family: they all went during the Feeding. But people I met along the way. It's how it was back then. Old families died and new ones got born from the chaos. It's why so many don't bother with a second name any more, I guess. It's not easy watching people who saved your life get sick and suffer. After the first few trips, though, I knew I wasn't really doing it for them any more. There's something about the Outside that hooks you. The Redoubt is a place surrounded by a wall that folks can't leave. Back in the Peace, they called that a prison. Not so many walls out here, you may have noticed. Out here . . ." He trailed off into a shrug. "At least you get to remember what it was like to live. Really live, I mean, not just exist. Back in the city, who gives a shit what you do? But out here, everything you do matters. If my old bones hadn't decided to screw me over, I'd probably never quit."

Layla peered through the viewport, seeing only anonymous shadows. "Have you ever had a crossing where you didn't lose anybody?"

His answer was spoken through pursed lips, a reflective arch to his brows. "Not yet. Usually, we'd expect to lose one or two per trip. Since Stave came back alone, though . . ." The words faded, and she watched him clench his jaw against more.

Sighing, Romer gave his back a final rub and moved to his bedroll. "No sense pondering shit like this. You go out and you come back, or you don't. And there's no way to predict who's gonna make it, so I hope you didn't piss any chits away betting on yourself." He settled down, turning onto his side with a soft mutter. "Remember what I said about saving the battery."

They moved on when it was fully light and long shadows had receded from the road. Stave set a punishing pace, insisting they run for the first hour, following the road until it left the buildings behind and curved into a broad swathe of grassland. The tarmac here was so cracked and eroded by vegetation that their route soon became a mere track through increasingly tall grass. Stave finally called a halt when it was no longer possible to discern the course of the road.

"Ten minutes," he told them, raising a flask to his lips. "Hydrate. You'll need it."

The absence of a whisper in his tone indicated he saw no threat in their surroundings. Eyeing the mass of tall, swaying stems obscuring the horizon, Layla wasn't so sure. It seemed thick enough to hide all manner of threats, and the way it hissed constantly in the wind was unsettling.

"Relax," Eylsa said, reading her mood. "Feeders like trees, but they don't like grass, no matter how tall. They stay away from places like this, even at night. No one's sure why. Something about the sound, maybe. Or—" she adjusted her pack, wincing in reluctance "—because it's such a bastard to move through."

"Single file," Stave said when the ten minutes were up. "I'm on point. Romer on drag. Stay in sight of each other at all times. Only run if I run."

Despite Eylsa's reassurance, Layla's nervousness increased as they commenced their trudge. In addition to the constant sibilance of colliding stems, she heard a frequent skittering of unseen creatures. "Rats and cats," Eylsa said. "Mostly rats. Used to be a few bunnies too, but you don't tend to see them out here any more."

The sojourn was mercifully brief, their progress slowing when a tall, pyramidal spire appeared above the swaying grass. The structure below came fully into view soon after, a dilapidated wooden building with a steep sloping roof and arched windows. It was liberally daubed with markings, black, red and white, all depicting the same thing.

"Crosses," Pitt said. "Icon . . . stuff."

"Yeah, early in the Feeding a lotta people gathered in places of worship," Romer said. "Mosques, synagogues, temples, you name it. Christian types painted crosses on the outside, thinking it would keep the evil out. They were wrong."

The church sat on a small rise, the surrounding earth a pale shade of brown, lacking vegetation. Unlike the garage, the windows were un-boarded and doors vanished, revealing a gloomy interior.

"How come nothing grows around it?" Luce wondered, scuffing a toe to the dry earth.

"They'd often ring the place with salt." Romer

grunted a hollow laugh. "Another superstition that didn't save them. Guess these holy rollers used more than most. I'd bet they hung garlic on all the doors and windows too. Silly bastards."

Venturing closer to the empty doorway, Layla made out what she initially took for some kind of bonfire. The pews had been dragged aside to make room for a conical assemblage of sticks shoved together in a tight mass. Perhaps the people cowering here had built it as a last resort, preferring death by burning to slaughter by feeder. But, moving closer, the nature of this thing became obvious when she saw the skulls littering the base of the pile. The roof had collapsed in places, allowing the elements to rot away the clothing, but the various trinkets these people had worn in life remained, watches, rings and jewellery forming a glittering carpet for the dead.

"It's a thing they do."

She jumped a little at the sound of Eylsa's voice. She stood at Layla's shoulder, squinting at the stack of bones with accustomed disdain. Layla couldn't tell if it arose from judgement of the feeders or their victims.

"Alphas, I mean," she went on. "Stack them up like this when they make a mass kill. Some think they're marking territory. I think they're just celebrating an achievement."

"Alphas did all this?" Layla asked.

"It's possible there was only one. Though they've been known to team up from time to time."

Scanning the bones, Layla found it incredible that one being could wreak so much carnage. "Have you ever seen one? An alpha?"

"Only from a distance, and that was as close as I ever want to get. Come on, girl." She jostled Layla's shoulder. "Airport's waiting."

Mercifully, once past the church, the grass grew a good deal shorter, allowing for rapid passage. Less welcome was the fact that it afforded Stave an opportunity to make them run again.

"Selection's starting to make more sense now," Luce panted at Layla's side. "Hope I don't piss myself."

By late afternoon, the grass gave way to a wide expanse of slabbed concrete. Weeds sprouted thick from the joins, creating a green grid a half-mile wide. Stave called another halt when they came to a line of posts. Beyond lay a sweep of cracked tarmac that stretched into the distance to either side. On the far side of the expanse rose a cluster of long, two- and three-storey buildings with an octagonal tower rising from its centre. Wrecks of a type Layla hadn't seen before dotted the swathe of tarmac like rust-coloured islands in a grey sea. Despite their unfamiliarity, she knew what they were. Strang's encyclopaedias were rich in aircraft illustrations and she also retained childhood memories of great metal birds leaving white scars across the sky.

"People really used to fly in those, huh?" Luce said, her expression both doubtful and fascinated.

"By the millions," Romer said. "All over the world, every day."

"What for?" Pitt asked.

"Same reason as us. Because they needed to get somewhere. They just went further and faster."

"No movement," Stave said, scanning the buildings with a small pair of binoculars. Lowering them, he turned to address the novices: "The safe house is on the roof of the main terminal. Ropes are hidden in a vent marked with blue paint."

Layla understood these instructions were imparted in case the veterans didn't make it. *Just how dangerous is this place?*

Stave led them across the runway at a rapid walk. Once again, he had chambered a round into the rifle and moved with the stock at his shoulder, tracking the weapon in concert with his gaze. With the sky beginning to dim, the runway felt vast, engendering an acute sense of vulnerability. Although they would see any threat coming, she had been left in no doubt how fast a feeder could move.

Nearing the terminal, they had to navigate a channel between two wrecked planes. The one to the right had been a passenger jet much like the others littering the runway, but the one to the left had a military look. Its wings had collapsed, borne down by the weight of four propeller engines. A ramp extended from its rear, providing access to the dark maw of its innards. Layla expended a short moment of fascination in the various markings on its fuselage, allowing her eyes to linger only briefly on the darkened interior. Honed scavenging instincts told her there would be plenty of valuable tech to harvest inside, assuming previous crosser parties hadn't already picked it clean. Given the pace Stave had set, she thought it unlikely. In there would be all manner of wires and circuits sure to earn a serious bounty from Velna and delight Taxo. As she tore her tempted gaze away, she froze in shock at seeing Stave halted directly to her front. He had the rifle raised and aimed at her head.

"Down!" he snapped, his finger already squeezing the trigger.

He fired before she completed her crouch, Layla feeling the rush of the bullets passing overhead, ears thrumming with the hissing snap of gasses escaping the suppressor. Two shots followed by the sound of a body colliding with metal, and something that resembled the whine of an injured dog, albeit coloured by an unmistakably human note.

Realising she had huddled into a tight ball, hands clamped to her head, she rose and spun, hand reaching for her blaster. A long pale shape lay at the base of the military plane's ramp. An arm, longer than it should be, extended to the edge of the shadow cast by the tailplane. Layla stared at the barbs protruding from the clawed fingers, estimating that it had been less than a foot from her when Stave fired. As she stared, they twitched, causing her to take a backward step and reminding her that she still hadn't successfully drawn her blaster.

Stave's bullets had torn through the feeder's body, two holes leaking dark fluid over the sinew and bone of its back. As Layla started to wonder how a being so reduced in muscle mass could move so fast, the feeder convulsed. The sharp ridges of its spine threatened to burst through the pallid skin as it folded in on itself, mouth opening to emit a torrent that was too dark and viscous to be blood. After that, it exhibited no further signs of life, but the body began to shrink, Layla hearing the dull crack of collapsing bone.

The mercury in the bullets, she remembered. *Just one pinch is enough.*

"Gamma," Stave said, head angled as he studied the feeder. "Pretty thin looking. Probably been dormant for a while. Explains why it attacked with the sun still up."

A sound came from the plane then, a faint clatter in the black shadow of its belly. It may have been a piece of dislodged wreckage, or another feeder. Either way, it was enough to make Pitt raise his blaster.

"Don't!" Romer grunted, lunging to push the

Riverbanker's arm down, but he was too quick on the trigger.

The shot echoed across the runway and the terminal buildings, taking a long time to fade. Layla saw flames begin to blossom in the plane's innards, Stave and the other veterans aiming their weapons in expectation of another feeder fleeing the fire. When thirty seconds went by and none appeared, Eylsa rounded on Pitt.

"Great work, genius!" Given the murderous glint in her eye, Layla fully expected her to shoot him. "You're a real fucking asset!"

"Wasting time," Stave cut in, voice hard with authority. He matched stares with Eylsa until, curling her lip in disgust, she backed away from Pitt.

"Might've got lucky," Romer said. They all turned to scan the terminal building. Layla's eyes roved the cracked and broken glass facade, seeing nothing of interest until she caught a vague shift in one of the reflections. It was soon followed by more. She couldn't discern any clear shapes, but gained an impression of many bodies moving rapidly on the other side of the glass.

"Then again," Romer sighed.

"Forget the roof," Stave said. "They'll be on us before we're halfway up. Cargo terminal."

"The tunnel?" Romer's face bunched in doubt. "No one's been near it in years."

"No choice." Stave tensed to run, but paused before

setting off, turning to fix Layla with a hard stare. "Pay more attention to your surroundings," he said before shifting his ire to Pitt. "Fire that thing again without reason, I'll take it and you can walk home alone. Now let's go."

Chapter Twelve

"Who the fuck put that there?" Romer spoke mostly in anger, but his voice held a worryingly shrill note. The object of his ire was the padlock on the metal door Stave had led them to. Set into a wall on the exterior of the cargo terminal, it had been concealed behind some artfully arranged wreckage. The door had a keypad lock of its own that Stave opened with a rapid, five-digit stab of his fingers. The padlock and the chain it was attached to, however, were evidently a new addition.

"Someone who wanted to mark their territory," Stave said, pointing to the symbol on the door, spray painted in red: an A within an inverted triangle.

"Can we shoot it off?" Luce asked.

Layla judged both chain and lock as too heavy to yield to a bullet, quickly confirmed by Stave after giving them a brief jangle. "We'd just be wasting ammo."

"We gotta get in there," Eylsa said. Her gaze flicked from the darkening sky to the now blazing plane wreck on the runway, leaking a thick column of black cloud into the fading blue of the sky. "Genius boy's fuck-up is gonna draw every feeder for miles."

"The roof," Romer said, fixing Stave with a hard, insistent glare. "There's no other option."

"They'd be on us before we got there . . ."

"I can open this," Layla said. Crouching at the lock, she removed her pack, undoing the straps to extract her pick kit. She felt Stave's eyes on her as she inserted a probe into the keyhole, surprised by the fact that her hands weren't shaking.

"How long?" he asked.

Layla worked the probe around the lock's interior, concealing a wince at the complexity she found. Despite its lack of rust, this was evidently a product of the Peace. "Few minutes," she said, not sure if she was lying.

"Stave—" Romer began, but Stave cut him off.

"Make it two," he told Layla. "Everyone else, eyes out and weapons ready."

Two minutes is impossible, Layla knew. Still, she said nothing and kept probing with her curiously steady hands, establishing the image of the lock's working in her mind. *Locks are simple things, really*, Strang told her once. *It's a lever encased in metal. To open it, you just have to find the right place to push.*

"Got movement to the right," Eylsa said. "Staying in the shadows, but I can see them."

"Type?" Stave demanded.

"All gammas, as far as I can tell. Counting three . . . make it five."

Standard arrangement, Layla decided with a sharp pang of relief. *Heavy mechanism, though.* Removing the probe, she plucked the two sturdiest picks from her kit and inserted them in the lock, one angled high, the other low. The instruments pressed into her palms as she exerted ever more pressure, grimacing with the effort.

"Movement left," Romer said, the words accompanied by the click of his revolver's hammer being drawn back. "More gammas. Counting six. Shadows are getting pretty long here, Stave."

"I'm aware."

Once again, Layla felt his eyes on her as she worked. She ignored him and altered the pitch of the lower pick a little, pressing hard enough for a trickle of blood to trace across her palm.

"Too long." Stave's hand descended to grasp her shoulder. "Leave it . . ."

The padlock's U-shaped shackle came free of its body with a loud snick, Layla quickly untangling it from the chain. "Got it," she said, a redundant statement since Romer and Stave were already scrambling to drag the door open.

"In!" Stave jerked his head at the revealed passage beyond. The absolute dark of it made Layla hesitate. *Stay in the light.*

"Move, girl!" A hard shove from Eylsa sent her sprawling into the shadow. "This is the only way in and feeders don't set locks."

She hauled Layla upright and pushed her again. After a few seconds of blind stumbling and colliding with rough walls, the veteran switched on her flashlight to illuminate the way ahead. The passage was a narrow channel of bare bricks with pipes and cables lining the ceiling. Layla's stomach plummeted at the sight of another door at the end of the corridor. Her dismay lessened when she saw that this door wasn't padlocked. It was also far heavier and thicker than the one outside, a solid mass of riveted steel with a keypad.

Eylsa punched in the numbers, the act rewarded by the sound of something heavy shifting within the door. Putting her shoulder to it, the veteran heaved, producing only a marginal shift in the barrier. Layla added her weight to the effort, quickly followed by Luce and Pitt. From the far end of the passage came the cacophony of many limbs pounding on metal. Romer and Stave had evidently locked the exterior door, but Layla had no idea how long it would last against such a weight of feeders.

Shouting, Eylsa redoubled her efforts and the steel door finally began to open, squealing on dry hinges. They burst into the room beyond in an untidy sprawl. Layla hissed at the sting of her cut palm scraping a concrete floor. Eylsa was first up, shouting into the passage now filled with the sound of pounding feet. "COME ON!"

Romer and Stave arrived in a welter of flickering flashlights, Layla and her fellow novices scrambling clear while the three veterans heaved the door closed. It sealed shut with a boom, followed by a loud clatter as Stave threw a lever to secure the hidden mechanism holding it in place. The pounding started instantly. It was muted into distant thunder, but Layla could hear the frenzied hunger in the rapid, overlapping thud of multiple limbs lashing at the door. Loud as it was, Layla was struck by the absence of any other sound. Feeders, it seemed, weren't especially vocal. Although the hammering failed to produce even a faint tremble to the door's steel body, she still found herself staring at it in dire expectation it might burst open any second.

"Don't fret," Eylsa said, helping Layla to her feet. "This was where they used to keep the valuable cargo. Nothing's getting through that without a thermal lance."

From the echo of her voice, Layla concluded this must be a sizeable space. Switching on her own flash-light, she played the beam over a row of wire-mesh cages. Some were empty, but others held pallets laden with boxes. Any hope that these might contain supplies was quickly dashed when Eylsa beckoned her closer, shining her flashlight at the opened box at the top of the stack.

"Pretty, isn't it?"

"Can't be," Layla muttered, squinting at the yellow gleam of the exposed metal. It was formed of close-packed bars, each one embossed with some kind of number.

"Oh, it's gold all right," Eylsa assured her. "Must be near a tonne of the stuff. Silver and platinum, too. My guess is some rich bastards got awful nervous in the latter days of the Feeding and starting moving their goodies around. Didn't help them much, obviously. Or us. No worth in stuff you can't eat or use any more. No matter how shiny." She shifted her flashlight to Layla's dripping palm. "That needs sorting." She pointed the beam to a nearby table and chairs. "Sit over there."

She duly sat while Eylsa used cotton wool and her bandage roll to tend the wound, ignoring Layla's protestations that it wasn't worth bothering over. "Anything that leaks blood leaves a scent for them to follow."

"No chance we're going out that way." Turning at the sound of Pitt's voice, she saw him standing close to the door. He spoke with a tense wariness, expectant of ridicule or criticism for his mistake. "I mean," he went on, "it'll be dark out there even when the sun comes up."

To Layla's surprise, any harsh reminders of his screw-up, or commands to shut his useless mouth, failed to materialise. Eylsa spared him a short, annoyed grimace before returning her focus to Layla's cut. Stave and Romer also had no opprobrium to offer. The immediacy of their forgiveness led Layla to conclude that bearing a grudge during a crossing was considered a dangerous indulgence.

"Every safe house has an escape hatch," Romer said. He pointed his flashlight beam into the deeper recesses of the vault, illuminating a ceiling vent.

"The door code is eight-four-nine-six-two," Eylsa said, tying the bandage tight about Layla's hand. "If you ever need it. We use it for every keypad lock out here, so it'll work on the exterior door. Though now the feeders have found this place, I doubt we'll ever come back here."

"They remember?"

Eylsa sighed a short laugh. "One thing you can't fault them for is memory. Once a safe house is blown, you can bet at least one will make a nest of it." Producing a small pair of scissors from her pack, she cut away the excess bandage. "All done. Check it tomorrow. Leave this on if it's not fully scabbed over."

"There's no stockpile here," Stave told them all. "So eat a ration pack. Then it's lights out and everyone gets some sleep. No watch tonight." His flashlight flicked towards the door. He didn't say anything else, but Layla knew the unsaid reason for not mounting a watch: *If they get through that, we're fucked anyway.*

The pounding on the door continued for hours. The others all managed to sleep, but Layla couldn't.

Although the vault lacked supplies, it retained some comforts, including a cushioned couch claimed by Luce after a round of rock, paper, scissors. There were also enough mats and sleeping bags for each of them. Yet, despite the warmth and the softness of the mat beneath her, Layla remained stubbornly awake. She knew it wasn't due to the feeders. *Come here, Layla. See what I made for you . . .*

"Finding it hard, huh?" Eylsa whispered. They had both bedded down as far from the door as possible, nestled between the rows of locked cages. Until now, Layla had thought her fully asleep.

"Had a . . . bad dream last night," she said. "Don't feel like watching a replay."

"Yeah. I get them too sometimes. We all do. Happens too often out here for it to just be down to stress. Heard some big brain in City Medical once say it might be due to atmospheric contamination. Something in the air, basically. What it is or where it comes from, who knows? My guess is the feeders give it off when they die. It wasn't enough for them to eat the whole world. They had to poison us too. But what do I know?" Layla heard her shift onto her side. "Don't worry about it. Adrenaline will keep you going. I never sleep much during a crossing, and this is my fifteenth."

"So, you've crossed with Stave before?"

"Ten times. We had a regular crew for a while. Me, him and a rat-faced little fucker called Ched.

There wasn't a hideout or a crawlspace Ched couldn't find. Saved our skin a bunch of times. Others we lost on the way, but the three of us always seemed to make it through. Till that last trip. I was slated to go, but twisted my ankle in training, so Rehsa went in my place. Only Stave came back. It's a measure of the man that he doesn't hate me for it. Rehsa . . . she was special."

"She drew something on the wall back in the village. Roses. She had talent."

"That she did. Smart too. Never met someone who'd read so much, and she seemed to remember it all. Could quote reams of Shakespeare at the drop of a hat. And the Bible, though she wasn't as fond."

"Do you know how it happened?"

"That's a question you don't ask. You go out, you come back, or you don't. Pondering the details isn't good for the brain."

"Sorry."

"Don't be. How would you know? We barely had time to teach you anything. When I passed Selection, they gave us two months of training. Two months. Can you believe it? After a while, as we lost more and more crossers, eight weeks became six, then four. Now we just drag you poor bastards out here and hope you can keep up."

She shifted again, falling quiet until Layla heard the soft rhythmic moan of her breaths as she slept. Her turn didn't come until the feeders finally stopped assailing the door. This time, she found Thorn waiting for her. He lay at the base of the wall, body broken and leaking blood the same wonderfully inviting shade of crimson. He begged as she advanced towards him, her movements slow as if to savour his fear. When Stave shook her awake, she had to hide her face in the folds of the sleeping bag to conceal her tears.

Chapter Thirteen

The vent was tight and took most of the morning to navigate. They had to push their packs ahead of them as they squeezed along the square metal channel. Repeated right and left turns brought them to a junction where a ladder ascended to a grate a dozen feet above. Eylsa went first, scaling the ladder, then drawing her pistol before slowly raising the grate.

"Clear," she reported after a quick look around.

They emerged into a wide space of vinyl floors, well lit by a long expanse of shattered windows. To one side sat rows of dusty seats beneath signs reading "Departure Gate" alongside a confusingly non-sequential set of numbers.

"Standard rules apply," Stave cautioned the novices when they had all climbed up. "Plenty of dark places in here and feeders are more active in daylight when they have a roof over their head. So stay vigilant."

As they moved through the terminal, Layla found it to be the least degraded structure so far encountered in the Outside, although there were patches of destruction. Wires dangled from the ceiling in places, bullet holes peppered the walls and floor in others, and their feet crunched shattered glass so often that Layla made a mental note to pick it out of her shoes when they next stopped. They passed a row of shops, including, she saw with bitter disappointment, a pharmacy with empty shelves. However, the jewellery store beside it remained well stocked with rings and necklaces, but no watches. What captured her attention most were the posters, particularly the people. They were everywhere, smiling out at her with gleaming white teeth and unblemished skin, hair luxuriously long or artfully short, bodies all honed to muscular or shapely perfection. Each one seemed filled with love for the things they held or wore, angelic beings raised to ecstasy by the treasures of a vanished world.

Once past the shops, they navigated a series of metal barriers and doorways before coming to a scene of familiar disarray. A field-sized expanse of floor spread out before them, every square yard of it littered with skeletal remains and luggage. Some bodies were intermingled with their possessions, as if they had died in the act of opening bags or suitcases. As they moved through the ugly mess of it all, Layla saw that many of the bodies retained a good deal of their clothing, the bones lacking the dark, weathered look that came from exposure to the elements. Neither she nor her fellow novices felt the need to ask what had happened here: a feeder pack had once enjoyed a feast.

They exited the terminal via a wide lobby before crossing through a maze of lateral roads marked with faded signs referring to buses and shuttles. Beyond lay a long straight road choked with the densest collection of wrecked vehicles Layla had seen yet.

"Running for the airport became kind of a ritual during the Feeding," Eylsa explained. "Even after every non-military plane in the world got grounded."

"Then why'd they do it?" Pitt asked.

"Panic and instinct, I guess. Airports always represented an escape during the Peace. You went there so you could fly away and escape your shitty life, even if it was only for a short while. Kinda makes sense you'd do the same when everything started falling apart."

Stave accelerated to a steady jog along the paved fringes of the massed wrecks. They soon veered away from the road, traversing more grassland, though this time it was thankfully of a more stunted variety. This proved to be the longest run yet, Stave allowing more rests than the previous day and keeping the pace manageable. Still, it hurt and, when he called a halt atop a bank overlooking a weirdly straight river, Layla sank to her knees and shrugged off her pack. Taking a deep breath, she noticed the smell pervading the surrounding air. It was too acrid for sewage, yet the nausea it birthed in her gut felt more acute.

"What's that stink?" Pitt asked, narrow features wrinkling at the acrid tinge to the air.

"The sweet fragrance of whatever shit they used to make in there," Romer said, nodding towards the other bank of the river. Following his gaze, Layla made out the narrow tubular towers and broad-domed cylinders of a chemical plant. Looking down at the river, she saw the uninviting rainbow-hued slick of something unpleasant scumming the sluggish water.

"You should be grateful for it," Romer went on. "The feeders hate it more than we do and won't go near the place."

"Take in a good amount of water," Stave said, kneeling to extract his flask from his pack, along with some other items. "Then put on your gloves and masks. Once we're in there, don't touch anything unless you have to and wash your gloves clean as soon as you can."

"Sounds delightful," Luce muttered.

Following Romer and Eylsa's lead, Layla, Luce and Pitt donned their masks and tightened each other's straps before pulling on the gloves. Layla found her earlier misgivings over the loss of dexterity less palpable now. If anything, they seemed flimsy protection against such a toxic environment. It was at times like these that she regretted reading so much of Strang's library.

Before starting off again, Stave checked them over, making sure the masks were secure. His careful inspection made it plain to Layla that crossers had been lost here before, and not to feeders. He then led them along the bank of the unnaturally straight river until they came to a part-destroyed bridge. It was of iron construction; the central space had vanished but the remaining structure retained a walkway on its outer edge. Crossing was a precarious but fortunately brief experience performed two at a time, the old metal letting out squeals of protests with every step. Bad as the air was, the sting of it still detectable through her mask, Layla relished a plunge into the polluted waters even less.

The route into the plant itself consisted of a once tarmac-covered road that had dissolved into a rutted, broken track. They were obliged to skirt several deep pools of water that appeared more choked with unfriendly substances than the river. Stave held up his hand to signal a halt when they came to a large metal container partially obstructing the road. It was much the same as those used for housing in the Riverbank, but extensively rusted with some kind of machinery attached to its roof. However, it was plain that Stave's attention had been captured by the symbol painted in red on its corrugated side: an A within an inverted triangle. Unlike the identical motif back at the airport, this one was accompanied by words: "PROPERTY OF THE AVENGING REMNANT".

"Avenging Remnant?" Eylsa asked, voice muffled by her mask but still comprehensible.

"Never heard of them," Romer replied, his own voice rendered into a growl. "Must be new."

"And fucking desperate if they've decided to set up here."

"They live in these?" Pitt asked, touching a hand to the container, his question earning a short laugh from Romer.

"It's a feeder trap," he said, pointing to the machinery on the roof. It consisted of a wheel and pulleys attached to the door. Unlike other containers, the door was just one section of steel, hinged at the top rather than the sides. "Feeder comes along at night, wanders inside, trips a plate in the floor, and the door comes down. They were used a lot in the Feeding, but there were never enough. And they only work with live bait."

He moved to the container, peering through a small hole in the rusted metal. After a short survey of the interior, he turned to Stave, face grim. "Fresh, and human."

"Then we proceed on the basis that they aren't friendly," Stave said, unslinging his rifle. "Weapons out. You too." He added to the novices. "Eyes on shadows and corners. I'm on point. Romer take drag. No talking unless you see something."

Following his steady, crouching progress through a gap in the wall, Layla found no reassurance in the feel of the blaster's grip in her hand. She worried about dropping it, or shooting at nothing like Pitt. The fact that Stave felt it necessary said a lot about the danger they faced here. *Human danger*, she concluded, recalling the symbol and Eylsa's words the morning they set off. *There's more than just feeders to worry about out there.*

Proceeding into the plant, she could feel the increased taint to the air, even through her mask. A good deal of the structure had collapsed, spilling whatever chemical foulness lurked the myriad pipes and tanks. Layla guessed years of rain had done a lot to dilute it, but plenty was sure to linger in the soil. Her acquired instinct for danger trilled a clear song of warning: *This is a very bad place.* Had she been here alone, the urge to run would have been irresistible, but still Stave kept to his unhurried, if tense, pace.

They heard the sound when they came to the long rusted snake of a fallen tower. It was distant but piercing, combining a hiss with a shriek rich in considerable pain. Stave held up a fist to halt them in place, crouching in the lee of the fallen tower until the sound faded. As it did so, Layla heard another noise: a faint but clearly human echo of multiple voices raised in laughter.

Eylsa shuffled closer to Stave, putting her head close to his to be heard through the mask. "Sounds like they caught one. Beta, judging by the pitch of the screams, maybe even an alpha. That's good. We scoot on by while they're entertained."

Layla saw a small twitch in Stave's eyes, the only sign of indecision she had seen in him. It was gone quickly, though, and probably missed by the others. "We need to know who this bunch are," he said. "And how many."

Eylsa's brows knitted in puzzlement. "This isn't a recon trip."

Stave's face hardened behind the mask, the unquestionable authority in his voice clear despite the obstruction. "This trip is what I say it is. Now let's go."

Their pace even slower now, they moved on, following the screams. Stave paused at the corner of every building as he traced a path deeper into the heart of the plant. Soon the screams reached a near-deafening pitch. It was as if each long, ugly shriek sank claws into Layla's head. Yet, the laughter that followed was worse.

Coming to a three-storey structure, blackened and hollowed out by fire, Stave darted his head through a gaping hole in the wall before leading them inside. Scouring the interior, Layla's gaze was drawn upwards by an ascending grid of overlapping steel girders. Peering at the upper reaches of the building, she saw it free of birds. Like the feeders, it seemed they wisely shunned this place.

The screams were so close now it was plain they were coming from beyond the mostly intact wall to their right. Gesturing for them to stay low, Stave crept towards a vacant window. It was broad enough for them to line out to either side as he came to a halt. He set his rifle down to reach into his pack, extracting a small circular wing mirror he must have scavenged from a wreck. Cautiously he raised the mirror to the lower edge of the window frame. Positioned at his side, Layla was afforded a clear view of what lay beyond.

Stave kept the mirror stable as he altered the angle, panning across a space between two buildings where a dozen people stood in a circle. They all wore long coats, each with a loose hood over their heads that covered the face down to the nose. A few wore goggles, but most viewed the spectacle before them through eye slits. The feeder at the centre of the circle had been secured in place by chains around its arms and legs, body stretched taut so that it was suspended above the ground. Still, it writhed and screamed. Eylsa's guess was proved correct in the overlong limbs and elongated head, baring a jagged array of teeth with every shriek whenever the long-coated figure at its side played a blowtorch over its skin. The pale flesh was blackened from its neck to its belly, emitting a steady cloud of smoke that made Layla grateful for her mask. This stench was surely worse than even the chemical miasma of this place.

The blowtorch wielder paused his torment, stepping back to raise the flaming instrument to his audience, who bayed with laughter. Layla heard a manic note to their amusement, noting the way their mouths gaped and teeth bared, almost as if they were sobbing.

"Witness this!" the man with the blowtorch called out. His voice was a ragged, grating wheeze Layla assumed to be the result of breathing the local air for an extended period. "Witness the only reward left to us in this world. Witness our vengeance!"

He continued to call out more invective as he lowered the blowtorch once again, but the words were smothered by the creature's screams. This time they were so loud, so piercing, Layla felt an irresistible compulsion to look away, fighting the rising tide of nausea. As she did so, she caught movement in one of the puddles littering the floor. Her gaze snapped upwards, fixing on a figure precariously balanced on a girder. He wore a long coat of stitched-together fabric and leather with a similarly fashioned hood on his head, given an insectile look thanks to the large round goggles concealing most of his face. He also had a crossbow at his shoulder, aimed directly at Stave.

She didn't hesitate or even think. The blaster's stock and barrel appeared in her eye line before she made a conscious decision to raise it. The flash and boom blinded and deafened her for an instant. When it cleared, she saw a smoking, bloody figure meeting the ground with a wet crunch.

Chapter Fourteen

Nothing happened for five seconds. Layla had time to take in the revealed face of the man she had shot, seeing the pus-leaking boils that covered much of it, and the reduced, blackened stubs of his teeth. Patches of ignited fabric littered his stitched-together coat, along with spattered blood. He didn't move. Not even a little.

The stillness was broken by the boom of Romer's revolver. Layla jerked her gaze from the corpse to see another man in a long coat collapse in a doorway, the crossbow he held discharging its bolt at the floor in a brief flurry of sparks. Luce fired next, another figure diving for cover behind a steel beam as the blaster shell peppered brick and concrete.

Rising from cover, Stave aimed his rifle through the window, firing one round into the head of the man with the blowtorch and another into the feeder. "Let's go!" he barked, running for a doorway at the far end of the building. Layla stumbled after him, her legs now seized by a treacherous numbness. She almost fell, but Eylsa caught her, grabbing one of her pack straps and dragging her along until she recovered her footing.

"Stay close!" she panted, head constantly swivelling about in concert with her pistol. They both ducked at the sound of another gunshot. Not one of theirs, but a flat boom from the right, raising dust and grit but inflicting no damage. Eylsa and Pitt both fired in unison, Layla glimpsing a hooded man with some kind of double-barrelled firearm slumping, bloody and smoking, into a pile of rusted metal.

They ran full pelt through a succession of ruined buildings, assailed on all sides by the echo of pounding feet and enraged shouting. Several times, Layla ducked at the whistle of crossbow bolts slicing the air. Luckily, from here on, the only gunshots she heard were their own. Stave's rifle coughed out another three rounds, and Romer's revolver boomed twice. She couldn't tell if they hit anything.

Exiting a structure that appeared to be mostly constructed of rusted pipes, they emerged onto a stretch of open ground, the centre of which featured a tall storage tank about thirty feet in height. Layla saw more figures running towards them beyond the tank, the tumult of shouts to their rear making it clear they were caught.

"There!" Stave called out, sprinting for the tank. Reaching the foot of a stairwell that snaked around the cylindrical structure, he crouched, rifle at his shoulder. "Go!" he commanded when Layla came to his side, jerking his head at the stairwell. Feeling no compulsion to argue, she started up. The metal stairs were even more degraded than the walkway at the bridge, shuddering violently as she climbed, closing her ears to the sharp squeal of ancient fittings under strain. Coming to a gap in the stairs, she paused, then ducked as something struck sparks from the side of the tank a few inches from her head. Looking down, she saw a dozen long-coated figures below, many bearing crossbows. Leaping across the gap, she clamped a hand to the stairwell's balustrade and hauled herself across. Turning, she offered a hand to Eylsa, who let out a snarl of refusal and gestured for her to keep moving.

A few more crossbow bolts chased her until she rounded the tank, scaling the last few yards to the domed summit. It was about fifteen feet across and edged by a two-foot high steel barrier. Crouching behind it, Layla risked a quick downward glance, glimpsing a burgeoning crowd of hooded people before a volley of projectiles forced her down.

She heard the sharp crack of Eylsa's pistol twice more before she appeared, quickly followed by Pitt and Luce. A cacophony of metallic thuds signalled a sustained barrage from their pursuers, the bolts careening off the surrounding barrier, some spinning in the air to land atop the tank. Layla stared at the top of the stairwell, hearing another salvo of suppressed shots from Stave's rifle, followed by a scream from below. Romer appeared first, grey-faced and crawling. Moving in a crouch, they hurried to drag him onto the curved roof, Layla seeing the bolt jutting from his upper thigh. His overalls were soaked in blood and his mask misted with rapid breaths.

"Lie still," Eylsa said, already unfurling a bandage. As she worked to loop the bandage around his thigh, Layla saw the bitter resignation in her eyes. *What do you think happens?*

Stave arrived, sprawling flat as missiles thrummed the air above his head. Turning on his back, he began to pound both feet against the bracket securing the stairwell to the tank's roof. It shuddered from his efforts but also from the weight of unseen bodies scaling it. Layla started forward to help, but Pitt beat her to it, both of them kicking at the bracket until it finally separated from the tank. The upper section of the stairs fell away, carrying a few of their pursuers with it, judging by the chorus of surprised yelps.

"Hope you break your necks, you fucks!" Pitt shouted, quickly jerking his back from the gap in the barrier when he was answered by a hail of bolts.

Stave crawled to Romer, Layla seeing him briefly close his eyes after he surveyed the damage. Whether it was guilt or annoyance, she couldn't tell.

"Pretty sure it missed the artery—" Eylsa began, falling silent when Romer cut her off with a harsh, agonised laugh.

"Small mercies, right? No way I'm walking out of here."

They continued to crouch, flinching from the bolts that occasionally spun into their midst after colliding with the tank's edge, until the barrage came to a sudden halt. Silence persisted for a few minutes until broken by a voice. It was female and, like the man with the blowtorch, rendered into an ugly rasp by exposure to the toxic atmosphere.

"You up there! Show yourselves!"

A pause as they all looked at Stave, receiving a firm shake of the head in response.

"Show yourselves!" the woman called again. This time Layla detected a manic shrillness to the sound, gaining the impression of a frayed self-control. "This is not your place!" she went on, Layla frowning at the accusatory, almost child-like peevishness she heard. "It's ours! We claimed it months ago! It's our . . . fortress. This is where we . . ." She trailed off, Layla gaining the impression of someone attempting to recall important information through a fog of confusion. "Where we fulfil our mission. Our mission of vengeance!" This was spoken with a sudden confidence, as if she had stumbled upon an important fact. She repeated it with increasing volume, the cry swiftly taken up by the unseen woman's companions. "Vengeance! Vengeance! Vengeance!"

"They're fucking mad," Eylsa observed.

"Constant exposure to this place can't be good for the brain," Stave agreed. He shuffled to the edge and poked his mirror above the barrier. "Counting over thirty. Too many to shoot. Too many to fight our way through." Moving to the opposite side end of the roof, he raised the mirror again, letting out a soft grunt of satisfaction.

"What?" Eylsa asked.

"Woodland. Only about twenty yards off."

"Still a long way to run with people shooting at you. Even if they are crazy. Still, it's likely to be clear of feeders this close to the plant." Layla found it notable that she didn't make any mention of the fact that Romer wouldn't be running anywhere anytime soon. Nor, for that matter, did Romer.

"We'd have to rope down in full view of those bastards," Pitt pointed out. "It's suicide."

Layla didn't see any fault in his reasoning, but Stave continued to stare into the mirror, brow creased in thought. Below, the raspy-voiced woman had begun to ramble.

"We're doing good work here, y'know! Saving the fucking world, actually. Not just grubbing around in the ruins like you lot. How many feeders have you killed? We've done a hundred of the fuckers!"

"Two hours till sunset," Stave mused, casting an appraising eye to the sky.

"No guarantee they'll leave just 'cause the sun goes down," Romer grunted. His face was slicked with sweat, tensing repeatedly against the pain. "Feeders won't come here even when it's dark."

"They caught one," Stave pointed out. "Which means there's a beta nest not far away." He shared a meaningful glance with the two veterans. "Those screams were awful loud."

"They'd still be cautious," Eylsa said. "There'd have to be something drawing them close."

"She's pretty loud," Luce said, jerking her head in the direction of the unseen woman.

"Yes." Stave settled his back against the barrier and flicked on the rifle's safety catch. "That she is. Get what rest you can. Nothing much is going to happen until it gets dark."

"You can join us, y'know! We're not ones for bearing grudges!"

The woman didn't let up for the next few hours, her rhetoric veering from threats to cajolery, then back again. She wasn't an especially gifted actor, and the threats sounded a good deal more sincere than the promises.

"Come on out so we can talk about it. Civilised, like. Maybe you've got stuff to trade. We do too."

"Oh, eat shit," Pitt muttered, blaster clutched in his lap. He had asked permission from Stave to try and shoot her, only to receive a silent frown of rebuke. Throughout it all, Romer got progressively worse. His skin shifted from grey to pale white, the bandage about his leg soaked through, although he refused to allow Eylsa to replace it.

"That's a waste. Save it."

Layla found the sight of him harder to bear than the woman's constant hectoring, although she noticed that it became less voluble as the sky grew darker. After another bout of unconvincing promises, she fell into a prolonged silence, prompting Stave to once again raise his mirror above the barrier.

"They're starting to drift off," he said. "Some look nervous. Not so crazy they can't get scared. Fear of the dark is a hard habit to break."

"That's good, isn't it?" Luce asked. "Fewer of them there are down there, the better, right?"

"We climb down in the dark and we'd be picked off by feeders within a mile of this place," Eylsa pointed out. "And you can bet these nut-bags will be back with the crack of dawn. They need to be gone."

"Oh, fucking stay up there, then!" came the cry from below, more childish than ever. "Got food, have you? How long's it going to last?" She laughed, a harsh cough of amusement.

"They're all edging back to the plant," Stave reported, mirror raised once more. He shifted his attention to the gap in the barrier where the stairwell had been, searching the shadowy trees beyond for some sign of movement. From the twitch of frustration in his brow, Layla concluded he hadn't found any.

"Just have to run and gun our way out in the morning," Eylsa said.

Stave didn't reply. After a few seconds of narrow-eyed contemplation, he moved to Romer's side, plucking the revolver from his holster. Cocking the hammer, he went to the barrier, jerking up to fire two rounds at the people below. The twin booms echoed long and loud, quickly followed by the clatter and clang of dozens of crossbow bolts striking the tank.

"You prick!" the woman screamed. Despite the damage to her throat, Layla gauged her voice as even louder than the gunshots. "We'll fucking kill all of you! We'll burn you down to the bones, you shits!"

Her diatribe was echoed by her companions, a collective chorus of unreasoning hate filling the air. Stave crawled back to the gap, reaching for his pack and extracting the night-vision goggles. Holding them to his eyes with one hand, he raised the revolver with the other and fired one more shot.

The woman's screams became wordless then, a torrent of incoherent rage accompanied by another flurry of bolts and increased shouts from her deranged companions. Layla kept her eyes on Stave's unmoving form as he continued to scan the trees. Then he stiffened. Shuffling closer, Layla peered over his shoulder at the woodland covering the ground beyond the faint track of the plant's perimeter road. It was almost fully dark now and she could see only the wavering shadows of treetops in the night-time breeze. Then, moving so fast she thought she might have imagined it, her gaze was caught by a pale flicker through the matrix of swaying branches.

"Get as low as you can," Stave said. Moving back from the gap, he lay flat on the tank's curving roof. "No one makes a sound until it's over."

The demented baying of the woman and her cohorts continued until it switched with jarring immediacy to terrorised, screeching panic. Fear quickly gave way to pain, shouts and guttural choking merging with the wet snaps and cracks.

Hearing a whimper, Layla's gaze snapped to Luce, teeth clenched and the onset of panic showing in the quiver of her features. Reaching out, Layla clasped Luce's hand, trying not to grip too hard. Meeting Luce's widened eyes, Layla forced a smile. It felt false, a tightening of her features that probably looked more like a grimace, but Luce found some solace in it. Entwining their fingers, she kept her gaze locked on Layla's until the ugly cacophony ebbed into silence.

The havoc raging below ended with a merciful quickness, but not completely. Judging by the moans and babbled pleas, the feeders had left some alive. Their helpless cries dwindled into the distance as Layla realised they were being dragged away. *Don't want to feed this close to the plant*, she concluded. She thought she heard the signature rasp of the spokeswoman among the forlorn, desperate calls of the captives, but couldn't be sure. As the last of the screams faded, she lowered her head to the metal of the tank and clenched her teeth against one of her own.

Stave made them lie still for another hour, clamping a hand to Romer's mouth when he began to let out some involuntary grunts of pain. Layla suffered a guilty spasm of worry over the blood leaking through his bandage drawing the feeders' notice, but realised it must have been smothered by the pervasive chemical stink. When finally satisfied the beta pack had gone, Stave removed his hand, murmuring, "Sorry."

"Don't . . ." Romer whispered back, ". . . worry about it."

"Double watch tonight," Stave told the rest of them. He tossed the night-vision goggles to Layla. "You and Luce first."

They sat together at the gap in the barrier. Layla scanned the trees with the goggles, seeing nothing and keeping it brief to spare the battery. After that they ate in silence until Luce muttered a question around a mouthful of oat bar.

"So, who?"

"Who?"

"Who're you here for? Must be someone, right?"

Layla finished her own bar and washed it down with a gulp of water. Seeing no particular reason to avoid the question, she said, "My . . . father. Got a lung infection. He needs anti-bios."

"Yeah. I guessed it would be something like that. Me, it's my sister. She's pregnant, y'see."

A certain rawness in her voice caused Layla to turn and see the tears coursing down Luce's cheeks, although her expression had hardly altered. "Complications, the doc says," Luce went on. "She'll need a C-section when the time comes. That's when they . . ."

"I know what it is."

"Yeah. Thing is, they haven't got the right stuff for that any more. Used up their last tank of that gas they use to knock people out months ago. They wrote it down for me. See?" Luce rolled up the sleeve of her overalls, baring her forearm. Layla had to lean close to make out the words tattooed onto her skin: "NITROUS OXIDE".

Predisilone, Layla thought, remembering the desperate, murderous look on Lenox's face. *Amoxicillin, clarithromycin, doxycycline.* "I . . . hope they have some to sell at Harbour Point," she said, unable to think of something better.

"They will." Luce patted her pack. "Got a pint of whisky in here to trade for it. Actual genuine Scotch. Grandpa kept it safe ever since the Peace, left it to me when cancer got him last year. The way I hear it, those greedy bastards at Harbour Point will sell me just about anything for a bottle of the real stuff."

She lapsed into silence, but Layla could sense she had more to say. "What?" Layla prompted, disliking the tension.

"Did you kill Lenox?"

Layla squinted at her but once again saw little point in a lie. "No. Nehna did. He tried to kill me in the Boneyard. Knew he wasn't going to pass Selection and wanted to improve his chances."

"Oh." Another uncomfortable interval until Luce spoke again. "I knew it would be bad out here, but not like this." She glanced over her shoulder at Romer, who had subsided into fitful unconsciousness a while back. "Odds are not all of us will make it. Just being realistic."

She met Layla's gaze, a need for understanding stark in the eyes above her mask. Her tears had stopped, but they still shone bright.

"OK," Layla said slowly, wishing she would get to the point.

"Nitrous oxide," Luce said. "You can remember it, right? Like I can remember whatever you need. Just in case."

A pact. That's what she wants. Layla looked away, resentful at being asked to undertake yet another obligation. But, after some grudging calculation, she realised it made sense. "Amoxicillin," she said. "Or clarithromycin. Or doxycycline. Any one of them will work. Can you remember, or do I have to ink it into your arm?"

A relieved smile played across Luce's lips. "Yeah. I'm good at remembering stuff. This—" she patted her arm "—was more of a . . . commitment thing, y'know."

"The Electric Palace Theatre in the Arts," Layla said. "His name's Strang, but speak to Taxo. He's the guy in the wheelchair."

Luce nodded. "Agri-Unit Twelve B. Her name's Una. Hard to miss since she's the only one pregnant."

"Una," Layla repeated, thinking: *Nitrous oxide. How heavy's that going to be?*

Chapter Fifteen

At dawn, Eylsa took Romer's rope and secured one end to a railing that had been part of the tank's stairwell. Layla had nurtured the shameful hope that the veteran might have bled out during the night. But he lingered, skin bleached and barely able to raise his head, but still fully aware.

"Stings . . . like a bastard," he said, voice reduced to a low mutter as his fingers teased the edge of his bandage. "Those mad fucks . . . smearing God knows what on their bolts. Hardly civilised . . . is it?"

He, Stave and Eylsa shared a smile before clasping hands.

"Switch," Stave said, holding Romer's revolver out to Layla and gesturing for her to hand over her blaster. She did so, then began to rummage in her pack for the remaining shells, stopping at a glare from Eylsa. They wouldn't be needed.

"Keep the top chamber empty . . . unless you know there's going to be trouble," Romer told Layla as she accepted the revolver, holster and ammunition from Stave. "Otherwise . . . you're likely to blow your foot off."

"Start down," Stave said, jerking his head at the waiting rope. "I'll be along."

No one said anything else, although Layla struggled to summon some parting words for Romer. In the end, all she could manage before taking her turn on the rope was a weak smile. He returned it, a glimmer of real gratitude in his eyes. It just made her feel worse.

Her descent was marginally less clumsy than at the wall. It seemed incredible that had been only three days ago. Once down, she and the others distracted themselves with a survey of the bodies. Layla counted twenty-two, all in various states of mutilation. Some were missing limbs; others had been torn from neck to groin. The only common factor was the relative dryness of the remains.

"No women," Luce noted. "Guessing they took her . . ." She swallowed a cough. "Alive."

"Beta packs are known to bear grudges," Eylsa said. "It was probably one of theirs back there under the blowtorch."

Luce frowned. "So they . . . care about each other?"

"So do dogs. Doesn't make them human."

"Makes them better than us, though," Pitt said, casting a dark glance at the top of the tank. "Couldn't Stave let him do it himself? In private, like."

"We have to be sure," Eylsa said. "Romer knows

every route and safe house. If an alpha found him . . .
We can't risk it. You all knew this was part of the
deal. So quit moaning."

Pitt, however, clearly had a hard time letting go of
a chewed bone. "Wouldn't have happened if we'd
kept going. Doing a recon was unnecessary. Romer
said so . . ."

"Get this, you little shit," Eylsa growled, rounding
on the Riverbanker. "When you've been out here
more than five minutes . . ."

Her blossoming rage died at the flat boom from the
tank's roof. They all stood in silence to watch Stave
descend the rope. He did so with unhurried ease, then
started walking, his expression as rigidly purposeful as
ever. "Let's go," he said.

An hour after departing the plant, Eylsa told them to
remove their masks, Layla feeling a thrill of unalloyed
pleasure at the first taste of clean air. They skirted the
woodland for most of the morning until it gave way
to grassland. It was shorter than the variety that had
surrounded the church, but thick. Several times Layla
came close to falling when her feet found a hidden
obstacle, mostly rusted pieces of metal weathered into
twisted abstraction. Soon they arrived at a partially
collapsed structure, a skeletal matrix of reddened steel
rising from the carpet of vegetation. Layla recognised
it as an electricity pylon thanks to the shards of cable
littering the area. They passed another a half-mile later,

this one marginally taller, and she realised Stave was using these remnants of the Peace as way markers.

The last of them rose atop a hillock overlooking a stretch of narrow river, possibly a branch of the one they crossed to reach the plant. It was looped across the flat land below the hill, enclosing a walled settlement. The wall appeared to be mostly fabricated from corrugated iron, reinforced in places by concrete slabs and piled rubble. Within it sat a squat building of dark stone, its architecture marking it as old long before the Feeding, and a trio of windmills, blades turning fast in the stiff breeze.

"No sentries," Stave said, lowering his binoculars after a prolonged scan of the settlement.

"Breached?" Eylsa wondered.

"No sign of damage to the walls."

"Bypass or check it out?"

"They were always pretty well stocked here. Be a shame to waste it. They might even have meds. Anything we find here we won't have to barter for in Harbour Point."

They exchanged a brief look of mutual agreement before starting down the hill.

"We don't get a vote, then," Pitt observed, keeping his voice too low for the veterans to hear.

Layla considered reminding him he was free to make his own way, but didn't. Despite Romer's acceptance of his fate, and Eylsa's apparently undiminished faith in their leader, the fact remained that Stave had led them into unnecessary danger. Following him, she couldn't shake the sense that he had been looking for something in the plant, something more than information about a newly formed group of lunatics. Also, she was pretty sure his search hadn't ended.

As they drew closer, Layla found that the settlement's wall was of sturdier construction than its ramshackle appearance suggested. It had been raised around a pre-existing fence, each section built between a series of tall concrete posts. A Peace-era sign stood outside its gate, faded lettering proclaiming it ELECTRICITY REGIONAL SUB-STATION WEST – MUNICIPAL POWER AUTHORITY PROPERTY – NO TRESPASSING. The words were defaced with a whitewashed symbol that resembled a lightning bolt.

"Spark Town, they call it," Eylsa said. "We come here to trade for batteries sometimes. Those windmills of theirs generate plenty of power and all the tech in the substation makes it easy for them to store it. The guy in charge of this place is always talking about sinking a waterwheel into the river. Or was. Guess they never will now."

"Luce, Pitt, stay here," Stave said, putting the rifle stock to his shoulder. "Eylsa, Layla, with me."

"Erm," Luce ventured. "What if you, y'know, don't come back?"

Stave waved vaguely to the right of the settlement. "Harbour Point is that way. Good luck."

Layla had followed Romer's advice about leaving

the revolver's top chamber empty, loading it with five of her remaining fifteen bullets. It was about the same weight as the blaster, but felt heavier as she drew it from the holster and fell in behind Eylsa and Stave, possibly because she knew it was a lot more lethal. Like the veterans, she kept the barrel pointed at the ground and her finger off the trigger.

Delivering a gentle push to the gate, Stave stepped back and raised the rifle when it swung open. Thanks to the faint but detectable odour of corruption staining the air, Layla knew what they would find before she saw it. The bodies were in a similar state of disarray to those back at the plant, but stiff and darkened with decomposition.

Eylsa and Stave moved in slow concert as they tacked their guns over the settlement's interior. Attempting to mimic them, Layla saw more bodies on the inner wall's parapet, and a denser cluster crowding the door to the old building. She couldn't tell if these people had perished in the act of fleeing the structure or seeking refuge within it. Glimpsing small corpses among the mass, she looked away.

"Betas," Eylsa said, crouching to cast an experienced eye over one of the bodies. "Heard of them over-whelming settlements before, but only in seriously big numbers, which is rare these days. I'd also expect more damage to the wall and the gate." She nodded to the chains lying on the ground near the entrance. "Looks like someone just let them in."

"Who would do that?" Layla wondered.

"It happens." Eylsa straightened with a groan. "Someone loses their mind, can't stand it any more, but wants to take everyone with them when they go. Maybe it was him." She nudged a toe to the body at her feet.

"We need to check inside," Stave said, moving towards the building. Layla saw a moment of conflict on Eylsa's face before she followed. *Doesn't think this is a good idea*, Layla decided. *Like the plant. Still following him, though.*

Entering the building entailed the unavoidable task of stepping on the carpet of bodies cramming the doorway. The two veterans crunched their way through without hesitation, Layla forcing herself to do the same while fighting an instinctive need to retch. Once inside, they switched on their flashlights, the beams playing over a space of improvised dwelling places rendered into disorder. Detritus littered a floor streaked with dried blood in between yet more bodies. Layla quelled another nauseous impulse upon seeing there were more children here than outside. Some were clutched in the arms of the adults who had tried to protect them, parent and offspring frozen in the moment of slaughter.

Stave insisted they stay together as they performed a slow and thorough inspection of the building. Beyond the living space, they found the banks of capacitors and relays that had once given it purpose.

It was inert, lacking even the faintest electrical hum, but Layla still refrained from touching anything. They discovered the settlement's stores, their ostensible goal, in what had been an equipment room. The door had been heavily secured, but the lock and chain lay in pieces on the floor. The contents were disappointingly sparse: just a few ancient cans and a water barrel. There were no weapons to be had, nor any of the batteries Eylsa spoke of.

Stave pronounced the place clear after checking the offices to the rear of the building. He sent Layla to fetch Pitt and Luce, then set them all to the task of rummaging the settlement for anything useful. When it came to consumables, the results were meagre. The few food cans Layla uncovered had all been pierced, and the spilled contents left to spoil. Also, despite forcing herself to search the bodies as well as the beds and lockers, she found no meds of any kind apart from an ancient packet of paracetamol. Luce uncovered a stock of clean water and Pitt found a store of car batteries hidden near the wall. Stave told him to cover them up again, saying another team might be sent to retrieve them later.

"Slashed the power lines to the windmills and smashed up the charging gear," Eylsa reported. They had gathered in the largest office, which appeared to double as the settlement's command post and library. A corpse was slumped head down on the desk, flesh dark with rot and part consumed by maggots. Despite the decomposition, they could make out the large hole in the side of his head.

"Shot himself," Eylsa concluded, frowning as she scanned the desk and the floor beneath. "No gun, though."

Shelves lined the walls, thick with books, most bearing completely unfamiliar titles. Layla resisted the temptation to take some for Strang, unable to justify the additional weight.

"No guns at all, in fact," Eylsa went on. "Anywhere in the whole settlement. Last time I was here, they had plenty. Someone gathered them all up."

"An alpha, right?" Layla said. "They look like us. Explains how they got in here."

"They look like us sometimes, but don't think like us. Underneath it all, they're just a bundle of blood-lust, like all their kind. And they shun other types. This—" Eylsa gestured to the destruction beyond the office windows. "—it's something new. I don't like it. We shouldn't hang around."

This she addressed to Stave, but he appeared distracted by the books. Layla watched him trace a finger along one section in particular, picking out the names of various poets on the spines until his hand stopped at a gap.

"Stave," Eylsa said.

Stave's hand closed into a fist. "Yeah," he said, moving to the door. "Time to move on."

Before following the others out, Layla lingered for

a closer look at his object of fascination. The gap between the books was large enough to have accommodated a couple of volumes, or one big one. Whoever had maintained this library had organised the books by both genre and alphabet. The book to the left of the gap bore the name "Betjeman" while the one to the right read "Browning".

"So, who's missing?" she muttered before an irritated snap from Eylsa had her hurrying to catch up.

They followed the road from Spark Town into a residential neighbourhood of mixed architecture: old terraced houses mingled with modern apartment blocks. Stave and Eylsa exhibited a similar level of wariness here as they had back in the tenements, keeping to the centre of the road and constantly scanning the passing windows and doorways. By late afternoon, Layla noticed that the streets became broader and the buildings taller. Many of them featured signs alongside their doors. Some featured symbols that vaguely resembled fruit or animals. Others proclaimed obscure names followed by meaningless abbreviations: PROMETHEUS MEDIA INC. or EXCELSIUS HYDROCARBONS GLC. The impression of grandeur was contrasted by the intensity of destruction that had taken place here. Every wall bore the telltale pockmarks of gunfire and many of the towering structures had been blasted down to their steel bones.

In the centre of this district, an array of ruined

military vehicles sprawled across a road junction. Tanks and personnel carriers, rusted and blackened, dotted the bisected roadway. They were all overgrown with weeds that sprouted through the cracked tarmac, putting Layla in mind of slain beasts surrendering to decomposition. Deep craters broke the road in several places, the legacy of weapons possessed of such power that Layla wondered how those who had striven to contest the Feeding could have suffered such absolute defeat.

"Welcome to the site of the last stand, kids," Eylsa said. "In this city, anyway. The Battle of Corporation Junction. Time was they'd have made a national park out of this place." She cast a sly glance at Stave. "Maybe, if you behave, our glorious leader will tell you all about it."

"You were here?" Pitt asked Stave. Layla expected him to ignore the question and issue a curt instruction to move on, but he surprised her.

"Echo Three," he said, approaching the rusted remnant of a weed-shrouded tank nearby. Following him, Layla made out the faded lettering on its turret: E-3. Below it was a cartoon figure too flaked and weathered to make out fully, but she thought it might have been some kind of duck. "Deadly Donnie, we called him," Stave went on. "Dug out of mothballs and handed over to a bunch of kids with barely three weeks' training. Still, he saved me when the air force started dropping thermobarics. Couldn't blame them for it, since the feeders had broken through every barricade by then. The bombs must've fried a few thousand all at once. They'd explode twenty feet from the ground, setting fire to the air. Some crews suffocated in their vehicles. Donnie was one of the few with a chemical warfare system, so we didn't. Melted the tracks, though. When we crawled out, there wasn't much of an army to fight for any more, but still plenty of feeders. We'd heard rumours about some kind of redoubt being built on the edge of the city, so that's where we went. Only two of us made it."

His face clouded, and he turned away from the tank. "That's enough ancient history. The day's getting old."

The next safe house consisted of a large, secured room on the third storey of one of the ruined buildings. The floors above had been blasted away, but this one remained remarkably intact. Eylsa called the refuge a "server room", it being filled with empty racks where tech had once resided, all long since pillaged.

"Places like this were how they ran the world during the Peace," she said, tossing each of the novices a can of beans from the well-stocked supply cache.

"How?" Pitt enquired around a mouthful of pickled onion, peering at a tangle of cables dangling from one of the racks.

"Wires, my lad," Eylsa said, then shrugged. "Until it all got wireless. It's complicated. Eat, then get some sleep. For tomorrow, we trade. Not something you want to do with dulled wits."

Layla confronted the subject of her ugly dream that night with a dispiriting lack of surprise. *Please don't!* Romer pleaded atop the tank, beautiful, silky red blood leaking from his leg wound as he tried to crawl away from her. This time, she could smell it, the scent reaching into her to stir a ravenous, painful hunger. Advancing towards Romer, she reflected on the peculiarity of her imagination, choosing to transform such a courageous soul into a coward. Tears and snot covered features moulded into a picture of gibbering terror as he babbled out hopeless entreaties. *I know things . . . I'll tell you all of it. Just please, please don't . . .*

Chapter Sixteen

For the first time, Stave had them up with the sunrise, running once again and avoiding the longer shadows cast by the ruins. The tall buildings of Corporation Junction soon gave way to a shopping precinct, the store windows bare of glass and their contents scoured clean years ago. Beyond this lay a river, though at first glance of the broad waters Layla assumed they had come to a lake. It dwarfed the reservoirs in the Agri districts, the wide arc of choppy, grey water stretching away to either side for miles. The bank was a long parade of railings and paved walkways. Plentiful vegetation sprouted all around, but wasn't so thick as to impede their progress. Some patches were dense enough to make Layla wary, but Eylsa and Stave seemed more relaxed here than elsewhere.

"They don't seem to like the smell of salt water much," Eylsa explained, inclining her head at the river.

"Salt water?" Luce asked.

"Yeah, it's tidal. Means it flows all the way to the sea," she added in response to Luce's puzzled frown. "Makes it a good place for settlements. Or it did until the boats began to sink. Lack of hull maintenance will do that after a while. Must've been thousands living on the river the first few years after the Feeding. These days, Harbour Point is the only one left."

Her words were clarified when Layla spied what she at first thought was an island in the middle of the river. Closer inspection revealed it as a collection of lashed-together boats and barges. Many were half submerged, and the only sign of life came from the flocks of gulls thronging the forest of masts.

They continued for another mile at a brisk walk until Stave raised a fist, bringing them to an abrupt halt. Gesturing for them to stay put, he put the rifle stock to his shoulder, moving slowly towards a patch of dense vegetation. Layla's eyes, now attuned to picking out objects of interest, quickly fixed on a grey shape lying among the weeds: *feeder corpse*. After a careful inspection of the body, Stave lowered his rifle and beckoned them closer.

"Gamma," Eylsa said, delivering a solid kick to the creature's deformed head. "Their skin darkens quick in the sun, so he hasn't been here long." Crouching for a closer look, her brows arched in surprise. "No wounds. Looks like his neck's broken."

"You said they fight," Layla pointed out, puzzled by the weighty glance Eylsa shared with Stave.

"They do," Eylsa agreed. "Tear each other to pieces when they're properly riled up. This thing isn't torn."

"An alpha then," Luce concluded, scanning the surrounding cover with wide eyes.

"That or a crosser with a really impressive skill set." Eylsa nodded to the body in admiration. "This is some real Van Damme shit."

"Van who?" Pitt asked, which brought a despairing sigh to the veteran's lips.

"Don't you kids get any education any more?"

"They don't usually come this close to the river," Stave said.

"Might do if they get hungry enough. It's weird, though. Like Spark Town was weird. Sooner we get there, the better."

After a short, intense scan of the jungle-like mass of growth fringing the path, Stave nodded. "We run the rest of the way."

He allowed no stops for the remainder of the morning, Layla reckoning they covered five miles by the time Harbour Point came into view. She had been hearing about the place for most of her life, a haven of riches where just about anything could be had for the right price. Initially, it went some way to living up to expectations, at least in terms of spectacle. The settlement was spread over a portion of the Riverbank, but the bulk of it had been constructed upon a bridge. A mammoth structure of huge suspension towers and a span about a hundred feet wide, it reached across the river before coming to an abrupt stop after a quarter of a mile. The huge piers that once supported the rest of it still stood, but the spans in between had vanished. The wall defending the bank-side compound consisted of wrecked vehicles piled on top of each other. The barrier of corroded metal had been augmented over the years with paving stones and sundry debris, but retained a solid, unassailable appearance.

Six people bearing a variety of firearms guarded the narrow entrance, with another four stationed on the wall above. They tensed at the sight of five running figures but relaxed in recognition at the sight of Stave and Eylsa.

"You owe me a pizza," a gruff-voiced, stocky woman with a pump-action shotgun informed one of her comrades. "I told you he'd be back." She revealed a set of gapped teeth as she clasped hands with Stave before exchanging a cordial nod with Eylsa. "How many did you lose?"

"One," Eylsa said. "Romer."

The woman curled a lip in sympathy. "Shit."

"Yeah."

"Well—" The guard took a small flashlight from the pocket of her heavily patched coat. "—you know the drill. Open wide."

"Still doing this?" Eylsa rolled her eyes before stepping forward to allow the woman to shine the light over her teeth.

"Old traditions are hard to break. And there's a lotta talk about alphas these days. You're good. Who's next?"

She subjected them all to the same inspection, then nodded to one of her colleagues to open the sturdy iron grate covering the entrance. "You newbies mind yourselves in here," she cautioned as they made their way inside. "Keep to Crosser Town and the market if you know what's good for you. And know this: you may start trouble, but we'll be the ones who end it. Any misbehaviour, we'll take your weapons before we kick you out and you don't ever get to come back."

With that, she signalled leave to enter with a jerk of her head and they proceeded inside.

The first thing to strike Layla was the smell, a heady, drool-provoking aroma of cooked meat and freshly baked bread only partially tainted by the commingled stench of unwashed bodies and clothing. The second was the noise arising from the chaotic flow of people. Market days in the Arts could get busy, but she usually only saw a crowd this dense on return days or at one of the mayor's assemblies. People clustered around stalls selling soup from steaming urns or roasted animals spitted above fire pits, mostly rats but with a few actual chickens. Others bought drink from carts proclaiming themselves purveyors of fine ale and spirits. Judging by the bunched features of their customers, Layla doubted the quality of the product, but that didn't seem to dissuade them from refilling their cups.

The people here contrived to be both disparate and familiar in appearance. Some bore extensive facial tattoos of intricate design, while others featured elaborate arrangements to their hair. The similarity came in their utilitarian clothing, weaponry and physicality. Most wore some form of overalls that allowed for easy movement. Everyone in sight carried guns or crossbows and all looked like they could run for miles without difficulty.

"Crossers," Layla realised, drawing a chuckle from Eylsa. Her cheeriness had returned now they were back behind secure walls.

"Didn't think we were the only ones, did you?" she said, jostling Layla's shoulder. "There're teams here from the Junkyard, the Crossroads, the Orange Farm, you name it."

"There's an orange farm?" Luce asked.

"Yeah. Weird thing is, they don't grow oranges there, or anything else as far as I know."

"We need to find a berth," Stave said, pushing into the crowd. "Stay close. Anyone talks to you, be polite but don't stop to chat."

They drew some curious glances as they forged their way through the throng, but most people seemed too intent on their meals or drinks to afford much notice to newcomers. Of the few that did pay attention, Layla discerned a distinct wariness in the gazes they directed at Stave. Once through the crowd, they came to an untidy array of tents and huts following the line of the wall. The dwellings had a more impermanent look than the sturdier constructions on the bridge. The smell also differed here, a far less pleasant melange of woodsmoke and exposed latrines.

"Welcome to Crosser Town," Eylsa said with faux grandiosity. "The one place that can make the Outside seem inviting."

She led them to a large, vacant tent formed of plastic sheeting tethered to the wall. The only furnishings consisted of bunks fashioned from wooden crates. Many of the surrounding dwellings were empty of people or belongings, indicating occupancy was determined on the basis of first come, first served.

"Leave your weapons here," Stave said, laying his rifle down on a bunk. "You're not allowed to carry them into the town proper."

"Won't someone take them?" Pitt asked.

"No one steals in Harbour Point. Crossers' Rules." Stave shrugged off his pack, placing it on the bunk before lying down to rest his head on it. "Rest for an hour, then we'll eat. After that, it's time to trade."

Stave spent a packet of tomato seeds to buy them each a bowl of meat stew flavoured with a mix of spices that seemed marvellous to Layla's inexperienced palate. She didn't ask about its origins, but it tasted too gamey to be chicken. Wolfing it down anyway, she chased it with a cup of cider Eylsa purchased from a nearby liquor stall.

"They'll try to gouge you," the veteran warned when the meal was done and discussion turned to their next task. "Don't take it personally. Being greedy as fuck is just how people are here. The trick is to give as little as possible while making them think they've cheated you. You can watch us at the Trade Ministry to get the hang of it. After that, kiddos, you're on your own."

The Trade Ministry occupied what had been the administrative offices for the bridge. Eylsa explained that, during the Peace, a transport facility of this size had required a small army to oversee maintenance and manage the thousands of cars and trucks that passed across it every day. The building was of purely functional construction, a two-storey concrete box distinguished mainly by the number of armed guards surrounding it, with more on the roof.

"They must have a lot of trouble here," Luce observed as they joined the line to the main entrance.

"There's more guns around than there used to be," Eylsa agreed, eyeing the guards. "Guess the boats have been less frequent recently."

"Boats?"

"Those who actually live here can get rambunctious from time to time. The goods they sell come from boats sailing up the river, mostly in summer. Sometimes, there are a lot of boats. Other times, especially in winter, not so much. When that happens, people start to get hungry, and hungry folk can be awful dangerous."

The line swiftly shortened and they soon found themselves in the building's main lobby. A man with a clipboard directed them to a desk behind which sat a bespectacled woman of slight stature and narrow, pinched features that gave her a bird-like appearance. Layla couldn't place her age. Her face wasn't especially wrinkled, but her gaze conveyed a sense of considerable experience, as well as intelligence. Of empathy, however, Layla saw no evidence at all. Her gaze narrowed in recognition at the sight of Stave and Eylsa, though she offered no greeting beyond a clipped, "State your business."

"Our inventory and offer," Eylsa said, pushing a folded piece of paper across the desk.

It seemed to Layla that the woman took longer than necessary to read the unfolded list. "We have no micro-processors in stock," she stated with toneless formality. "Also, the price of the medicines you require has now doubled. You will either have to halve your requirement or double your payment."

Eylsa raised her eyes to the ceiling, taking a calming breath. Layla couldn't tell whether this was the bargainer's artifice she had alluded to or genuine anger. She suspected both. Eylsa cast a questioning glance at Stave. Receiving a nod, she turned back to the woman. "We don't have any more seeds, but we can provide information. Specifically, the location of a number of car batteries."

The woman's eyes blinked slowly behind her lenses,

Layla noticing that one of them had a small crack in it. *These people are no richer than we are*, she realised. *They just happen to live in a more convenient place.*

"Acceptable," the woman said after another brief examination of their list.

"Spark Town," Eylsa said. "Looks like it got overrun a couple of weeks ago. Might've been an alpha, so tell anyone you send to be careful."

The woman didn't acknowledge the advice, instead dipped a pen into an ink pot and went over the list, putting crosses next to some of the items and ticks next to others. Despite having to read the letters upside down, Layla was sure she made out the word "Amoxicillin", marked with a tick, before the woman added the sheet to a pile on her left. "The goods will be available for collection this afternoon."

"Afternoon?" Eylsa frowned. "Doesn't leave us much time to get clear before nightfall. We usually pick up right away."

"Afternoon," the woman repeated. Her tone was as uncoloured as before, but Layla detected a certain relish in the slight raise of her brows. "The manner and time of your departure is a matter for you. Though I would recommend you stay the night, thereby affording you the opportunity to engage in local commerce."

Outside, Eylsa produced a half-dozen seed packets from her pack and handed them out. "Don't say I never give you anything."

"Thought you didn't have any more," Luce said.

"Makes me a big fucking liar, doesn't it?" Eylsa smiled. "Here endeth the lesson, kids. The market is that way." She nodded towards the bridge before starting off towards Crosser Town. Stave had already taken his leave. Apparently, the veterans felt no need to acquire personal goods here.

"So," Luce said to Pitt, "what're you here for? If it's meds, maybe the three of us—"

"It isn't," he cut in, before shouldering his pack and walking away.

"You're thinking it too, huh?" Luce asked Layla, face dark as they watched him disappear into the dense maze of buildings covering the bridge.

"Thinking what?"

"Had to be Romer and not him, right?" Shrugging, she brightened quickly, looping her arm through Layla's and tugging her into motion. "Any idea where to look?"

"Start at the market and go from there, I guess."

The market took the form of a precinct formed amid a rectangular arrangement of shipping containers, repurposed into shopfronts. Hand-painted signs proclaimed various wares and services for sale. Layla's interest was piqued by the sight of a small man wielding a soldering iron amid a pile of circuit boards. Taxo would have found a lot to talk to him about. She resisted the impulse to linger and kept scouring the signs until her gaze alighted on one that read ANGEL'S

PHARMACY. An additional, smaller sign offered a customer advisory: No Oxy – So Don't Ask.

"Don't tell me." The woman behind the counter held up a hand as they approached, her smooth brows furrowed in calculation. "The Redoubt, right?"

"Is it that obvious?" Luce asked.

"You lot tend not to have so many tattoos." The woman laughed. "And there's a particular cut to your clothing. Like it's all made by the same person." She laughed again. After the blank efficiency of the bird-like official at the Trade Ministry, Layla found her warmth disconcerting. "What can I do for you girls?"

"You go first," Luce said. She still had hold of Layla's arm so she could feel a small tremble. *Afraid she might have done all this for nothing*, Layla concluded.

"Amoxicillin," she told the store holder. "Or clari-thromycin, or doxycycline."

"Someone back home got a touch of the wet lung, huh?" The woman offered a sympathetic wince.

Layla looked hard into the store holder's eyes. "Do you have any?"

A small dimming of her smile, but the sympathy remained. Layla was surprised to read it as genuine. "One of the three," the woman said. "Doxycycline. But it's expensive."

"I have rapeseed." Layla fished into her pack, laying the three seed packets out on the counter.

The pharmacist looked at the offering but didn't take it. "Not enough. The goods came off a boat that stopped coming, so it's unlikely there'll be any more. Might even be the last course of anti-bios to be had in the Harbour. You want it, I need four times that, and more varieties." Seeing Layla's face harden, she added, "You're welcome to try elsewhere, of course. I'll even hold it for you, but I can pretty much guarantee you'll be back within the hour." She spoke with an air of apology, the sympathy still shining in her eyes. *Is she actually being kind?* Layla wondered.

"This is all I have," she said, putting her remaining seed packets on the counter. It came to about twice as much as her initial offer and prompted a predictable response.

"Not enough."

Layla reached into the pack again, placing all her blaster shells alongside the seeds. The pharmacist's brows arched in approval but also expectation. *I could just take it*, Layla thought. *Come back tonight when it's quiet. Kill her and take it.* But her honed instincts told her that would be a very bad idea. Affable as she was, there was a steeliness to the pharmacist that warned against unwise notions. Besides, Layla's experience at the plant had revealed a salient fact: she really didn't like killing people. Gritting her teeth, she placed five revolver rounds on the counter. It left her with three plus the five already loaded.

With the warmth of her smile now fully returned, the pharmacist swept the goods off the counter. "Be right back," she said, before disappearing through a door. In the six or seven minutes it took her to re-appear, Layla contended with the suspicion she might not be coming back. She had begun to debate the wisdom of vaulting the counter when the pharmacist returned.

"Sixty pills," she said, place a small plastic bottle in front of Layla. The adhesive label was yellowed and faded, but Layla could make out the printed letters: "Doxycycline – 100 mg – x60". "Enough for a full course. Hope it does the trick." The pharmacist winked and turned to Luce. "What about you, hun?"

Luce had been told to bring back two one litre tanks of nitrous oxide which, to Layla's annoyance, attracted a far less steep price. "Boat came in last year stuffed with it," the pharmacist explained after Luce handed over half her seed packets. "Salvaged off a military ship they found abandoned out at sea. People use it to get high, mostly. You girls stay safe now. But if you're looking for fun, the dock is the place to go. Just make sure you keep together."

Chapter Seventeen

Despite Layla's reluctance, Luce insisted on going to the dock. "I just wanna see it."

Layla had pocketed the pill bottle rather than risk consigning it to her pack. The hard lump pressed against her thigh, constantly reminding her of its worth. Worried someone might have witnessed the transaction in the market and followed with thievery in mind, she constantly checked their surroundings as Luce tugged her ever deeper into Harbour Point. The dwellings consisted mainly of stacked containers, with a few modified buses and trucks. Every street was a narrow alley, mostly free of people, though they did squeeze by a few patently annoyed locals before emerging onto a walkway affording a view of the river. The redundant pylons rose through a haze covering the water, enhancing the sense of vertigo. Looking down, Layla saw water sloshing around the wooden hulls of several motor boats moored at a makeshift jetty. She guessed the drop at about sixty feet. Looking to her right, she saw a procession of cranes dangling cables over the edge of the bridge. The space between the cranes was taken up by more containers, modified like those back at the market, but selling only one product as far as Layla could tell. People thronged around each one, mostly locals but with a few crossers mixed in. What sounded like an accordion and a fiddle cast music over the scene. No one was singing, but all were drinking.

"Look," Luce said, nodding to something in the crowd. Layla soon picked out Pitt's wiry form, engaged in an animated discussion with a large man in oil-stained overalls. "Wonder what he's buying." Luce started towards them, obliging Layla to follow.

Pitt was too focused on whatever bargain he was attempting to strike to notice their approach. But, from the tension of his lean features, Layla could tell he was struggling to keep his temper in check. "I told you," he said. "I haven't got anything else to trade."

"Then go find some," the oil-stained man replied. He had an extensive beard, liberally soaked in liquor, that parted to reveal an incomplete set of yellow teeth. "Passage for an unskilled hand is not cheap, son. You'd be taking up space I could use for cargo." He raised a clay cup to his lips, taking a long drink. Layla could tell he was enjoying watching Pitt struggle to quell his anger. "Or," the large man went on, leaning closer, "maybe there's another arrangement we could come to."

Pitt's face became very still, jaw tightening. Seeing the smirk beneath the large man's beard, Layla knew this was not a sincere offer, just a chance to indulge more cruelty. "Don't worry," he said. "I won't be asking too much. Just a daily cock-sucking. Pretty sure a little shit like you has done worse."

Pitt's hand reached into the pack resting on the upturned oil barrel that separated them, forearm flexing as he gripped something. Layla remembered she hadn't seen him leave his blaster behind in the tent.

"You treacherous fuck!" she said, stepping forward to deliver a hard slap to Pitt's face. "This is what you're here for?"

Too surprised to do more than stare at her, Pitt failed to react when the oily man, laughing now, shook his head and disappeared into the crowd.

"What the fuck is it to you?" Pitt demanded, rounding on Layla, then blinked in confusion at her sudden lack of anger.

"Nothing much," she said, resting against the oil drum. "But you pulling that blaster causes trouble for the rest of us."

Her calmness, however, wasn't matched by Luce. "People back home are relying on us," she said, voice low and face set in a glower that made Layla worried she was about to launch herself at Pitt.

"Your people," he replied. "No one's waiting for me back in that shit hole."

"Luce," Layla said, seeing her tense for a lunge.

"Get some drinks. Since you're the one who can pay for them."

"Riverbank's done for me now," Pitt muttered a short while later. He regarded the cup he held with miserable eyes, the third he had drained in about an hour. Layla drank only half of one, a bitter but strong brew that left her tongue slightly numbed. Luce had silently matched Pitt drink for drink, her glower still in place.

"The Fury," he said, rolling up a sleeve to bare a tattoo on the underside of his forearm. It wasn't especially well rendered, but Layla discerned the vague outline of a car. "Named ourselves after an old Plymouth Fury we found rotting in the Boneyard. There were six of us to begin with, but we grew in time. The other gangs got older or did each other in, left room for us. It's how it is in the Riverbank. You fight your way up until there's no one left to fight." A thin, bitter smile flickered over his lips. "'Cept, of course, there's always someone coming up the ladder behind you."

"So you got knocked off the top rung, huh?" Layla asked. "That's why you joined the crossers."

"Wasn't me at the top. That was Jules. Meanest little bitch you could ever meet. Even worse than you two. When we were on our way up, she really was something. No odds too long. No bastard too big. I was there the night she bit off Jelly Boy's ear, and he was fucking huge. But . . ." He paused to take another drink, nostalgia draining from his face. ". . . she was always way too fond of the solv, and got awful hard to be around when she couldn't get it."

Layla had never partaken herself, but knew the solv by reputation. They sold it in shadowy corners in the Arts, small jars of chemical solvent, one sniff of which could send you into oblivion. The crushers were always hard on those caught dealing in it, so hard in fact that even Velna wouldn't sell it. But harsh punishments never made the demand go away.

"Then when she did get it she'd have all these great ideas," Pitt went on. "About bringing the gangs together, taking over the whole city. Like the crushers wouldn't have shot us all to pieces in five minutes flat. Her dreams did for her in the end. She called every crew in the Riverbank together for a nice friendly chat where she'd announce her grand plan. They all rushed her at once. Wasn't much left by the time they were done. Not much left of the Fury either, just me and a couple of others. They ran off to the Garrison. I chose Selection."

His eyes slid towards Layla, wary with a glimmer of contrition. "All that stuff I said, it wasn't personal. I just needed to make it through."

"Where were you going to go, anyway?" she asked. "The Feeding happened everywhere."

"There's places I heard about. You have to cross the sea to get there, but they're better than here."

"How could you know that?" Luce said.

"Where d'you think all the stuff they sell here comes from? Besides, anywhere has to be better, or at least it can't be any worse."

"Good people got eliminated in favour of you," Luce said. "People with families in need."

"At least they got a fucking family. I told you, there's nothing back there for me."

"Hey," Layla said gently. She cast a meaningful look at the surrounding drinkers as their increasing volume began to attract attention.

"How many boats have you tried?" she asked Pitt.

"Three," he said, returning his focus to the cup. "Price is too high."

"Then suck some cock, like the man said," Luce suggested.

"Fuck you."

"Never in a million years." She afforded him a final glare of contempt before turning to Layla. "I'm done here. We're telling Stave."

"You do that." Pitt snorted a laugh. "You think he gives a shit about dragging a load of stuff back to the city? You're dreaming, girl. Why d'you think he led us into the plant, or Spark Town? Whatever he's out here for, it isn't us."

"I'd still trust him over you." Luce drained the last of her liquor and stepped back, affording Layla an expectant glare. "You coming?"

Layla pushed her half-full cup towards Pitt. "You're wrong, about there being nothing for you back there.

Come back with us and you'll be a crosser. That's
something, right?"

"For how long? The Redoubt's dying, even I can
see it. All we're doing is prolonging the misery. There's
nothing there for you either," he added as they started
to walk away.

Pausing to regard the resentment on his face, Layla
wondered why she had no anger for him. *Because he's
making sense? Or because, if it wasn't for Strang, you'd be
doing the same thing?* "Offer them some of your blaster
ammo," she said. "Seems to fetch a decent price here."

"Treacherous little turd!" Luce fumed. "Stave's gonna
beat his brains in."

Layla wasn't convinced. She felt sure Pitt wasn't the
first crosser to try something like this, and his suspicions about Stave's actions echoed her own. It seemed
more likely that he or Eylsa wouldn't do much of
anything, especially given the locals' dislike of trouble
within their walls.

As they made their way back through the market
where the vendors were busy shutting up shop for the
night, she paused at the sight of something on the
counter of the tech repairman's stall. A box, filled to
the brim with discs, some loose but others in cases. Her
gaze flicked over titles and actors she had heard Taxo
talk about but never seen. The thought of presenting
all this to him on her return brought a smile to her
lips, cut short by the tired interjection of the repairman.

"You're from the Redoubt, right? One seed packet per disc."

Layla didn't look up from the box, her gaze snared by the item on top. The cover had been ripped at some point, removing the title. But the remaining image showed a dark-haired woman carrying some kind of absurdly large weapon while holding a little girl in her arms. Both their faces were raised to stare at some unseen horror. Even though Layla had never seen this film, she knew the plot intimately thanks to Taxo's endless recitations. He could even recite the dialogue off by heart.

"I don't . . ." she began, intending to see if the repairman would accept Nehna's knife as payment. Parting with it would hurt, but leaving this behind would be worse.

"Here," Luce said, handing the repairman a seed packet.

"You don't have to," Layla told her.

"Sure I do." Luce smiled, her anger dimmed now. "Down payment for carrying one of these tanks back for me." She pulled Layla into a tight hug. "They're heavier than I thought they'd be. Come on—" She led Layla away, now clutching the disc. "—I'd really like to get drunk."

They found the border of Crosser Town alight with a revelry that contrasted with the quiet intoxication of the dockside drinking dens. A large man with a tattooed face stood atop a stack of crates playing an electric guitar, an instrument rarely played in the Arts since the amp drained batteries so quickly. The chords thrummed across a crowd lost to dance, mostly crossers but with a few food-stall vendors and other Harbour folk mixed in. There were other distractions besides the guitarist. They made their way past a shaven-headed man juggling knives and a woman breathing fire from a bottle of something even more potent than the local ale. There were also storytellers, veteran crossers regaling the youthful compatriots with tales of the Feeding or the Peace.

Spying Eylsa waving to them through the crowd, they found her seated at a table with a small group, all fellow veterans, judging by their age. "Where's Genius Boy?" Eylsa asked, having to shout above the music.

"Trying to buy himself a place on a boat," Luce shouted back. "He's skipping out on us."

Eylsa fulfilled Layla's expectations by responding with a faintly amused grimace. "Yeah, thought he might."

"You're not going after him?" Luce asked.

"What for? Can't force someone to cross and he's got nothing worth bringing back."

Except his blaster, Layla thought, but chose not to say.

"Take a seat, kiddos." Eylsa gestured to the empty bench at her side before getting to her feet. "I'll get some drinks, then introduce you to the only people here worth knowing."

After Layla's third cup of ale, followed by a smaller dose of something described as apple brandy, but she suspected would be better employed as paint stripper, Layla's awareness began to dull. Eylsa had told her the names of the people they drank with, three from the Junkyard and two from somewhere called the Lock, but she found she couldn't recall them. Talk was mostly an exchange of crossers' tales, narrow escapes and commemorative toasts to those lost. Spark Town's fall heralded a grimness of mood, soon alleviated by the more welcome news that the chemical plant was now free of the Avenging Remnant.

"Those mad fuckers nearly got me a few months ago," the Junkyard crosser seated next to Luce said. A tall, rangy man a few years younger than the others, Layla noticed that Luce afforded him more attention as the night progressed and her alcohol intake increased. "Had to hide in a tanker overnight until they'd gone. Think they'd forgotten I was there." He chuckled. "Not gonna miss them."

"You were crossing alone?" Luce asked.

"We vary it," he said. "Groups in winter, solo in summer. Feeders are more active when the weather warms up."

"Impressive." Luce raised her cup to him. "No way I'd go out alone. Not even sure I'm gonna do this again once we get back."

"Everyone says that, but almost everyone goes back out. The Outside, it gets under your skin. Taste of freedom kinda thing. Once you've had it, you want more."

As their conversation continued, Layla found herself ignored, not that she minded. The stew Stave bought had been her only meal today, and the liquor sat uncomfortably on a denuded stomach. With her head increasingly fuzzy and guts starting to roil, she leaned close to a distracted Luce, whispering, "Be back before dawn."

Luce responded with a grin of surprising shyness before hefting her pack and pushing it into Layla's arms. "Watch my tanks, OK?"

Accepting the pack, Layla started towards Crosser Town. Nearing the outlying tents, she heard a softly spoken collection of words that struck a faint chord in her memory.

"*Oh rose thou art sick . . .*"

Turning, she saw a group of people clustered around another storyteller. *Not stories*, Layla thought as she lingered on unsteady legs to listen. *Poetry.*

. . . the invisible worm that flies in the night
Hath found out thy bed of crimson joy
And its dark secret joy
Does they life destroy.

I know that, she realised through her liquor-induced

haze. *One of Strang's books.* She couldn't recall which one though, and wouldn't have minded hearing some more, but the speaker appeared to be done. A tall woman in crosser's overalls with long dark hair, she raised her hands in modest acceptance of the applause afforded by her miniature audience before walking away. Layla caught only a small glimpse of her face, but saw no one she recognised.

Time for bed, she decided, resuming her unsteady course into Crosser Town. She found Stave already sleeping. Sloughing off her pack, she collapsed onto her own bunk, hand reaching into her pocket to grasp the pill bottle. She fell asleep to the sound of guitar music and distant laughter.

Chapter Eighteen

Unfortunately, the liquor didn't kill the dreams. This time she was back in the office in Spark Town, but instead of a rotted corpse behind the desk, it was Strang. He wore an expression of severe disappointment she would never expect to see on his real face. But, for all its falsity, she still found it hurtful.

"Who sits between Betjeman and Browning in a poetry section?" he demanded.

"What?" Layla squinted at him, distracted by a burgeoning headache and a strange sense of pressure around her mouth.

"A poetry section in a library!" Strang shouted, slamming his hands on the desk for emphasis. "Who sits between Betjeman and Browning?"

"I don't know . . ." Layla began, then trailed off when she realised she did, actually. *Oh rose thou art sick . . .* She remembered it now. An illustrated plate in one of his favourite books: *Songs of Innocence and Experience*. But who wrote it?

"Blake! William Blake!" The name emerged as garbled, smothered gibberish, the pressure around her mouth becoming painful. She tried to speak again, hoping to dispel Strang's disappointed scowl, but, with shocking suddenness, he transformed into Stave. He leaned close, fixing her with a stern command in his eyes, hand tight on her mouth. It was the smell of his breath that made her realise she was no longer dreaming.

"Get your gear," Stave instructed in a terse whisper.

"What is it?" she whispered back when he removed his hand.

He went to his own bunk, hauling his pack onto his shoulders and hefting the rifle. "Feeders are inside the walls," Stave said and nodded to a still sleeping Eylsa. "Wake her. Keep it quiet." He moved to the tent flap, crouching with the rifle at his shoulder. It was still dark outside and a quick glance around the tent revealed no sign of Luce.

Questions tumbled through Layla's mind, competing with mounting fear and the nagging sense that her nocturnal realisation had been important. William Blake, the poet missing from the library shelves in Spark Town, author of the poem she had heard only last night. She pushed it all away and went to Eylsa. It required several seconds of shaking to rouse her, Layla dodging a flailing punch when the veteran came awake with an angry groan.

"Feeders!" Layla hissed at her, catching hold of her arm. "Get up!"

Eylsa shrugged off her confusion with impressive swiftness, pulling on her boots and assembling her gear far more quickly than Layla managed. "How the fuck did they get in?" she asked Stave, crouching at his side with her pistol in hand.

"Same way they got into Spark Town, I'd guess."

Eylsa's eyes tracked back and forth, a grimace passing over her face. Layla saw and heard nothing out of the ordinary, but the two veterans plainly did. "The gate?" Eylsa asked.

"Pretty sure it's already fallen. The walls too. We'll head for the docks."

"Shouldn't we warn people?" Layla asked, checking to make sure the pill bottle was still in her pocket before reaching for her pack.

"This place is already gone," Eylsa told her. "Just doesn't know it yet. We start shouting we'll just draw the feeders to us." She flicked an impatient hand, urging her to hurry up. Layla began to pull on her pack, then stopped at the sight of Luce's. *Watch my tanks, OK?*

Leave it, Layla decided. *Too heavy . . . Her name's Una.* Swallowing a sigh, she went to Luce's pack and extracted the tanks. They weighed about a kilo each, not especially burdensome, but she knew she would feel it after a few days. *Just take one?*

"Layla!" Eylsa grunted.

Stuffing both tanks into her pack, Layla tightened the straps and pulled it on.

"Gun out," Eylsa said, gesturing to the revolver holstered at Layla's hip. "You're going to need it."

They departed the tent in a crouching run. Any doubts Layla had about her colleagues' judgement were dispelled by the sight of a body sprawled from a hut a few yards on. She also heard the sound of running feet, too swift to be human. The screams began when they got to the edge of Crosser Town, a shriek of surprised agony, quickly cut off, immediately followed by more, then a flurry of gunshots as flashlights flickered to life among the tents.

"Luce . . ." Layla murmured, seeing the first feeder erupt through a canvas wall, recognising the elongated skull and limbs of a beta before it sped away too fast to follow. The urge to go back was a small, instantly quelled fluttering in her chest. *She's gone*, she decided, hating her own ruthless cowardice, even though she knew it to be true.

Stave and Eylsa started running then, Layla sprinting in their wake. They pelted through the line of food stalls and into the narrow alleys of the town proper. Layla entertained a dim hope that the feeders would be fully preoccupied with the plentiful prey in Crosser Town, but the rapid thud of inhumanly fast feet on the metallic rooftops proved her wrong. They made it to the market as the Harbour dwellers began to issue from their homes. A crowd of them milled about in the square, many barely clothed, some armed, most not. The sight of three fleeing crossers provoked a barrage of shouted questions. Stave ignored them, but Eylsa spared a breath for a brief response: "Feeders inside the walls!"

Their exclamations of doubt and shock transformed into screams when a beta landed in their midst. Layla caught a blur of slashing limbs and a flash of red before tearing her gaze away and following Stave and Eylsa into another alley. She closed her ears to the sounds of slaughter and kept running, encroaching panic causing her to rebound from the metal walls several times. Up ahead, she heard the suppressed snap of Stave's rifle, two shots followed by the louder crack of Eylsa's pistol. Layla didn't pause to look at the feeder corpse in her path. Hurdling it, her fear surged when she found the alley ahead empty. Rounding a corner, she gasped in relief at finding both veterans on the dockside. Less reassuring was the fact that they had come to a halt.

Feeders were on the upper platform, three betas gorging themselves on recently killed prey. Layla shuddered with an involuntary chill at the sight of their pale bodies heaving as they drank, faces buried in the wounds they had gouged into their victims. They were too preoccupied with their glut of nourishment to notice Layla and the others, but the thunderous cacophony of many more sweeping across the rooftops of Harbour Point made it starkly clear their reprieve was only temporary.

"Left," Stave told Eylsa quietly before nodding to Layla. "Right."

Crouching, he trained his rifle on the feeder in the centre while Eylsa trained her pistol on the one to the left. The revolver felt lighter than before as Layla raised it, although the sights trembled with annoying violence as she fought to align them on the head of her allotted target. Gripping the weapon with both hands, she locked her elbows and fired the moment Stave did. Her bullet sheared away the top of the feeder's skull in an explosion of red and white. It collapsed instantly, coughing out a short gout of blood before subsiding into animated twitching atop the corpse it had been gorging on. Stave had also felled his target with a single shot, while Eylsa was obliged to put two additional rounds into hers before it lay still.

"The ropes," Stave said, starting forward at a run. "The ladders are too slow."

As they made their way along the platform, Layla spared a glance at one of the bodies now entwined with the fallen feeders, making out the oil-smeared overalls and weathered features of the boatman Pitt had haggled with only hours earlier.

"Stop gawping!" Eylsa snapped, Layla turning to see her leap from the platform and catch hold of one of the ropes dangling from the crane arms looming above. Stave had already done the same and was nimbly descending to the dock below. Holstering her revolver, ears now filled with the cacophonous drumbeat of a great many feeders approaching, Layla leaped for the nearest rope. It was a thick cable of dense cord, thankfully dry, her hands finding purchase easily. It swung with alarming energy as she made her inexpert descent, leaping clear when she judged the distance to the dock as less than ten feet. From the ache of her ankles when she landed, she had miscalculated the drop.

"Wait!" Eylsa called out to a boat pulling away from the dock, water churning and smoke blossoming from its narrow stack. The lone occupant paid her no heed, spinning his wheel to point the bows towards open water before gunning the engine to maximum speed. The few other boats were all busily following suit, apart from one occupied by a skinny figure waving at them with manic urgency.

"Get the fuck on!" Pitt shouted as they pounded towards him across the wooden planking.

"Thought you'd left," Eylsa greeted him as she hopped aboard.

"Would have if I'd known how to work this thing." He gestured at the wheel and engine controls. "One of you better or we're fucked."

"What happened to the owner?" Eylsa asked as Stave moved to take the wheel.

"Didn't want passengers," Pitt said with a shrug. Layla noted he had his blaster in hand.

Stave put one hand on the wheel and another on the throttle. "Cast off," he said, jerking his head at the ropes attached to the bows and the stern. Eylsa hurried forward while Pitt and Layla went aft.

"What kind of knot is this?" Pitt griped, fingers plucking ineffectually at the overlapping cord.

"I've got it," Layla said. Crouching, she drew Nehna's knife from her ankle and set about cutting through the rope. It came apart after some energetic sawing, Stave spinning the wheel and pushing the throttle forward the moment it did. The boat heaved over the wakes left by the other craft, sending Layla and Pitt into an uncomfortably intimate sprawl.

"Sorry," he muttered, removing his hands from her hips. Rising, he offered her a hand, brows raised in a question. "Luce?"

Layla began to shake her head, then opened her mouth to shout a warning as she saw the pale shape descending from the sky. There must have been over twenty feet between the boat and the docks, but the feeder covered it with ease, long limbs enfolding Pitt's torso as it sank its many teeth into his neck.

The revolver bucked in Layla's hand, blasting the feeder's head into bloody chunks. She didn't remember drawing it. Pitt collapsed to the deck, blood seeping through his fingers, while Eylsa hurried aft to help Layla shove the beta's corpse over the side. Unearthing her bandage from her pack, Layla applied a thick wad to Pitt's wound, holding it there as Eylsa looped another around his shoulder and chest to secure it in place. He babbled for a time, drool-flecked nonsense spilling from his lips until, to Layla's relief, he slipped into unconsciousness.

A boom loud enough to shake the boat drew her gaze back to Harbour Point, seeing an orange ball of flame rise above the container stacks. It was followed by three more, each explosion more powerful than the last. Falling debris peppered the water to the rear of the boat while flames took hold in the town. They rose high in the space of only a few minutes, wavering red tendrils reaching into the sky.

"Someone managed to get to the fail-safe," Eylsa said.

"The what?" Layla asked.

"Pre-set napalm charges in case they got overrun. Lot of settlements have them. They're intended to create enough of a diversion for at least a few to escape, and kill as many feeders as possible."

Layla blinked tears in the acrid smoke gusting across the river, watching the fire consume the docks. The containers didn't burn, instead transforming into blackened husks as the inferno ate their contents. "All those people . . ." she said.

"Better burnt than eaten." Eylsa slumped onto a duckboard, sagging with exertion and despair as she regarded Pitt's unconscious form. "Or turned."

Chapter Nineteen

"Reckon we've got about half." Eylsa looked up from the contents of her pack, face drawn in grim acceptance. Deprived of the opportunity to share their cargo out among the team, they were forced to leave a good portion of it behind. "Including all the meds, so that's something. Techies won't be happy, though."

"Can't be helped," Stave said. "Coming back with something is always better than nothing."

He had steered the boat downriver, following the shifting tide. When dawn began to glimmer above the banks, he turned towards shore. Layla had asked if they could follow the river home, but Eylsa said it curved away from the Redoubt by several miles. Also, judging by the increasing sputter of the small diesel engine, it seemed likely they would soon run out of fuel.

Hearing a whimper from Pitt, Layla fitted the tarpaulin more tightly around his neck. He had begun to shiver with fever during the night, sweat-beaded skin growing paler with every passing hour.

"How long?" she enquired of Eylsa. "Until he . . ."

"No way to know. Sometimes they die. Sometimes they don't. Sometimes they turn. Sometimes they don't. There's no way to know which type either. Whatever happens, what you're doing isn't a kindness." She had said this once already, touching her pistol to make her meaning clear. In response, Layla sat closer to Pitt, dripping water over his brow and calming him during the infrequent moments of waking. He seemed so much younger now, his face tensing in fear during the brief instances of awareness. With the burgeoning daylight, Layla noted how his eyes had changed colour, the irises taking on a yellow hue. His agitation increased as the sun rose above the horizon, though he calmed when Layla raised the tarpaulin to shade him.

"Thirst . . ." he croaked when his shudders abated. His eyes seemed to glow beneath the covering as he stared at Layla in plaintive need. "Thirsty . . ."

She put her flask to his lips, though he managed only a few gulps before choking. *He's not thirsty for water*, she knew, watching the fear overtake him once more. He wept for a while before calming, though this time he didn't fall back into a stupor. Swallowing, Pitt fixed his unnatural gaze on Layla, addressing her with a steady, controlled rasp: "I can see . . . your blood flowing . . . in your veins. It's almost . . . beautiful."

She began to draw away, but he caught her wrist, moving too fast to see. Her hand went to her revolver, but stopped when he spoke again. "You know . . . what's to be done. I'd rather it was . . . you. If that's . . . OK."

Layla fought down a surge of anger, looking away. *This isn't fair!* Her shameful cowardice returned with a vengeance, urging her to twist her arm free of his grip and tell Eylsa to take care of it. But she didn't.

"OK," she said.

Pitt made a sound that mixed a human sigh with something far more guttural and animalistic, releasing her wrist and slumping into the arch of the boat's bows. "You ever . . . make it back . . . to the Riverbank," he said, each word now emerging as a mangled grunt. Layla couldn't tell if it was because his teeth were growing. "Be sure . . . to tell them . . . Pitt said they can . . . all go fuck themselves with a rusty knife."

"I'll tell them," she said, forcing a smile. She got to her feet and angled the tarpaulin to keep the sun off him as she reached for her revolver.

"Here," Eylsa said, pushing Pitt's blaster into her hand with an apologetic wince. They needed to save the good ammo.

Layla was grateful that Pitt's awareness had faded again when she trained the weapon on his head. Instead of subsiding back into unconsciousness, he began to jerk and spasm, his body emitting a series of cracks and crunches that told of transforming limbs. Seeing his hands morphing into pale, wriggling spiders, the fingers lengthening into barbs, Layla dragged the tarpaulin aside and shot him in the head.

It was fully light by the time Stave moored the boat alongside a heavily overgrown bank. After they leaped ashore, he tied the stern rope to a tree. "Someone might need it," he said in response to Layla's inquisitive frown.

"Course home?" Eylsa enquired. They huddled in a tight cluster, speaking in whispers while darting constant glances at the trees crowding the bank. Layla didn't need her to explain that there was no prospect of returning the way they had come.

"The tracks," Stave said.

"Too straight. And the tracks take us past the refinery. Pretty thick with feeders last time I went near it."

"Won't be now." He nodded back towards Harbour Point, where a column of smoke rose above the trees, a dark stain upon the sky which showed no signs of thinning. "Most of them are going to be otherwise occupied."

"I've seen places fall before, but not like that. Way too quick. Almost like they had help."

Oh rose thou art sick . . . Layla wasn't sure why she didn't say anything about the poetry-reciting woman. Maybe they'd laugh at her. It seemed like an outlandish connection between a missing book and a poem she half heard when drunk. But, as she continued to ponder the wisdom of speaking up, the two veterans had already started moving.

Upon clearing the trees, Stave struck out across a series of open fields. Layla was glad he didn't make them run. Luce's tanks were an ever more present burden, provoking the guilt-tinged notion of dumping one, or even both. The sight of Pitt's head blasting apart dispelled the temptation with a flare of self-loathing. She deserved this pain and more besides.

The fields eventually gave way to a curious landscape of low, undulating hills where the grass grew tall in places and short in others. The recurrent slopes and shallow gulleys seemed unnaturally compacted, making for ground that was both annoying and nerve-wracking to navigate. "This is some weird country," she commented during a rest stop.

"Golf course," Eylsa said, nodding to an overground mound. Peering closer, Layla recognised it as some kind of vehicle beneath the shroud of greenery, a squat conveyance with small wheels, almost like a child's go-cart. "People with nothing better to do would come here and hit little balls with sticks," Eylsa elaborated. "Ride around on those in between holes to save the bother of walking. Cost them a fortune to do it, too."

Layla had read about golf, and other odd games played during the Peace, always finding them so far removed from her experience that they seemed like fiction. But, looking at this expanse of arable land given over to something so frivolous, the sheer scale of the change wrought by the Feeding struck her with a new potency.

"How many people were alive back then?" she asked. "Do you know?"

"A lot," Eylsa said. "Billions. But only a few of them played golf."

"Eight point five billion," Stave said. "So many some scientists worried we were going to eat our way through the whole world. Then the feeders came along and did it for us." He took a final gulp from his flask. "Time to move."

Beyond the golf course lay a cluster of large houses. They were arranged around the faint outline of a branching road, each structure rising above an enclosing jungle of vegetation. To Layla, they possessed a picture-book quality, high sloping roofs with small turret-like towers at the apex or corners. As they drew closer to one, a number of car wrecks became visible amid the undergrowth. Counting six of different types and sizes, Layla concluded several families must have lived in each house. The observation provoked a suppressed laugh from Eylsa before she put a cautionary finger to her lips.

They circled the house before going inside, weapons drawn and eyes flicking to every shadow. Entry was gained via a planked-up window on the building's side. Stave reached behind the boards to throw a hidden catch before removing the covering. He spent a short interval scanning the interior with the rifle at his shoulder before nodding to Eylsa and hauling himself inside. Clambering in after them, Layla was struck by the orderliness of the place. It was dusty but otherwise unspoiled. Marble floors caught a full gleam from the partial light leaking through the boarded-up windows, outlining tables bearing various ornaments and framed pictures on the walls.

Stave replaced the barrier on the window, securing it in place with a bolt. Gesturing for Layla to stay put, he and Eylsa made a careful ascent of a broad staircase sweeping in an elegant curve to the upper floor. They returned a few minutes later, the three of them making a thorough inspection of the ground floor. Layla found the lack of destruction jarring, as if she had climbed through a window into a moment from the Peace, albeit shorn of inhabitants. Her gaze flicked over bronze statuettes and paintings, some of which she recognised from Strang's books on art history. The fact of finding them here seemed a wonderful discovery until she peered closer and saw that they weren't true paintings but printed reproductions.

"You can't buy class," Eylsa said, casting a caustic look around a room furnished with leather sofas and, taking pride of place in the centre, a grand piano. "I'd bet a week's ration chits none of the fuckers who lived here could play a single note."

They ended the tour in the kitchen, a space so extravagantly large and rich in sinks and cupboards, Layla wondered why the inhabitants needed the other rooms. She checked the extensive store room, finding it empty of threats, the shelves piled with the dust of long-rotted food.

"Just leaves the basement," Eylsa whispered to Stave with a grimace. "Do we have to?"

"Not if you're OK with making the return trip on an empty stomach," he said. Moving to a sturdy door at the rear of the room, he punched a sequence into the keypad that had been fitted in place of the lock. He turned on his flashlight as the door swung open. Keeping it pointed into the shadows below the revealed set of stone steps, he rested the rifle's fore stock on his arm and started down.

"Why so cautious if it's sealed?" Layla whispered.

"Foundations give way over time," Eylsa murmured back. "Always possible one of them might have crawled in there."

Her own flashlight in hand, Layla kept close to Eylsa as they followed. The steps ended after about a dozen feet, the three beams gleaming on a multitude of bottles sitting in rows of floor-to-ceiling shelving. Layla started at the sound of a heavy click, then blinked as light flooded the cellar, provided by a quartet of halogen bulbs dangling from the upper shelves.

"Batteries still got some juice after all this time," Stave observed, lowering his hand from a switch box.

They inspected the walls, revealing patches of misaligned brickwork, but no unwanted intrusions. The bedrolls and supplies, all covered in a liberal coating of dust, lay beneath a wide vent at the far end of the cellar.

"How long since you were here last?" Layla asked, lifting a bedroll to shake it free of dust.

"Three years, maybe," Eylsa said. "Or it might be four." Layla noticed that she seemed preoccupied with the bottles. Directing a questioning glance at Stave, and receiving a shrug in response, Eylsa grinned and began to tour the shelves. "Think I'm in the mood for something in a Chablis."

"You should take one," Stave advised Layla. "There's people back home who'll pay a lot for good wine."

"Yeah," Layla agreed. She wasn't sure why she said what she did next, but the words were out before she thought to stop them. "Like Velna. You know her, right? Mean old crow with a shop in the Arts. Buys and sells just about anything."

His only reaction was a small narrowing of the eyes before he turned away to prop the rifle against the wall. "I've heard of her," he said, groaning a little as he removed his pack.

She sold you something, you fucking liar. What was it? This time, she managed to cage the words. Something was starting to come together in her mind. Spark Town. William Blake. The gamma with a broken neck they found near Harbour Point. It all felt like spokes on the same wheel, but she couldn't see it all yet. She also wasn't entirely sure she wanted to. *Home.* She reached into her pocket to grip the pill bottle, a new mantra filling her head. *All that matters is getting home.*

"Montée de Tonnerre, Grand Cru," Eylsa announced with a note of triumph. She returned from the shelves, blowing cobwebs from a bottle. "I'm guessing whoever lived here paid an expert to stock this place." She plucked a trio of upended wine glasses from a shelf and sat on a bedroll to peel the foil from the cork. "Care to join me?"

The wine wasn't like any liquor Layla had tasted before. A mix of dry and sweet that slipped down with delightful ease and had her extending her glass for more.

"Girl's got taste," Eylsa said, pouring a refill.

Smiling, Layla drank again before the guilt hit her like a hard punch to the chest. Suddenly, the wine tasted bitter, swallowed hard past a constricting throat. "Romer dead," she said, her voice coloured by a welling sob. She didn't care if they heard it. "Luce probably dead. Pitt definitely dead, because—" Layla let out a grating laugh. "Because I killed him. And we're sitting here drinking *fucking* wine."

"That we are," Eylsa sighed. She held her glass up, angling it to study the sunlight yellow liquid inside. "And excellent it is, too."

Layla wanted to throw the rest of her wine in Eylsa's face, accompanying the gesture with a loud "Fuck you!" But she didn't. Instead, she set her glass down on the concrete floor and huddled onto her bedroll. For a while, no one said anything. Eylsa continuing to drink wine Layla guessed she would never have been able to afford during the Peace, while Stave disassembled the rifle for cleaning.

"People die out here," Eylsa said finally, voice duller than usual, which Layla assumed to be the result of consuming almost the whole bottle herself. "It's shit. But that's how it is if you do this job. And it's not like no one told you, is it? Selection is hard for a reason. Killing is the price we pay for all the goodies we bring back, like those pills in your pocket. Death." Layla heard the bitter smile in Eylsa's voice as she added a final mutter. "It's the only real currency out here."

Layla woke to the sound of music. At first she thought it a lingering remnant of a dream, but then realised that, for the first time since descending the wall, she had experienced a dreamless night. *Maybe the wine?* She smothered the question with the need to address a far more urgent concern. *Where's the music coming from?*

Jerking upright, she wiped grit from her eyes to find herself alone in the basement. Eylsa and Stave were gone, and so was their gear. *Cut me loose?* Layla wondered. Perhaps her whining last night had persuaded them she wasn't worth the trouble any more. *But why the music?*

Pulling on her pack, she drew the revolver and made for the stairs. She found the door unlocked and the kitchen also empty, but the music louder, coming from the front of the house. Her tension abated when she remembered the grand piano in the big room with the leather sofas. Still, she kept a two-handed grip on the gun as she made her way along the hall. The music stopped as she entered, Stave looking up from the piano with an arched eyebrow.

"Finally, she appears," he said. "Thought you might sleep the day away."

"Should've woken me," Layla said.

"Looked like you needed a rest. And the trek today isn't particular long. Just one more safe house and we're only half a day from home."

Holstering the revolver, Layla looked around the room. "Where's Eylsa?"

"Rummaging the house across the street for anything worth taking."

"On her own?"

"Way she wanted it. Besides, all the years we've been coming here, we've never found a feeder in any of these houses. Always wondered if they had an aversion to the smell of money."

Different all of a sudden, Layla decided, watching him return his focus to the piano. The faint smile on his lips conveyed a fond familiarity, as did the way his fingers traced over the keys. He tapped out another tune, intricate and fast, also familiar.

"Mozart," Layla said. "Right?"

"That's right."

"I thought you were a soldier."

His smile broadened a little as he continued to play, the tune shifting into something more ominous. "I was a conscript. There's a difference."

Layla had never been adept at music, despite Cuhla's attempts to teach her, but had heard enough of it in the Arts to recognise true expertise. She thought the current tune might be Beethoven, but wasn't sure.

"Ouch!" Stave said, wincing as he struck a particular key. It hadn't sounded bad to Layla, but clearly he had a more discerning ear. "I did my best to tune her, but she's an old girl. Surprised the strings haven't snapped years ago."

He played on, and Layla was content to let him for a while. Sinking onto one of the sofas, she sat back, letting the music wash over her. She did this sometimes back home, on the roof listening to the sound of Cuhla's cello drifting over the Arts.

"Where'd you learn that?" she asked when the piece came to an end.

"From my mother, at first. Did my ten thousand hours and got a scholarship to music school." He paused, tapping out a series of lighter notes before continuing in a brisker tone. "That's where I met

Rehsa. She was studying literature. I'm not exaggerating when I say she was the single most intelligent person I ever met in my life. She could've studied anything and excelled. Physics, medicine. Anything. But she chose books. 'Words, my love,' she told me. 'That's where the true power lies.' Halfway through our first term, the news started talking about a spate of unexplained animal attacks. Then they started talking about massacres. Then cities going dark. Then whole countries. Soon enough, we both found ourselves in uniform."

"She was there, at Corporation Junction. She was the one who made it to the Redoubt with you." Layla shifted, uncomfortable despite the softness of the sofa. "I'm sorry. For losing her. I guess it was . . . hard."

Stave glanced at her, brows creased.

"I'm not good with words," she said.

"I think you do all right, all things considered."

It all came together then, each spoke of the wheel guided into place by his story. More than that, it was his expression when he spoke of his wife. This was a man still in love. "I guess Rehsa must've known poetry?" she asked. "If she studied literature, I mean."

His smile returned, fingers resuming their melodic course over the keys. "Oh yes. She had a liking for the romantic rather than the modern."

"Like William Blake? He was a romantic, wasn't he?"

Stave stopped playing, his smile now gone. "He's

classed as a romantic," he said, voice toneless now. "But Rehsa always said he deserved a category of his own: Mystical Theologism. That was going to be the basis of her thesis; how the uniqueness of his voice and vision defied categorisation."

"'The Sick Rose'," Layla went on. "That a favourite of hers, maybe? I'd guess it was in that book she took from the Spark Town library. Funny thing, I heard a woman reciting it in Harbour Point just a few hours before it all went to shit. Didn't get a proper look at her face. Kinda wish I had, though."

Stave let out a sigh, his finger descending upon a single key. This time she could hear the discordancy of it, a dry thrum of aged twine.

"She didn't die out here, did she?" Layla got to her feet, moving to the piano, staring down at him. "She got bit and you couldn't kill her. That's why you never crossed together before. You knew if it came to it, you couldn't do what I did for Pitt."

Stave said nothing, continuing to tap the same key, his rhythm slow and steady.

"Spark Town," Layla said, stepping closer. "Harbour Point. It was her. Not sure how she got in, but once she did, she could wander the place at will. What I don't get is the betas. It's like they're working with her, but we were told that never happens. Any thoughts to share?"

He kept tapping the same key until she slammed her hand down next to his, the blare of overlapping notes echoing in the room. Stave didn't speak until it faded. "I don't know about the betas," he said. "I didn't know . . . what she had become. But yes, she got bit and I . . . couldn't. She begged me to . . ." He trailed off, shaking his head, eyes closed and swallowing hard. "I just couldn't."

"But you knew she turned. You came out here to look for her. That's why you made us go into the plant. That's why you insisted on checking out Spark Town."

"I left her while she lay dying." Stave opened his eyes, staring up at Layla. She had never expected to describe this man as pathetic, yet now he was, that and more, a guilt-stricken coward begging for understanding. "I couldn't watch her . . ."

He faltered when Layla quick drew the revolver and pressed the barrel to his forehead. "Romer's dead because of you. Harbour Point . . ."

"I didn't know that would happen." She saw no fear in his unblinking stare, just the same need for her to comprehend his weakness. "I didn't know she had gotten in. But you're right. It's all on me."

Kill him and I don't get home, she thought, still not shifting her finger to the revolver's trigger. It was an arguable point. Who knew what other missteps he would make in his search for his wife? And what did he intend to do when he found her?

"I saw you at Velna's," she said. "What did you buy?"

His smile returned, and she was tempted to shoot him just for that. "Something that's going to wash away all my sins, Layla," he said.

She flinched at the sound of the board being lifted from the side window. Eylsa had returned. "She doesn't know, does she?" she asked Stave in a whisper, receiving a fractional shake of his head in response. The revolver barrel left a red circle on his skin when she removed it. "Keep it that way. From here on, no more fucking around. We just get home. Understand?"

Before she received an indication of agreement, Eylsa came through the door cheerfully brandishing a bouquet of wires. "Copper!" she said, hair and shoulders dusted with grime and powdered plaster. "They had solar panels and one of those wall batteries." She began coiling the wires. "This'll stop the techies moaning too much. We should check the other houses."

"No time," Stave said. Closing the piano lid, he reached for the rifle and got to his feet. "Should've been on the tracks by now. Time we went home."

Chapter Twenty

The tracks offered the straightest route they had taken so far, but also the most nerve-wracking.

"Every year, the woods grow thicker and the shade deeper," Eylsa said, voice hushed as they followed the twin lines of rusted metal atop rotted sleepers. They kept to the relatively clear gap between the two separate tracks, the shingle that underlaid them busy with weeds that grew dense enough to obscure the rails in places. Eylsa's gaze constantly roved the forest to either side. "There's a reason we don't often come this way."

They were required to skirt a number of trains. Some had tumbled onto the verges, but others still sat atop the tracks. Most were freight haulers, but some were formed of passenger carriages. A few of these had evidently been occupied for a while after the Feeding, bulked out with improvised fortifications and additional shelters. From the shattered windows and overgrown state of the defences, it was also clear they hadn't lasted long.

"Helluva way to go," Eylsa said when they paused alongside a carriage with ladders propped against its sides and a lookout post rising from its roof. "Stuck on a train at the end of the world."

Layla considered scaling one of the ladders for a look inside, but opted against it. *Just another place filled with bones*, she thought, recalling the airport.

They started to move on, then stopped when a loud boom echoed across the tracks. Layla joined the others in crouching and drawing her weapon. However, as the sound faded, her eyes tracked over woodland undisturbed apart from the agitated flutter of birds.

"Fuck was that?" Eylsa said, and Layla was shocked to see her pistol shaking in her grip. *She really has done too many trips.*

"High-ex, whatever it was," Stave replied. He continued to pan the rifle over the trees for a few seconds longer, then lowered it. "As to what or where." He shrugged and straightened. Layla searched his face for signs of deceit, but saw nothing. If this connected to Rehsa, he didn't know how. Jerking his head, he started off at a brisk walk, both of them following closely.

They covered another mile before the next unexpected event, but this time it wasn't an explosion, but a dog. Catching a flicker of movement in the bushes to her left, Layla hissed in warning. All three of them halted to train their weapons on a reddish-brown shape emerging from the undergrowth about twenty feet away. The animal was so different in appearance from the mangy, vicious denizens of the Undercut that Layla thought it might be from a separate species. For a start, it was about twice the size. Also, instead of milky, unseeing eyes, it regarded them with a bright inquisitive gaze, tongue lolling from an open mouth in a manner that resembled a guileless smile. Its coat was free of matting or sores, its tail long and swaying gently. All in all, it exhibited no sense of threat, but hard-learned instincts were difficult to break and Layla still found herself raising her revolver.

"Don't," Eylsa said, putting her hand on Layla's forearm, easing the weapon down. "She's harmless." Sinking to her haunches, she extended a hand to the dog, fingers open and palm displayed. "Hello, you. What you doing out here, hun?" The dog tilted her head from side to side as Eylsa continued her coaxing. "You're not out here alone, are you? Don't look hungry enough."

The dog inched closer, nose twitching as it drew near to her outstretched hand, then darting back in alarm at the sound of Stave's voice. "Daylight's burning, Eylsa."

"This girl's got an owner, I reckon," Eylsa said, arm still extended. "Too clean and well fed. Friendly too, ain't ya, girl? Noticed how she doesn't bark? Means she's awful smart."

"No time," Stave said, voice hardening with insistence.

Grimacing in annoyance, Eylsa rose, causing the dog to retreat a few paces. "Best if you go on home now," Eylsa told her as they resumed walking only for the animal to keep pace with them along the verge.

"Could be tracking us for somebody," Layla suggested, still conflicted over whether to shoot it. *Too loud*, she reminded herself, casting a wary glance at the surrounding woods. *Have to get close enough to cut its throat.* But the dog never approached more than a dozen feet, maintaining its placid tail wag and decidedly non-hostile expression throughout the day. After a while, Layla's concern eased, though the animal's presence remained a perturbing distraction until Stave came to a halt, the reason obvious in the form of a bridge spanning a narrow gorge up ahead.

"Seems intact," Eylsa said. "I made it across OK last time I was here."

"Doesn't mean we will this time," he replied.

The bridge looked sturdy enough to Layla, despite the extensive patches of rust covering its riveted iron girders. Vegetation had spread from both banks to lace vines through its crossbeam arches, although the span itself showed no gaps.

"Getting late," Eylsa pointed out as Stave continued to scrutinise the bridge. To Layla's eyes, the sky hadn't dimmed all that much. They probably had another hour of true daylight before the shadows started to lengthen. But she remembered Eylsa's hands shaking and heard the strain in her voice. The dog might have provided a welcome diversion, but that had been temporary. Eylsa's nerves, stretched over years and now tested to their limit, were starting to fray.

Thoughts of the dog drew Layla's gaze to the verge, but it had gone. *Back to whoever feeds it*, she thought, though she couldn't imagine anyone living among these trees.

"We'll take it slow," Stave said, starting forward. "Single file. Keep to the edge and eyes on the tracks. Watch out for gaps."

Only a few steps onto the bridge were enough to convince Layla that Stave's caution was justified. The rails had been laid atop a platform of sheet iron, thick with moss and extensively rusted. The corrosion was so deep she could glimpse the fast-flowing river below. Consequently, they were forced to walk on the relatively intact base of the left-hand arch. The walkable surface was only a few inches across, meaning they had to adopt a one foot in front of the other gait, which made for slow progress.

"She didn't follow, then?" Eylsa said, casting a regretful glance at the far end of the bridge.

"Couldn't see her," Layla said. As last in line, she was obliged to halt when Eylsa did. "Guess she's gone home, wherever that is."

"Was kinda hoping she'd follow us all the way back." Eylsa turned to resume progress. "Would've been nice to have a dog again."

"Pets aren't allowed."

"Oh, screw that. After fifteen crossings, if I want a pet, I'm having a fucking—"

Her words ended in a gasp of surprise and pain as a patch of rust to the right of her foot exploded. A claw punched through the degraded metal like wet paper, sinking its barbs into Eylsa's ankle. Seeing the snarling face of a beta through the hole below, Layla drew the revolver, but Stave had already opened fire. A salvo of bullets shredded metal and flesh, the feeder losing its grip to tumble from sight. Layla couldn't hear the subsequent splash over the sound of Eylsa's screams.

"FUUUUCK!" She slumped onto the span, clutching at her ankle, blood seeping through her fingers. Hearing an alarming crack of strained iron, Layla began to reach out to her, only for another claw to erupt through the rust to her right. Layla pivoted and fired in the same motion, the bullet raising a red plume as it hit wide of the flailing limb. Incredibly, the feeder kept clawing its way up, scattering red fragments as it emerged into the light. Before she fired again, Layla saw the all too human squint of pain on its distorted face. *Hates the sunlight*, she realised. *But still keeps coming.*

Her next bullet took the feeder in the throat, sending it thrashing onto its back until the metal gave way under its weight and it fell from sight. The crack of Stave's rifle snapped her gaze to the left, watching ejected cartridge casings arc as he loosed off short bursts at the dozen or more feeders now climbing into view.

"Layla . . ."

Her gaze shifted to Eylsa, lying with a bloodied hand outstretched, her face bleached and terrified. Before Layla could reach out, the veteran convulsed, a fountain of red erupting from her mouth as her body arched like a bow. A red ball forced its way through her sternum, recognised as a feeder's fist when the fingers opened to latch onto what remained of Eylsa's torso. She disappeared in a cloud of powdered metal as the feeder dragged her down. Layla could see it perched on the upper beams of the bridge support, head and jaws worrying as it feasted on its prize. She shot it twice, sending both predator and prey tumbling into the speeding current.

Turning back to Stave, she saw him crouched, tossing a magazine aside as he slotted his second into the rifle. A feeder clambered onto the crossbeams above, unnaturally long arm reaching out for Stave's neck. Layla shot it in the chest, but it held on, dark fluid frothing from its mouth as it convulsed. Aiming for its head, Layla pulled the trigger on an empty chamber.

"Shit!" She began fumbling for the bullets in her pockets, crouching and snapping the revolver's cylinder open to slot them in place. Hearing the snap of Stave's rifle again, she looked up to see him putting a round through the head of the feeder still clinging onto the beams. As it tumbled from view, he shifted his aim, blasting another beta crawling along the base of the arch. The rest kept coming, leaping from beam to beam to avoid the hail of bullets as Layla joined Stave's barrage. She hit one, three shots catching it in mid-leap, before the revolver clicked empty once more. She was out. The abrupt silence of Stave's rifle made it clear he was, too.

"Jump!" he told her, nodding to the large rent in the span left by Eylsa's demise. The rushing water below was deeply uninviting, but so were the fast-approaching feeders.

"Both of us," she said, suffering a jolt of shock at Stave's expression when she turned back to him. Instead of the tense concentration of combat from moments before, she saw a nervous expectation, even acceptance.

"They won't kill me," he said, voice absurdly calm save for a small tremor. "Not if she sent them."

She reeled back as a feeder latched a claw to his shoulder. But instead of the expected explosion of blood and flashing teeth, it took hold without sinking its barbs into his flesh. Another descended to enclose his legs in a tight embrace, both creatures bearing him up and away as if he weighed no more than an infant. The others continued to advance on her, all exhibiting the same squinting detestation of daylight, but a ravening hunger shining bright in their eyes. Stave they wouldn't eat. Her, on the other hand . . .

The closest one lunged for her, a sound that resembled an old saw blade meeting thick wood emerging from its gaping maw. Layla threw the revolver at it and jumped.

Chapter Twenty-One

A brief sensation of weightlessness as bridge, woods and river revolved in a chaotic swirl, then the water gripped her like an icy fist. The shock of it rendered her incapable of struggle in the churning current. Layla willed unresponsive hands to catch hold of the rocks that scraped and thudded against her before the irresistible force dragged her on. She regained some measure of movement when her lungs began to burn, jerked into motion by the adrenaline surging through her veins.

The current eased, and she found herself drifting, gazing up at a roof of dappled light as her feet raised clouds of silt from the riverbed. Flexing her legs, she pushed for the surface, breaking through with a shout, swiftly cut short by her instinctive gulps for air. The weight of her pack almost bore her under again until her flailing hand caught on something. Gripping tight, she saw it was a tree branch extending from the bank, just far enough for her to grasp. Grunting with the effort, Layla hauled herself into the shade of over-hanging foliage. Reaching the muddy shore, she managed to crawl halfway from the water before exhaustion dragged her down, her cheek slapping into mud. Unable to do more than lie there and shiver, the world slipped into hazy unimportance as she spiralled into oblivion.

She was woken by something wet fluttering at her fingers. Groaning, she flicked them, which succeeded in banishing the sensation, but only briefly. The moist insistence of it brought the realisation that a living thing was touching her flesh. Sputtering mud, Layla jerked upright, hand going to the knife on her ankle, then pausing when she found herself staring into a pair of dark brown eyes.

The dog's mouth opened wider, tongue lapping over her chops, before she let out a short huffing sound. It was much softer than a bark, and sounded weirdly like a question, the impression emphasised by the way the animal's eyes tracked over Layla's mud-caked form.

"I fell in the river," she told it, then laughed at the absurdity of offering an explanation to a dog. The laugh went on longer than it should, diminishing into a series of short, choking sobs. *Stop that!* Layla pounded a fist against her thigh in reproach, dragging in a series of breaths. *Not the first time you've been alone*, she reminded herself, continuing to take in air until she felt strong enough to move.

"I'm guessing," she said to the dog as she struggled onto firm ground, "you don't happen to know where the nearest safe house is?"

Receiving another quiet huff in response, she nodded. "OK then. Guess I'll have to find it myself." Looking around, she saw only the wide curve of the river and a great many trees. She could follow the river back to the bridge, but going anywhere near it seemed like an extremely bad idea.

They didn't kill him. The memory of Stave's capture replayed in her head, bright and strange. *He wasn't afraid. Or as afraid as he should've been. They won't kill me. Not if she sent them.*

She shook her head, deciding all of that was too much to think about right now, then froze in the grip of another, far more urgent realisation. There was nothing in her pocket. Looking down, she saw the fabric ripped, exposing a patch of chilled, bare flesh, and no sign of the pill bottle.

"No!"

Feverishly, her hands explored every pocket and fold of her overalls, finding nothing. Sobbing, Layla took off her pack and rummaged it deep. She told herself she must have switched the pills to the pack last night. But she hadn't. Luce's two tanks of nitrous oxide remained, along with a few supplies, but no pills. They were now floating serenely downriver.

Layla slumped onto all fours, heaving in anticipation of either uncontrollable weeping or throwing up.

Surprisingly, neither happened, because she remembered something. *The list. The list Eylsa handed to the woman at Harbour Point.* Amoxicillin had been on that list. Meaning either Eylsa had it, in which case it was gone for ever, or it was still in Stave's pack. Stave who had been dragged off by a pack of betas to fuck knew where.

She let out a sob, hating the sound of it. The weakness it held. She raised her fist, intending to deliver another punch to her thigh, then stopped when the dog gave another huff. Looking up, she found it had retreated a short distance, regarding her with an unmistakable air of expectation. Darting forward a few feet, it huffed and drew back once again.

Does it actually want me to follow it? Layla halted the laugh in her throat, worried it would summon panic. A few more darting retreats from the dog, however, convinced her that it actually was trying to get her to follow. The notion of doing so seemed ridiculous until another thought occurred: *Where else have you got to go? Wander around the woods until it gets dark, maybe?*

"OK," she sighed, getting to her feet. "But if you take me to some kid trapped in a well, I'll fucking kill you."

After following the dog for a time, it occurred to her that she no longer had any real idea where she was in relation to either the river or the tracks. *Should've scratched arrows on the trees or something*, she berated herself through a mounting fugue of fatigue. She had stumbled several times already, losing sight of her four-legged guide, though it always came bounding back into view. After about an hour, Layla began to discern a track of sorts beneath the carpet of ferns. It was faint, just a line of marginally impacted ground, but it told of a path repeatedly walked by human feet. It was also clear that the dog was following its winding course through the trees with diligent attention. The only deviation came when, instead of proceeding into a gap between two tall, thick-trunked pines, the animal opted to move around the one on the right. Her vision dimmed by her body's demands for sleep, Layla kept plodding along the track. She stopped when the dog rushed into her path, letting out its loudest huff yet.

"What?" Layla grunted, waving a hand and trying to edge around the animal, whereupon it fastened its jaws on her sleeve and began to tug her off the track. "Hey!" Layla wrested her arm free, the violence of the motion bringing her to her knees. Muttering an obscene rebuke to the dog, she began to rise, pausing when she saw the line of thick twine stretched across the path. It was about two inches off the ground, meaning her foot would surely have caught it.

Rising, Layla traced the twine to the trunk of the tree to her right, where it disappeared into a thick patch of ferns. She began to edge forward for a better look, keeping well clear of the twine.

"Another stray. Terrific."

Layla froze. The voice came from behind. Female, clipped, and none too pleased to see her.

"I have a gun," Layla said, surprised and gratified by the fact the lie was uncoloured by any betraying uncertainty.

"Me too, sweets," the unseen woman replied. "But mine's pointed at you and yours is nowhere to be seen." A short pause in which Layla felt herself to be appraised, then: "Turn. Slow. Keep your hands in sight. Won't get any pleasure from shooting you, sweets, but that doesn't mean I won't."

Hands raised, Layla turned. The woman stood a dozen feet away, her face concealed in the hood of a camouflage-patterned waterproof. The assault rifle she had trained on Layla's chest was different to Stave's, smaller with a shorter barrel, and lacked the extensive repairs and modifications. From the way she held it, stock tight against her shoulder, Layla had no doubt of the woman's expertise. There was small comfort in the fact that her finger was off the trigger, but Layla knew that was just a standard safety precaution.

"Redoubt?" the woman asked.

"Yeah," Layla replied.

"Your lot never travel alone. Where's the rest of your crew?"

"Dead." *One captured, actually.* Layla thought best not to say so. Relating something so unbelievable struck her as deeply unwise. "Feeders. At the bridge."

"In daylight?" The tone of the question held a note of doubt, but not as deep as Layla expected.

"Yeah. Pretty weird, huh?"

"More than weird, sweets. But there's been a lot of weird lately." The assault rifle's barrel dipped a few inches. "You don't really have a gun, do you?"

Layla shook her head.

The woman gave a soft grunt and lowered the rifle all the way. "Name's Riann," she said, inclining her head and turning away. She didn't give any indication Layla should follow, but she did anyway.

"Layla."

Another grunt, the woman pausing to crouch at the patch of ferns, pulling them away to reveal what looked like a six-inch square of clay encased in clear plastic. "Tenth of a kilo of C4," she said. "One more step and I'd be talking to a woman with no legs. You're lucky Tricks took a shine to you. She doesn't with everyone." Hearing her name, the dog came to the woman's side, tail wagging fast and ears flat.

Looking at the explosive strapped to the tree, Layla remembered the boom they had heard on the tracks. "You set traps for them."

"More of a discouragement exercise than anything. They can be pretty smart, learn to avoid certain places. Apart from the ferals. I get one or two of those dumb shits every month." She looked up, Layla catching a glimpse of her face for the first time, bright eyes in narrow, aged features that jarred with the trim vitality of her body. "C'mon then," she said, rising and resuming her trek. "You look about ready to drop."

"I'm fine," Layla said. Despite this woman's lack of hostility, she still thought it prudent to affect an air of strength. It lasted about five minutes of traipsing in her wake on increasingly numb legs before Layla fell flat on her face.

"Well shit," she heard Riann mutter before the void closed in.

She awoke on a bed in a darkened room. The comfort of the mattress, smell of clean sheets and the absence of any obvious gaps in the roof above her head provoked tactile exploration as Layla convinced herself she wasn't dreaming. Once satisfied that the tight weave of the fabric she fondled was real, she rose from the bed, eyes exploring the shadows until they alighted on her pack. A quick check of her ankle also revealed Nehna's knife was still in place. Her shoes had been removed and sat alongside the pack. Pulling them on, Layla went to the door, opening it to be greeted by a gust of warm air tinged with woodsmoke and a drool-provoking scent of roasting meat.

"Come on out," Riann called, tone faintly amused. "Supper's waiting."

Pushing the door open all the way revealed a large room bathed in the light and warmth emanating from a brick fireplace. Riann sat before it on a padded leather armchair. Shorn of her hood, Layla saw she had long hair that seemed a shade too dark for a woman of her age. She didn't turn as Layla emerged from the bedroom, her attention fixed on the spitted carcass of some small animal roasting over the fire. Tricks rose from her side, hurrying to greet Layla with a flurry of tail wags and licks to her hands.

"You'll have to forgive my trusty companion," Riann said. "Rarely gets a chance to make new friends. Join me." She gestured to the chair opposite hers. "I trust you've got no problem with eating cutesy bunnies."

"None," Layla said. Instead of taking the chair, she lingered for a more thorough examination of her surroundings. The room featured two windows on opposite walls, both covered with black fabric, Layla assumed to prevent any light leaking into the outside. A number of curious objects adorned the remaining space, twigs twisted into a circle and interlaced with twine.

"Dreamcatchers," Riann said, still not turning. "The one superstition I haven't been able to shake. I like to think they help. Did you dream, by the way?"

"No," Layla said, her eyes fixing on the three guns hanging above the fireplace. One was the assault rifle Riann had been carrying when they met. Above it sat a bolt-action rifle with a large scope and, above that, a long-barrelled shotgun.

"Stop dithering and come sit," Riann snapped, her patience evidently wearing thin. "Can't tell me you're not hungry."

Her stomach quickened by the scent of the roasting rabbit, Layla moved to the chair and sat. It wasn't padded like Riann's armchair, and creaked a little under her weight.

"Sorry about that," her host said, running a hand over Tricks's pelt as she came to her side. "Haven't got much in the way of excess furniture. Don't get many visitors. Any, in fact."

Seeing her face in full for the first time, Layla found it the handsome, slightly wrinkled visage of a woman somewhere between fifty and sixty. She wore an olive-green tank top that left her arms bare, the toned, sculpted muscles a stark contrast to her apparent age. Riann's eyes were closed as she drew in the smell of her cooking, lips curving in appreciation. "Sprinkled on some wild thyme and a little of the salt and pepper I've been saving," she said. "Hope you appreciate me pushing the boat out like this."

"I'm . . . grateful," Layla began, coming to an abrupt halt as Riann opened her eyes and turned towards her. *Her eyes.* They caught the gleam of the firelight well, so well in fact that it was as if they glowed. Layla's gaze shifted again to Riann's arms, tracking across the hard muscle, the skin painted a yellow hue where it was touched by the fire's glow, but pale where it wasn't. Too pale.

Layla lunged for the rifle above the fireplace, hauling it clear of the bracket it rested in, whirling to train the barrel on Riann's chest, her finger squeezing a trigger that refused to budge.

"The safety," Riann said, pointing to the lever above the pistol grip.

Before Layla could put her thumb to the lever, something blurred across her vision and the rifle was plucked from her hands. Her gaze snapped to Riann, standing a few feet away, rifle cradled in her arms and brows drawn into a reproachful squint. At her side, Tricks let out a distressed whine. "That was hardly polite," Riann said.

"Fucking alpha!" The words sputtered from Layla's lips as she retreated, eyes flicking around the room. *Door! Where's the door?*

"Not exactly." Riann crouched to calm an agitated Tricks with a rub to the head before setting the rifle against the stone flank of the fireplace. "I like to think of myself as kind of an omega," she said, sinking back into her armchair. "It's a long story. I'll tell you all about it over dinner if you like."

Layla's panicked gaze had finally found the door, which, of course, was on the other side of the room. No way she could get to it before this thing did.

"I won't stop you leaving," Riann told her. She wrapped one hand in a cloth and lifted the spit from the fire. "Reckon this is about done. Dark outside," she added when Layla jerked towards the door, faltering to a halt before she got halfway. "Awful lot of my little inventions out there, too. So you might want to wait until morning."

Spitted rabbit still in hand, she rose and disappeared into the shadows at the far end of the room, Layla hearing the opening of drawers and rattle of cutlery. "Don't have much to offer by way of liquid refreshment," she called from the dark. "Just water. It's sterilised, though."

A lamp blazed into life, illuminating a table and chairs in a small kitchenette. Two plates complete with knives and forks sat on the table, along with a glass jug filled with water and a pair of tumblers. Setting down a roasting tray, Riann took up a knife and fork to slice off pieces of rabbit flesh. "Seriously, sweets," she said, not looking up from her task. "If I was gonna eat you, don't you think I'd already have done it? How many feeders have you seen cook their own meal?"

Layla's eyes flicked to the door and back again. Then they snapped to the guns over the fireplace. Neither was a viable prospect. Moving on stiff legs, she walked to the table and sat down. She had to swallow several times before she could get the words out.

"If you're not an alpha," she said. "What the fuck are you?"

"An omega, like I said. One of a kind, end of the line sorta thing. As far as I know, anyway." Riann set a portion of steaming meat in front of Layla, then extended her right arm, displaying a series of numbers tattooed into the too pale flesh. "More precisely, I am Subject Number Six-nine-seven-oh-three." She grinned at Layla's baffled expression, pouring each of them a glass of water before sitting down. "I did say it was a long story."

Chapter Twenty-Two

"I guess you're too young to properly remember it." Riann stared into the fire as she spoke, one hand stroking Tricks's fur. The meal had been a tense but mostly wordless affair. Layla had stared at her plate for a full five minutes, mind racing with all manner of dire possibilities. Was the food drugged? Poisoned even? She also suffered a persistent suspicion that, at any second, this thing would launch itself across the table at her. Eventually, Layla's hunger defeated her doubts. Picking up her fork, she wolfed down the slices of roast rabbit while trying to keep her eyes on Riann. She seemed to find it amusing.

When they were done, Riann tossed a few scraps to Tricks, who had been sitting at her side in well-behaved suffering for the duration of the meal. After washing the plates in the sink, Riann towelled her hands dry and resumed her seat at the fire. She started talking when, after another bout of fearful dithering, Layla took her place on the rickety wooden chair.

"The Feeding, I mean," Riann went on. "Looking back, the strangest thing about it all was how long it took. You'd think it was all over in a few days, but, in reality, it dragged on for months, until what you might call the final acceleration. I didn't get to see that, myself. They never let us watch the news."

"They?" Layla asked. Her voice was still raw with fear and her eyes kept returning to the door. She wondered how dark it was now, and if she could reach her pack before she made it out. The flashlight was probably useless after her dunking in the river, so spotting any traps would be impossible.

"Do me a favour, sweets," Riann said with an apologetic smile. "As my old recovery group counsellor used to say, save any questions until the end."

She held Layla's gaze until she responded with a jerky nod, then continued her story. "As to who 'they' were, I never found out what they were called. Some kind of institute, maybe. But there was an improvised feel to their set-up that made me think they'd been cobbled together in response to the Feeding. I rarely saw faces since they wore full PPE most of the time, except when they were gawping at me from the other side of a glass wall. But there were all colours of the rainbow, many accents. I'm pretty sure they were a collection of experts from all over the world, summoned by the UN or something similar to find a cure."

A cure? Layla nearly spoke it, but the question caught in her throat. Riann heard it though, rolling her eyes in admonition before speaking on. "That's right, sweets. A cure. I got bit, y'see? Early on in the Feeding. It's always bothered me that, to this day, I can't remember who or how." The thin lines around her eyes crinkled as she winced. "I had what they called substance abuse issues back then. Doesn't help with recollection, but it's not just that. Something about getting bit changes you in more ways than just the obvious. My life before the bite is a distant thing. I know the basic facts, remember certain events pretty well, but the details are vague. More than that, I don't feel it. I remember getting divorced, and know I cried my eyes out that day, but it's like watching a scene from a movie of someone else's life. After the divorce, there was the whole economic crash thing. Then the whole not having a fucking job for ages thing. No wonder I drank. No wonder I smoked dope." She paused for another wince. "No wonder I ended up on the meth-head express after a while. That's how it was back then for a lotta folks, sweets. Don't let anyone tell you different. Things could be great for some, but real shitty for others." Her face clouded a little, her hand moving to her neck. "Anyway, I was telling you about my bite.

"Best as I can establish, it happened at Joey's. It was a bar-cum-diner with a none-too-discerning attitude towards customers. Joey was an enterprising owner. He'd let the dealers do business on his premises as long as they kept it quiet and kicked him back a slice.

I remember walking through the doors, scoring from some scumbag. I think his name was Kurt. Doesn't matter. I think I went outside, and I'd guess that's where the feeder got me. I do remember a lot of flashing lights and sirens, so I guess I wasn't the only one. After that, it's all just a big grey bank of fog until I woke up in a sealed white room with a glass wall, an IV in each arm and my neck hurting like a bastard.

"People in masks would come in from time to time, nurses or doctors or whatever, always accompanied by a soldier in full bio-warfare gear pointing a rifle straight at my head. I was strapped to the bed, couldn't move, nor talk much more than a mumble because they had this muzzle-type thing on my face. I noticed how the medics would avoid looking me in the eye, but whether it was guilt or fear, I never knew. I like to think it was guilt, 'cause they hurt me, sweets. That shit they pumped into my veins felt like acid burning its way through every nook and cranny of my body. I screamed a lot, begged for pain meds, as much as the muzzle would allow. Tried desperately to get one of them to actually say something, but they didn't. Not once.

"I've no idea how long it lasted. Might've been a week or a month, but after a while the pain lessened, became what you might call manageable. And I felt . . . different. Stronger. I'd strained against the straps holding me to the bed before, finding it useless. But now I felt them give, just a little. I stopped then, not wanting to let them know. Because, while my body had clearly changed, so had my mind. All of a sudden, it was like I could see *everything*. Every pore on the few inches of skin above the medic's masks. Every bead of sweat and tiny little hair. And it wasn't just the details, it was how they moved. I found I no longer needed them to talk to me because it was like they spoke with every gesture. Anger, annoyance, attraction. It was all there, as if they had thought bubbles floating above their heads.

"And then there was the smell. At first, it was disgusting. The room got cleaned and disinfected every day, but it still stank. Chemicals mixed with the sweat of people, and each one told a story. I could tell which medic was menstruating. I could tell which of them had had sex the night before. What they'd had for breakfast. And the more I sensed of them, the less disgusting it became, until soon it was like a new drug. And the most intoxicating variety was fear. They reeked of it more and more each day. I had no idea what was happening beyond the walls of that room, but their stink and their movements told me the story well enough: things were really going to shit out there, and they were running out of time.

"The pain was still bad, the stuff in the IVs still hurt, but by now I found I could manage it without screaming. Hunger was a frequent visitor, but every two days they'd add a bag of plasma to the IV drip and it would go away. I began to realise how bad things were getting beyond that room when one of the nurses attaching the bag fell to her knees and started crying. 'This is so fucking pointless and cruel,' I heard her say as the soldiers dragged her out. She never came back, and I noticed, day by day, there were fewer people on the other side of the glass wall. At first, there had been a dozen or so. After a while, about half were left. Not long after that, just one. Unlike the others, he didn't wear a white coat or scrubs or a uniform. Just a nicely tailored suit. He was maybe fifty with a short grey beard and these piercing blue eyes. The kind of eyes that feel like they see into you. Except he wasn't seeing into me, I was seeing into him. I couldn't smell him through the glass, but I could *see* him. See him with my new eyes, and you wanna know what I saw, sweets? There was no fear in this one, just lust and envy. It was like he glowed with it, a need just as fierce as any I'd ever felt for booze or drugs. He wanted what I had.

"I measured time in intervals between sleeping, but sleep isn't really what it was. It was more like a coma, a period of complete nothingness then a sudden waking, with no grogginess or headache or needing to piss. It was pretty jarring at first, but I got used to it. Anyway, I started counting the number of sleeps in my head, and there were five between the time Suited Guy disappeared from behind the glass wall to when he turned up in my room. I'm sure I'd been left alone all that time. Abandoned really. Whatever this experiment was, it looked like it had lost its importance. My IVs emptied and my hunger grew. I still slept my coma sleeps but had a sense they were longer now, each waking briefer, and the hunger more acute. I understood later it's a feature of . . . what I am. If we can't find prey, we sleep the deep sleep until it comes along. Hibernation kinda thing. So, I've no real idea how long I lay there strapped to that bed until Suited Guy's stink woke me up. He stank like a man who hadn't washed for fuck knows how long, armpit and crotch odour. It was probably the most wonderful smell I'd ever known.

"I strained against the straps, finding my teeth were a lot bigger than they had been seconds before. Suited Guy should've been scared, but he kept standing over me, that longing desire blazing out of him. 'Allow me to introduce myself, my dear,' he said. 'Ranulf Weisserman, at your service.'

"'Never fucking heard of you,' I said, but it came out like a snarl as I jerked my head at him, trying to bite despite the muzzle. He still wasn't scared, though.

"'I have created many things in my life,' he told me. 'But none so beautiful as you. You are a true miracle, my dear. The only one I have seen in a life-time of searching.'

"Then he smiled and undid my straps and I tossed him across that room like he weighed no more than a rag doll, and me barely a hundred pounds at my heaviest. I threw him hard enough to put a crack in the glass wall, heard a good many of his bones break, then I was on him, ripping his suit and shirt to get at his neck. He was gonna taste so *fucking* good."

Riann stopped talking, lowering her gaze to Tricks. The dog's head rested on Riann's lap, brows arched and ears flat as if she sensed distress. "Couldn't do it," Riann said, snatching at the dog's neck fur. "Don't know why. I was so hungry, and he smelled so good. But I couldn't. Even had my teeth pressed into his skin. But I pulled back. Weirdest thing of all, sweets, he lay there, all broken and bleeding, and begged me to do it. 'Please.' He said that, clutching at my leg, weeping and desperate. And that's where I left him.

"Things get hazy after that. It may have been the hunger, or the after-effects of all that shit they pushed into my veins, but it's mostly a blur. I recall running through an empty building. Everyone who worked there had fucked off, papers and equipment all scattered about. Outside there was a bunch of army trucks and a fence, and beyond that, woods. I ran and ran through the trees, not really getting tired, only stopped when the hunger became too much. I know I slipped back into the coma sleep for a while. When I woke, I was standing over the corpse of a deer with its throat torn out and I wasn't hungry any more. I wandered about for a long time. The confusion was so bad I didn't have any clue where I was, and everything looked and felt strange now, like I'd landed on another planet.

"I met a few people who ran off when they got a

good look at my eyes. Some shot at me. After that, I kept to the woods, feeding on whatever dumb animal was unlucky enough to cross my path. I reckon it was well over a year until I got some part of myself back. I was looking up at a road sign and realised I could read the words. Since escaping, I hadn't been able to read. The letters would get all jumbled up and dance around. Now I knew what they meant. It was a sign welcoming me to a city. Not much was left of it, from what I could see. A few more weeks of wandering brought me here." Riann waved a hand at the wooden walls. "My cabin in the woods. There were a lot of tents pitched around it then, all stocked with military goods, but no actual soldiers apart from a few bodies. Looked like all of them had blown their brains out. I guess they were using it as some kind of base. Left behind plenty of weapons, long-life ration packs too. Yes," she added, seeing the surprise on Layla's face, "I can eat real food too, though; to keep the coma-sleep at bay I do need to hunt every now and then, rats and rabbits mostly.

"Took me a long time to figure out what they'd done to me, and even now I'm not sure I get it all. Best as I can reckon, I was on my way to turning into what you folks call an alpha, but the stuff they pumped into me stopped it, just not all of it. I can do what they do, but still think like us, mostly at least. Makes for a lonely existence, but I don't mind that much. People stumbled by from time to time, all keen to move on when they understood what I was. After a while, I realised I could just go back to sleep when things got boring. Don't hunt for a while and let the hunger send me off to bye-byes for a time. Last time I did that, I got woken up by this one's scent." She ruffled Tricks's fur. "Had yourself an owner then, didn't ya? She was how he found me. Turns out she's been trained to find us, specifically alphas. Her owner was certainly a capable fellow. I'm no expert, but I'd guess he'd been special forces or some such before the Feeding. Real good liar, too. Made out that his settlement had been overrun and he was just looking for a place to rest. But these eyes, sweets." Riann turned to her, the firelight forming two bright circles in her irises. "Best lie detector ever made.

"I let him stay, mainly out of curiosity to see what he'd do. One day, he tried to stick a hypo in my neck. Guess the intention was to take me off to be studied somewhere. I'd like to say I just broke his arm and let him go, but that would be a lie. Didn't eat him, though. Still can't seem to do that with people. Before I snapped his neck, I asked him if he'd ever heard the name Ranulf Weisserman. He said he hadn't, but I knew he was lying. Probably could've gotten more out of him, but I was fairly annoyed. Didn't like the lies, and all the pretending to like me. It was insulting." Her lips pursed in faint regret. "Would've been good to know how he found me, and where exactly he was from. Still, kill in haste, regret at leisure. But—" She let out a small laugh and planted a kiss on the dog's nose. "—got me a bestie out of it, anyway."

She lapsed into silent contemplation of the fire, while Layla's thoughts contested with the lure of the door and the story she had just heard. Unable to think of anything else, she said, "Are you going to let me go?"

"You're free to leave anytime, sweets," Riann told her with a chuckle. "I wouldn't recommend it just now, though. She's gotten all riled up lately."

"She?"

The glowing eyes slid towards Layla, narrowing in appraisal. "Remember what I said about these being a lie detector? You know who I mean. The big bad she-wolf who took up residence in the refinery. Got a new-made scent about her, but she's awful smart. The way she's got those feeders at her beck and call, never seen that before."

"Rehsa," Layla said. Clearly, there was no point in dancing around this. "Her name's Rehsa. She used to be a crosser, like me."

"Makes her even more dangerous. She'll know what you know."

"More. This is my first crossing."

Riann's arched an eyebrow. "Then, like I said, I wouldn't recommend venturing out."

"I have to. She captured someone, the man leading our team. He has something in his pack. Medicine. I can't go back without it. You said she's at the refinery. Where is it?"

Riann's eye's narrowed again, Layla knowing they saw her determination. "You're getting tired again," Riann said, jerking her head at the bedroom. "Rest up. We'll talk more tomorrow."

Layla began to argue, but realised it was true. Her head was starting to fog with another wave of fatigue. She worried again the food might have been dosed with something, but this felt like the natural tug of sleep. Getting to her feet, she started for the bedroom, then paused. "Thanks," she said. "For helping me. And . . ." She trailed off.

"Not eating you? Yeah, you're welcome, sweets. Sleep tight."

Chapter Twenty-Three

The refinery had a similar appearance to the chemical plant, but covered an even larger area. Its perimeter had long since been swallowed by encroaching vegetation, along with many of the outlying buildings. The inner precincts remained mostly uncovered. The dense cluster of towers put Layla in mind of the fairy-tale castles in the books Strang would read to her as a kid. But instead of gleaming white walls and banners fluttering from minarets, this was all dark, rust-streaked metal. The kind of castle an evil sorceress might call home. They stood atop a wooden platform constructed about the trunk of the tallest tree within walking distance of the cabin. Riann explained it had been here since her arrival, ascribing its construction to the long-vanished soldiers.

Layla tracked the binoculars over the office buildings, thinking them the most likely place for habitation. She saw only darkened windows and doors, bare of even a flicker of movement. Further out, she found a row of railway tank cars sitting on the tracks that skirted the complex. The scene was entirely lifeless apart from the occasional flutter of birds among the trees, the small flocks always keeping to the upper branches.

"You can't smell 'em, but I can," Riann said. Layla found it hard to get used to the woman's uncanny facility for sensing thoughts. She insisted it wasn't actually telepathy, just an instinct for subtle shifts in posture, expression and, most of all, scent. "Even from here. I've found nests before, but never one as big as this. Feeder packs rarely number more than a dozen. I reckon there's at least sixty in there." She paused, raising her face a little, nostrils twitching. "More now, and they got that new-made whiff about them."

"All those who got turned at Harbour Point," Layla said, lowering the binoculars. Looking at her, Layla didn't need any special abilities to discern Riann's opinion on the likelihood of success. "You're about to tell me it's suicide, right?"

"Was gonna go with 'you'd be dumb as a fucking stump to go anywhere near that place'." Riann sighed and took the binoculars from Layla. "Still," she said, reaching for the iron pegs set into the trunk to commence the climb down, "seeing as you're set on it, I may have a few things that'll help."

She accessed the cabin's basement via a concealed entrance at the rear of the building, hauling away a dirt-covered tarpaulin to reveal a door. After pulling it open, she led Layla down a deep flight of steps where a far more substantial barrier waited. "Used to have a keypad on it," Riann said, revealing a rectangle of hinged steel about ten inches thick as she pushed it open. "Ripped it out." She stepped into the unlit space beyond without pause before letting out a faint laugh of realisation. "Here," she said, Layla catching the large, baton-sized flashlight she tossed from the gloom. Switching it on, Layla followed, playing the beam over a row of stacked crates lining the wall of a room about twenty feet long by ten wide.

"My theory is this place was some kind of secret military hideout long before the Feeding," Riann said. "End of the world bunker type thing." She moved towards a bench set against the far wall, patting a hand to the stacked crates. "Guns, ammo, food. Sorry to say as regards your intent, sweets, but no medical supplies beyond field dressings. They did have some plasma, but I threw it in the river. Didn't like the temptation of it. I guess those soldiers that didn't take the coward's way out took all the good stuff when they ran off. Left plenty of other gear behind, though. Some of it will be of help to you, but what I want you to see is all my own invention."

At the bench, she took a glass jar from a shelf, one of about a dozen, all seemingly identical. "Take a look," Riann said, handing the jar to Layla. Seeing nothing remarkable about the object, Layla removed the lid, with some effort. It was tight, revealing a grey, granular substance. Sniffing it, she found the aroma less than pleasant, but not especially potent.

"What is this?"

"Eau d'Riann." Laughing, Riann took the jar back and scooped out a dab of the substance with her finger. Taking hold of Layla's arm, and rolling her eyes at the instinctive flinch, Riann began to apply the stuff to Layla's skin. It tingled a little, but didn't seem to cause any adverse reaction. "To mere human noses, it ain't much," Riann said. "But to feeders, this is a heady brew. They're always keen to avoid me, though some linger for a second and do this weird lying flat, eyes down pose before scurrying off. Early on I noticed how, if the wind was right, I could always smell 'em before I saw 'em. Which means they could smell me, and didn't like it. This—" she gave the stuff on Layla's arm a final smear and withdrew her hand "—keeps them away."

It didn't take long for Layla to deduce the ingredients of this particular ointment, Riann laughing again at the resulting, involuntary grimace of repugnance. "It's mostly blood, sweets," she said with a sly grin. "I bleed surprisingly easily, but heal so fast it's no trouble. There's about a quarter-litre of dried blood in each jar, mixed up with rendered animal fat. Cover y'self in this and you'll smell like me. I made it for her." She jerked her head at Tricks, who had followed them into the basement and was now busily engaged in sniffing the crates. "Feeders know to steer clear of me, but they'd be awful interested in her. It worked all right, but she hates it, always jumping in streams to wash it off. Hence my recourse to booby traps of late."

She opened a drawer in the bench and extracted something else. "Best if you take this, too. I'd give you a rifle, but since stealth is your object, this'll work better."

The pistol was marginally smaller than Romer's lost revolver, but felt lighter when Layla drew it from its holster.

"Fifteen shot mags," Riann said, tapping the three spares tucked into pouches on the holster's harness. "Loaded with what I think are titanium-tipped nine mills. Never had cause to shoot a feeder with 'em, but I'd guess they were specially developed to do just that."

Layla had practised with Eylsa's pistol enough to work out the basics of operating the handgun. She ejected the magazine and worked the slide, finding it smooth and well oiled. She repeated the action several times, keen to ingrain what muscle memory she could. As she did so her eyes strayed to a spread of documents pinned to the cork board above the bench, a mix of maps and photographs. These showed mostly anonymous forests or hills, sometimes buildings, and appeared to have been taken from high in the air. The maps were more confusing, crammed with elevation lines and small numbers, and also heavily annotated in red ink. The handwriting was large, clumsy, and difficult to read. Most of the characters consisted of question marks, although she did make out one name: "Weisserman".

"My special project," Riann said. "Sometimes I get a yen to try to find that institute, or whatever it was. It was easier in the early days when there were a lot more abandoned military camps about. Raided government buildings, too, but they weren't much use. Gotten a good deal harder to find anything useful since everything started to rot."

"Did you ever find it? The institute?"

"Not yet. Kinda got bored with it a while back and let it slide. Best as I can gather, it was probably somewhere around here." She pointed a finger to a spot on the largest map, the various place names meaningless to Layla. "That's about two hundred miles north of this city. Not an easy trek. Haven't worked up the energy to make it yet."

"What do you expect to find when you get there?"

"Answers, maybe. What exactly did they do to me? Did they ever find an actual cure? That kinda thing. Though, if I'm honest, I mostly want to get my hands on Weisserman again. Got a terrible sense of unfinished business when it comes to him. Might've let it go if he hadn't sent someone after me. But we make our own choices, I guess. Anyway, back to the matter at hand."

Riann pushed aside a covering of documents to unpin another map, this one all clean, narrow lines. As she set it down on the bench, Layla read the framed words at the top:

EXCELSIUS HYDROCARBONS INC.
Proposed Refining Facility – Revised General
Layout Plan V.6.

"Found this in a city council office years back," Riann said. "Thought it might come in handy. Seems fairly accurate, though some of the smaller buildings have fallen down since." She reached into the drawer again to extract a stub of red crayon. "Your best bet is to start here once the sun's fully up." She marked a point just short of the railway line describing a broad curve around the refinery's right side. "Trees are thin there and they'll all be keen to stay in the shade. From here." She drew a line from the X into the heart of the complex, following a course through the increasingly dense maze of buildings before coming to rest on a large rectangular structure. "It's a straight line to the place where they kept all their road vehicles. I've a sense that's where she holds court, so to speak. If your friend's still breathing, that's where he'll be. Move fast but quiet, sweets. Most of them will be sleeping, but they'll wake up real quick if they get a whiff of you, so avoid dripping water. Reapply if you notice any gaps on your skin."

Surveying the map, Layla experienced a muted pulse of surprise at her own resolve. Attempting to sneak into a place crammed with feeders, under the sway of an alpha no less, seemed just as suicidal to her now as it had yesterday. Riann had already told her how to get to the Redoubt. It was closer than she thought, easily done in a day. But, apart from a couple of circuit boards and the nitrous oxide for Luce's sister, she would be returning with nothing. Even so, there was still no doubt in her mind she would do it. *Amoxicillin. It was ticked on the list, so it's still in his pack. Unless it was in Eylsa's.* She pushed the thought away. If that was true then there was no point to any of this.

"Why are you helping me?" she asked Riann.

"Why wouldn't I? Just common decency, sweets. Besides, Tricks likes you."

Layla found it surprising that, while this woman's power to detect lies was inarguable, it turned out she was a pretty poor liar herself. The tell was there in the slight tension of her jaw and sideways flick of her eyes. "It's more than that," Layla said. "I do this and you get something out of it, right?"

Riann's brows gave a rueful twitch. "You sure you didn't get bit, y'self? Seems you're awfully perceptive." She went to one of the crates, opening it to extract a brick-sized object wrapped in clear plastic. She placed it on the bench before retrieving a pair of smaller objects from a separate crate. "Not a good idea to store them alongside each other," she explained before naming each one in turn, starting with the brick. "One kilo of C4." Her finger moved to an object that resembled a blunted pencil. "Detonator. And this—" She pointed to a small circuit board attached to a screen no bigger than Layla's thumb. "—is a timer."

"You want me to blow something up," Layla said.

"Not just one thing. All of it. The entire refinery, and when it burns, hopefully it'll take *her* with it." She met Layla's gaze, entirely serious now. "She's not right, sweets. She smells *all* wrong. And what she's doing with all those feeders bodes ill, don't you think? Two settlements fallen already. How many more? How long until she's outside the walls of your city? Seems a dead cert she's smart enough to find a way in. She's gotta go. You know I'm right."

"It's not just that," Layla said, seeing a glimmer of something unexpected in the unnatural glow of the woman's eyes. "You're scared. She frightens you."

"You're fucking right she does. Sooner or later she's gonna catch a trace of my very particular scent and curiosity is gonna lead her here. I could run, of course, but I shouldn't have to. I was here first."

"Then kill her yourself."

"Why, when I have you to do it for me? Besides, this is your chance to get your meds."

"If I say no?"

"Then take the pistol and good luck. The jar stays with me, though."

The certain knowledge that there was no stealing from this woman drew Layla's attention back to the refinery layout. "OK," she sighed. "Where do I put it?"

Chapter Twenty-Four

They set out shortly after dawn, Layla roused from a fitful sleep that testified to the uselessness of Riann's dreamcatchers.

Thorn had returned to torment her this time, both of them wandering the smouldering ruins of Harbour Point, the smoke thick enough to obscure the sun.

"You have to admit, Layla," Thorn said with a faint chuckle, "it does seem to follow you. Death, I mean. The list keeps on growing. Me, Romer, Pitt, Luce, Eylsa." He kicked at a pile of ash. "All these poor bastards. And Strang, of course. Even if you get those meds to him, what then? What are you going to do when he gets another infection? Or instead of a cough that won't stop, it's a lump that doesn't fade. He's old. It's going to happen. To him and to Taxo. Then poor little Layla is all alone again."

Part of her wanted to spit defiance at the taunting, faux sadness on his face. *This isn't you! Thorn would never say that!* Except, that wasn't quite true. Thorn, she had always known, was a depressed soul at heart. Every opinion was an expression of his innate pessimism. Every observation laced with barbed cynicism. She had thought him wise in his misery, a truth teller confronting the reality of life in the Redoubt. Now she just saw a bitter young man who had failed in his one attempt at escape.

"You cowardly, lazy piece of shit," Layla told him. "Couldn't make it through Selection, so you just gave up. Didn't even think about trying again, did you? Nah, just take a tumble off the wall and fuck everyone else."

"Did I tumble?" he asked. The smoke roiled in the sky above, turning it black, Thorn's eyes glowing in the resultant shadow. "Or did you push me? I saw it, Layla. That look on your face when I came back from Selection. That judgement. You knew you could do better. It was hard to take. And then when I fell, you just left me there . . ."

"Fuck you, you self-pitying prick!"

Her words had no effect, Thorn shifting to a new topic without pause. "Didn't you ever wonder just how she got into Spark Town, or Harbour Point?" he asked, and as he spoke, she realised it wasn't him any more. Now he wore Pitt's face, and instead of taunting cruelty she saw a deep, almost desperate need for understanding.

"Think about it, Layla," he continued, moving closer. His features blurred, smearing, then reforming until it was Eylsa speaking, though the plea for comprehension remained undimmed. "She would have been recognised," Eylsa insisted. "So how come none of the guards at Harbour Point happened to mention to Stave that his wife had turned up a few hours ago? Think about it!" Eylsa lurched towards her, reaching out with hands that had become claws. "Think, you stupid bitch!" The barbed nails dug deep, rending flesh and grinding against bone. "Think . . ."

Layla's shout of pain woke her, revealing the fact that she was sprawled on the floor, having tumbled out of bed. She blinked, seeing just the gloomy bedroom and Tricks outlined in the doorway, tail wagging and head cocked as she voiced a curious whine.

"Rise and shine, sweets!" Riann called from the next room. "Time to make shit go boom boom!"

Riann had constructed a shower stall to the rear of the cabin, cobbled together from equipment left behind by the soldiers. An electric pump hooked up to a car battery sucked unheated water from a canvas tank, assailing Layla with a forceful and painfully cold deluge as she scrubbed her skin with a coarse brush.

"Gotta get as much of your own stink off you before we apply the magical ointment," Riann insisted. "Scrub up good now."

Once washed and towelled dry, Riann handed Layla the jar and she began to apply a thick coating.

"Everywhere." Riann accompanied the instruction with a pointedly intimate glance. "Gotta get those smell centres." When Layla had covered everywhere she could, Riann took the jar and saw to her back.

"There," she said, with a final slap to Layla's buttocks. "How's it feel?"

"Not too bad. A little itchy."

"That'll probably get worse as it mixes with your sweat. Not much to be done about it." She tossed Layla a clean set of army fatigues. "Get dressed and let's be on our way."

Getting Tricks to stay behind proved a difficult task. Riann was unwilling to chain her up and the dog clearly keen to come along, repeatedly rising from the sitting position she had been commanded to whenever they began to walk away. Finally, Riann fixed the animal with a hard stare that succeeded in freezing her in place. The voice that emerged from Riann's lips was the least human sound Layla had heard her make, the single word coloured by a grating quality that recalled the feeder on the bridge. "Stay!"

This time, Tricks remained where she was when they started towards the trees, head down and ears flat.

Riann avoided the tracks when approaching the refinery, leading Layla on a serpentine course through the woods. "Best not to be obvious," Riann said. "Given her minions' willingness to hunt in daylight, and all." She paused for a second, nostrils twitching. "Not scenting any, which is good. If they're out, they're far away."

She carried a machine gun today. It had a box of belt-fed ammo instead of a magazine and must have weighed twice as much as her rifle, although it seemed to cause her no strain at all. "This is Glenda," she said, patting the gun. "Named her after my first girl-friend. She had a helluva vicious tongue."

When the first glimpse of rusted metal appeared through the trees, Riann's demeanour shifted, all traces of emotion leaving her face. She began to move with a hunched but fluid grace, faster and quieter than Layla, through the undergrowth. *This is a predator*, Layla reminded herself, finding she had to struggle to keep up. *Smart and kind and brave, but still . . . inhuman.*

Riann came to a halt at the base of a shallow incline, pointing the machine gun's barrel at the procession of tank cars sitting on the tracks at the top. "Here it is, sweets," she told Layla, her voice once again shot through with that grating note. "Your moment to shine. Mask on from here. Your skin is covered, but they can still smell your breath."

Donning her mask, Layla tightened the straps, then paused before starting up the slope. The moment required some kind of farewell, but all she could come up with was a statement of the obvious. "I guess I'm never going to see you again."

Riann's features were now a mostly emotionless

mask, Layla thinking that her skin had also gotten a shade paler. After staring at her for a second or two, her mouth formed a smile, revealing teeth that were longer and sharper than they had been moments before. "Maybe in your dreams," she said. "Now go get what you came for and fry that bitch."

Quickly scaling the slope to the row of tank cars, Layla drew the pistol and checked the underside of the nearest one before crawling under. A quick survey of the buildings beyond revealed no movement. Re-holstering the gun, she shrugged off her pack and extracted the first of Riann's three bombs.

"Those cars have been sitting there since the Feeding," she had explained back at the cabin. "Oil gets all claggy after it's sat for a long time. Doesn't mean it won't burn, though, if you give it a big enough kick."

Layla pushed the device into a gap between two of the large pipes tracing across the tank's belly. As she began to tap in the sequence to activate the timer, she was annoyed to find her hands shaking. Clenching her fists, she took a series of deep breaths, then tried again. A few taps and the number 30 appeared in red digits on the screen.

"Thirty minutes, sweets," Riann had said. "Any longer than that and you ain't coming out."

Rolling clear of the tank, she drew the pistol again and made for the gap between the two closest buildings.

Riann had sketched her a map of the complex, but Layla felt no need to reach for the folded paper in her leg pocket. The route was clear in her head as she made her way through the leaf and brick maze of the refinery's outlying structures. Coming to a corner, she found the junction of pipes where Riann had told her to place the second bomb. *The pipes trace all through the complex like veins. I'm hoping for a chain reaction kinda thing.* After placing the device against the large valve wheel at the heart of the clustered tubes, she set the timer for twenty-five minutes and moved on.

Navigating a rusted jungle of degraded metalwork, Layla emerged onto a roadway. According to the map, the other side was supposed to be occupied by an administration block. Instead, she found herself confronted by a tumbled mass of piled bricks and concrete. It barred the direct route to the vehicle bay and forced a detour through the castle-like structure the map named as the "Crude Oil Thermal Treatment Centre". She would have preferred to skirt it, but the surrounding undergrowth was far too thick. Fortunately, the ground-level walls had fallen in several places, allowing for easy access. Less welcome were the many bricks that clacked and clattered as she made her way inside, each sound echoing long in what was evidently a cavernous interior. It was as she clambered over a pile of rubble, trying hard not to dislodge more than she had to, that she saw the first feeders.

They lay in a sprawl directly in her path, all betas,

their pale bodies entwined in an ugly parody of sleeping
kittens. Layla trained her pistol on the head of the
nearest one, once again fighting a pang of anger at her
trembling hands. The feeder failed to rise. It twitched
a little, as did the others, but otherwise all were un-
reactive and immobile. *It works*, Layla thought, eyes
flicking to the caked gunk on her gun hand. With the
image of red numbers counting down in her mind,
she traced as gentle a course as she could around the
sleeping feeders. Once clear of the bricks and treading
a flat concrete floor, she looked upon an interior domi-
nated by a huge structure consisting of a cylindrical
tank affixed to a towering metal box. Riveted valves
and pipes festooned it like mechanical cancer, casting
an intricate matrix of shadows across the floor. And
everywhere there were shadows, there were feeders.

Layla make a quick decision not to count them,
since what difference would it make? If only two or
three woke up, she was dead anyway. Stepping around
them, gun still gripped in both hands, she saw most
were betas with a few gammas. These lay closer to
the light than the others, indicating a hierarchy of sort
among these monsters. It also made it clear that Rehsa's
influence extended to both varieties of feeder. *Maybe
not entirely*, Layla thought, recalling the body of the
gamma they had found on the riverbank approach to
Harbour Point. *Its neck was broken. Punishment, maybe?
A demonstration to keep the others in line? Is that how she
does it? Simple fear of death.*

Getting all the way to the far end of the building required five full minutes in which Layla felt she could hear the numbers on the bombs ticking down. Even so, she paused upon reaching a doorway beyond the huge monolith of oil-burning apparatus. It was open, revealing only shadow. Riann's elixir birthed a sudden itch under her left armpit. *Mixing with sweat.* The thought stirring another reminder: it won't last for ever.

Resisting the impulse to reach for the flashlight dangling from her pack, she aimed the pistol into the gloom and stepped through the door. A few seconds of blinking and her eyes adjusted enough to perceive a long, rectangular space of metal storage racks. Most were empty, but some had been tipped over to spill a variety of technical looking bric-a-brac on the floor. Layla concluded it must have been the parts store for the giant machine in the main chamber. Some additional squinting revealed no pale, slumbering forms, but no door. However, she did perceive a definite lessening of shadows off to the left. Moving deeper, she found a collapsed section of wall. The gap was mostly filled with debris, but there was just enough room for her to scrape through if she removed her pack. Pausing to holster the pistol, Layla shrugged the pack into one hand and began to edge herself into the gap.

A sniff.

The sound was subtle, but unmistakable. Layla's gaze jerked towards the source, heart pounding at the sight of a pale form crouched in the shadows less than six feet away. With the left side of her body wedged into the gap, the pistol was now a hard lump of unreachable metal against her ribs. She was frozen in a curious pose, one hand still holding the pack, almost as if she were offering it to the feeder. Scenarios flicked through Layla's head with blurring speed. Keep trying to force her way through? No, it would be on her before she managed another inch. Pull herself clear and draw the pistol? Same outcome. Throw the pack at it? Might distract it. Worth a try.

But she didn't do anything except watch the feeder watch her, kept still by a singular but important real-isation: *It should have attacked by now.*

The feeder edged closer, revealing itself as a beta as its head dipped into a beam of light. Its flattened nostrils flared in an elongated face, eyes narrowing. Some kind of recognition seemed to dawn then, because it drew back a little and lowered its body to the floor.

Eau d'Riann, Layla thought. *Thinks I'm an alpha.*

She was debating the wisdom of continuing to push her way into the open when the feeder shuddered. Shaking its head in confusion, it jerked forward before coming to a halt less than three feet from Layla. Seeing its face clearly, Layla clenched her jaw against a gasp of shock. It was a distorted face. An inhuman, deformed face. But the angle of the cheekbones and the curve of the brow summoned a dreadful recognition.

"Luce?" The name emerged as a thin, near inaudible whisper that barely misted her mask, but the feeder heard it. Eyes narrowing and nostrils flaring once again, it crept even closer. The horrible sense of familiarity surged when Layla looked directly into its eyes and saw an echo of the same curiosity she remembered when watching Luce look upon the Outside for the first time. *I knew it would be bad out here, but not like this.*

Layla crushed the resultant welling of pity and grief. *She's dead. This is a thing. A thing that needs to die.*

It appeared that the creature formerly known as Luce detected the sentiment, her posture losing any impression of subservience as she drew back a little. With the itch under her pits getting worse by the second, Layla knew this thing was now drinking in a far more potent brew of human fear. Perhaps it had already scented some remnant of Layla as she passed through the main hall, wakened by a faint, familiar redolence. Judging by the hungry glimmer in her narrowed eyes, it had also triggered a hunting instinct.

"The tanks, Luce," Layla rasped through her mask, raising the pack. "For your sister, remem—"

Luce lunged, closing the distance between them in a blur. Layla had time to draw the pack towards her, holding it up like a shield, then the feeder was on her, barbed teeth rending and biting.

Chapter Twenty-Five

It took Layla a few seconds to realise two principal facts. The first being that, despite the feeder's jaws busily snapping bare inches from her face, she wasn't dead. The second was that her view of the creature was partially obscured by a thin but rapid stream of mist emerging from her pack. *The nitrous!* she realised, watching Luce rear back, shaking her head in confusion. *She punctured the tanks.* Layla lunged, shoving the pack and its gushing cloud of vapour into the feeder's face. She had no idea how quickly nitrous oxide affected humans, but the reaction it produced in a feeder was jarring in its suddenness.

Luce thrashed at her, a single powerful swipe of her extended arms. The barbed claws failed to catch Layla's flesh, but she suffered a hard knock from the flailing forearm that sent her sprawling. She scrambled upright, still holding the pack towards Luce. The feeder's struggles had now transformed into a weak spasm. Letting out a soft, throaty sigh, she collapsed, slumping onto her side, mouth slackened to reveal many teeth flecked in drool. The eyes widened and contracted several times, then closed.

Sucking air through the mask's filters and hoping they caught the gas, Layla drew the pistol and aimed it at the shadowed depths beyond Luce's unconscious form. She thought she might have heard a faint scuff in the darkness. Maybe something. Maybe nothing. Either way, she wasn't inclined to stay and find out. *Time*, she reminded herself, the red numbers ticking again.

She quickly checked the pack, finding one tank punctured, its contents apparently exhausted. The other was scratched but intact. Casting the damaged one aside, she checked the pack's hardy fabric. It was torn in places, but not enough to spill the contents. Rushing back to the gap in the wall, she stopped and turned to regard Luce. *Can't leave her like this.* The decision was unhesitant and coloured by as much by mercy as it was pragmatism. There was no telling how long she would be out, and would resume the hunt when she woke, raising a ruckus when she did.

Kneeling at the creature's side, Layla drew Nehna's knife from her ankle. Pressing the point of the blade to base of Luce's skull, she tried to push away memories of a scared girl who had sacrificed herself for her sister. Luce weeping the night before they descended the wall, grieving herself. That night atop the gas tower when they joined hands to ward off rising panic.

"It's not her," Layla whispered, though it felt like a lie. Still, it didn't stop her thrusting the knife as hard as she could into Luce's spine. A sob escaped Layla's lips as the thing that had been her friend, albeit briefly, convulsed and died. It was a small sound that failed to echo long enough to attract the notice of any nearby feeders.

Squirming free of the gap in the wall, she crouched amid a patch of thick vegetation, donning the pack once more and trying to get her bearings. The structures nearby were in such a reduced state that she found she couldn't reconcile any of it with her memorised map. Resorting to Riann's sketch didn't help, and it was only when her eyes fixed on the tall, rusted tower off to the right that she managed to orient herself. *Turn right at the main distillation tower*, she remembered. *Then twenty metres past the gas treatment plant to the vehicle bay.*

She placed the third bomb amid the overlapping rusted tube work of the gas treatment plant, setting the timer for fifteen minutes and moving on at a run. Nearing the vehicle bay, she forced herself to a walk and surveyed the exterior of the long, warehouse-like structure. Like the thermal treatment building, it featured a number of gaps in its walls, each one a gloomy ragged triangle that might have concealed a dozen feeders. With no time to indulge in indecision, she chose the closest gap. This time, she unhooked the flashlight before entering, casting the beam around to reveal only concrete walls, bare except for flaked and faded paint.

The interior of this structure was cleaner than the first, free of piled bricks or other detritus. *This is where she lives*, Riann had said. Despite the vacant silence, Layla didn't see any reason to doubt her judgement. *Maybe Rehsa's fond of good housekeeping*, Layla thought, fighting down the perverse impulse to laugh. She turned off the flashlight before venturing inside, pointing the gun down a long corridor, head ringing with a question that managed to blot out the image of the red numbers. *Where is he?* More importantly: *Where is his pack?*

The corridor was interrupted by a series of doorways, Layla aiming the pistol into each one and seeing only bare rooms. By the time she reached the end, her pulse pounded and her breath had shortened into near panicked gasps. *WHERE?!*

The knowledge that she could spend far more than fifteen minutes, less than that now, searching this entire building, summoned a shout of frustration. She clenched her teeth, slumping against a wall and quelling the increasing babble in her head with a mantra. *I can't go back without it. I can't go back without it . . .*

Then she heard it. A faint echo from the doorway to her left, the soft chink of metal on metal. It might be nothing. Just another portion of this ageing, unmaintained structure falling apart. But there was regularity to it that told her otherwise.

Entering the doorway, she noticed something she had missed on her first pass: a small semicircular gap in the corner of the far wall. It was a few feet off the ground, but she could see a flat surface beyond. Once again, she had to remove her pack before crawling through. She pushed it in first, assuming any feeder waiting on the other side would lunge for it. Nothing happened, and she squirmed her way in, quickly scrambling into a crouch atop a damp metal surface, the pistol fanning right and left as she blinked in surprise. *A pool?*

The water lapped under a raised steel barrier, filling a space about forty feet square. Workbenches, like the one she stood on, lined the walls, leading her to conclude this must have been the vehicle repair shop. The rusted bulk of a tanker truck rose from the water below a ceiling festooned with dangling chains. A few feet above the truck, suspended amid a web of chains, was Stave. He sagged, apparently unconscious. He twitched every few seconds, sending a faint rattle through the matrix of iron links.

Layla suppressed the impulse to rush for him. Instead, she turned the flashlight on and shone it into every shadowed corner of this place, tracking the pistol with the beam. Satisfied they were alone, she pulled her pack on and leaped onto the bonnet of the tanker. The sound was loud enough to make her wince, but not pause. She was too close now and further delay intolerable. Stave hung about three feet above the roof of the truck, Layla looking up at bruised and slackened features. Reaching for his leg, she felt his skin, finding a pulse in the hollow between heel and ankle bone.

"Stave," she hissed through the mask, shaking his leg. The movement provoked a jerk, then a groan. His eyelids fluttered but failed to open. She tried again with the same result, her eyes fixing on the padlock at the centre of chains coming together around his midriff. Reasoning that he might come round if she were able to slap him, Layla shrugged off the pack and rummaged for her lock picks. *Gotta be quick*, she told herself, surprised to find that her hands weren't shaking when she inserted the picks.

"Don't!"

Her eyes snapped up to meet Stave's, now glaring down at her in stern command. She saw the pain etched into the lines around his eyes, but also an unwavering resolve. "Leave it," he croaked, his chains rattling as he swivelled his head to scan the repair bay. "How did you . . . get in here, Layla?"

"Doesn't matter." She reached for the lock again. "Need to get you down. And get your pack . . ."

"I said leave it!" His croak became an angry rasp, chains thrashing as he jerked his body. "You need . . . to get out . . . of here."

"I need your pack," she told him. "The meds. I lost them. I need yours. Where is it, Stave?"

Something like humour showed in the expression that twisted his face. An attempt at a wry smile, she thought. "As it happens," he said. "I need it . . . too." His eyes flicked to the truck cab beneath them. "In there. You'll find a . . . metal tube. Bring it. Be quick."

Luckily, the truck cab's windows were open, so she didn't need to manoeuvre the door open. Crawling inside, she was forced to resort to the flashlight again to find the pack. It sat in the sleeping compartment at the rear of the cab, seemingly untouched. Jamming the flashlight between her neck and shoulder, she undid the straps and began extracting the contents. She tossed aside Stave's mask, batteries and circuit boards until she found the pill bottles at the bottom. Alongside them lay the metal tube he had asked for. It was about seven inches long with a screw cap on one end. Lacking the time to inspect each bottle, she consigned them all to her own pack. Shoving the tube into her fatigue pocket, she climbed back onto the roof.

"Open it," Stave instructed, eyes flicking between her and the wall behind. Turning, Layla saw the water lapping around a half-opened door. "Hurry!" Stave grunted.

Unscrewing the cap, Layla upended the tube, allowing a plastic object to fall into her palm. A syringe with a stopper on the needle, its contents concealed within a covering of electrical tape. "This is what you bought from Velna," Layla realised. "What is it?"

Looking up, she found Stave grinning. "Medicine," he said, his grin evaporating at the sound of sloshing water. Looking back at the half-opened door, Layla saw a fresh agitation to the pool's surface. "She's coming," Stave said. "You have to do it now."

Layla gaped at him. "Do what?"

"Inject me, Layla. Do it!"

The sloshing was louder now, with a rhythmic quality that told of something making their way through it. With a final glance at Stave, his face set in stark, desperate entreaty, Layla bit the stopper on the needle and spat it away before sinking it into his ankle and thumbing the plunger.

Stave's response was fast, and ugly. Jerking in his chains, he let out a series of loud, painful grunts, veins standing out in his neck, eyes bulging. Still, he managed to fix them on Layla and gasp out a final order. "Go!"

Pulling on her pack, Layla turned to the hole she had come through, but the increasing disturbance to the water told her she wouldn't make it. Instead, she climbed to the other side of the truck cab, lowering herself into the water. It came up to her waist, shockingly cold and, she knew, dissolving her protective covering whenever it touched her skin. She began to make for the raised steel barrier, then froze at the sound of squealing hinges.

"You're awake," a soft voice echoed, female and suffused with a cautious note of affection. "How do you feel?"

Crouched next to the deflated rubber of the truck's

tyre, Layla heard Stave's chains rattle some more before he coughed out a reply. "Shitty."

"They weren't supposed to hurt you." The voice's echo changed as its owner moved, Layla surprised by how utterly human it sounded. She heard regret and guilt, both unmistakably genuine. "But it won't matter soon," Rehsa continued. A brief surge of displaced water, then the thud of feet landing on the cab roof. A pause followed, during which Layla began to edge towards the barrier, staying low in the water. Repeated upward glances revealed Stave's dangling, twitching body, but no sign of Rehsa. Layla stopped her progress when her arm came into view, pale but, like the voice, apparently human.

"My wonderful man," Rehsa said, her tone wistful now as she reached up to play a hand over Stave's chest. "You came to rescue me, didn't you?"

Stave's chains rattled violently as he jerked, flinching from her touch.

"And you have, my love," Rehsa continued. She moved closer to him, and Layla saw her face for the first time. It was still the face of the woman who had responded with modest, uncomfortable smiles to the cheers of the crowd when she returned from a crossing. But Layla felt there to be a disconcerting perfection to it now, flawless skin and a symmetry that hadn't been there before. She was undeniably beautiful, fascinatingly so, and Layla found she had to force herself to look away. Turning back to the door, red numbers ticking loud, she calculated the wisdom of slipping under the water and swimming out.

"Do not fear me, Steven," Rehsa told her husband, a catch in her throat as she faltered into silence. When she spoke again, her tone was sombre, but laced with a hard note of certainty. "I know it's hard to believe, but this is the best thing that could have happened. I can see it in you. The fire Blake spoke of, the fire that must be seized. The same one that burns in me, that blazed to life when I was bitten. I understand it all now."

Mad as fuck and an alpha, Layla concluded, sinking lower. *Bad combination*. The brackish appearance and shiny oil scumming the water's surface repelled her, but so did the prospect of burning alive in the next few minutes. She lowered herself until the water covered the mask up to the eyes, then slowly began to inch herself along the side of the truck as Rehsa's voice resumed its sorrowful echo.

"I met one of the old ones, you see? One who walked this earth long before the Feeding. Imagine it, Steven. A being that has seen the rise of Napoleon and the fall of the Berlin Wall. Such knowledge he had. Such wisdom. All that has happened is an aberration, he told me. The emergence of the lesser breeds, the Feeding, all a freak twist in the natural order, as much a calamity for our kind as it was the prey. But also, a great and marvellous opportunity. For now, we can remake the world. Now we can make it ours."

Stave grunted something then, chains rattling.

"What is it, my love?" Rehsa asked, concern now supplanting the melancholy in her voice.

"Not . . . you!" Stave said in a choking rasp. "Didn't . . . come for . . . you! Who you . . . used to be!"

A faint laugh. "I'm still me. All that I was, remains. But I am . . . evolved. Perfected, you could say. And soon you will be too."

"You . . ." Stave's voice was a tremulous rasp now, shot through with suffering, but Layla could still hear the palpable hate in it. Now she understood the true impetus behind this, his last crossing. He hadn't done it out of love. Quite the opposite. "You . . . are an . . . animal!" he spat at the creature that had been his wife. "Something . . . wearing her skin. You are . . . a mockery . . . of everything she was!"

Another laugh, though this one sounded forced to Layla. Annoyed at allowing herself to be distracted, she concentrated on continuing towards the steel barrier. Six or seven feet and she'd be out.

"Could a mere animal do what I have done?" Rehsa asked. "All of it I did knowing it would force you to come looking for me. So that we might be together again. We have shared dreams, you and I. Another gift of my evolution. I have tasted your grief, your longing. I called to you, and you came. This world has changed on a fundamental level. It now belongs to the feeders. To live in it, to thrive even, you must adapt. *We* must adapt. I will not allow what we shared to die."

"And . . . when you've . . . eaten everything . . . that can be eaten. What then?"

"Haven't you been listening? I said we must adapt. Our food supply must become sustainable. A domesticated breed of human, controlled, corralled. For that to happen, they must first be scattered, the pitiful communities they've built destroyed. In time, I will offer them refuge, a beneficent ruler who can keep the feeders at bay. They will love me, and offer their blood willingly, an honourable sacrifice for their queen, and the king that reigns at my side." A pause, then she raised her voice, the unmistakable note of being directly addressed bringing Layla to a frozen halt.

"And will you not love me, my young friend? Wouldn't it be better than the misery you call life? Come on out. All this eavesdropping is quite rude, don't you think?"

Layla fought down the instinct to stay still. Ticking red numbers, and the terror of having been discovered, making her reach for the pistol. She managed to draw it by the time the water directly to her front erupted into white. Layla quelled the resulting flinch, aiming the pistol into the raised curtain of liquid, finger tightening on the trigger, then stopping as a face loomed before her.

Eylsa!

It was undoubtedly, inescapably her. The same knowing cast to the eyes and ready smile, one eyebrow cocked as if to ask a question. *You really going to shoot me?*

The moment of confused hesitation lasted barely a second, Layla rejecting the impossibility of what she was seeing and pulling the trigger, only for her hand to explode in pain as something blurred across her vision. The pistol was whipped away to shatter against the wall. A vice closed upon Layla's neck and she felt herself lifted from the water. She bucked and flailed, lashing punches that didn't land, then scratching at the hand that held her.

"Enough!" A hard, choking shake, then Layla felt her windpipe close. She tried to fight on, but, starved of oxygen, her muscles failed and she hung limp in the monster's grasp. Through a darkening crimson fog, she saw Eylsa's face loom closer, nostrils twitching. "Now that's a curious scent," she said, Layla dimly aware that her voice was not Eylsa's voice. "Where did you pick it up, I wonder?"

"REHSA!"

Eylsa's face jerked upwards at Stave's shout and as it did so, it changed. Layla heard a grind of bone and squelch of sinew as flesh remoulded into Rehsa's features. *Think about it, Layla*, Pitt had said in the dream, and now she understood why. *This is how she got into Spark Town and Harbour Point. This is why the guards didn't recognise her.*

Rehsa crouched, then leaped clear of the water, taking Layla with her. She shouted in pain as they landed on top of the truck, but her closed throat allowed no sound to escape her lips. Unwilling to let her die just yet, Rehsa loosed her grip a little as she peered closely at Stave's greying, red-eyed features.

"He's dying," she said, and Layla felt her grip tighten again. Rehsa's features transformed once again as she dragged Layla closer, the perfected, flawless mask of beauty shifting into a veined, animalistic mask. "You did this? What did you do?" Layla felt her upper spine compress as she was shaken again, a rag doll in the grip of an angry dog. "What! Did! You! Do?!"

"Rehsa . . ."

The shaking stopped at the sound of Stave's pitiful groan. Rehsa's face resumed its human-like state as she swung back to him, eyes wide with concern.

"Cyanide," Stave told her. "We all . . . carry it now . . ."

Letting out a grunt of rage, Rehsa slammed Layla down onto the truck's roof. "I was going to turn you," she said, releasing her grip to leave Layla stunned and gasping. "Now, I'll just throw you to my dogs."

Through eyes clouded by pain, Layla watched her shatter the lock on Stave's chains, pulling it apart like a piece of flimsy cardboard. She caught him as he fell, sinking to her knees. "Foolish, foolish, man," she said, smoothing a hand over his shuddering brow. "Don't fret, my love. I'm going to save you. The gift cures all."

Layla shuddered in instinctive revulsion at the sight of the teeth extending from Rehsa's mouth, jagged spikes that looked more like metal than bone. Pulling Stave close, she sank them into his neck. Seeing her eyes close in apparent blissful union, Layla willed movement into her body. The surprising but welcome realisation that she could move her legs made it plain her spine hadn't been broken after all. She succeeded in flopping onto her front, groping for the edge of the truck roof. How many minutes left? Five? One? The certain knowledge that it would be better to be under water very soon kept her moving. Her fingers latched on to the roof's edge and she dragged herself towards it.

A loud, guttural hacking sound sent a shudder through her, almost jarring her hands loose. It was similar to the disgusted exclamation of a child tasting something awful, but greatly magnified. Layla wanted to ignore it and keep crawling, but found she had to look.

Rehsa had retreated from Stave, her perfect face red from mouth to chin. She stared at his body, now drained of all movement, with a mix of horror and accusation. "M—" she stuttered, casting a spatter from her lips that was too dark to be blood. "Mercury . . ."

The vast boom of an explosion shook the building

then, providing a curiously apt accompaniment to the sudden, back-arching convulsions that took hold of Rehsa. She jackknifed across the truck roof, a gout of black fluid erupting from her mouth with every bone-cracking shudder. Layla thought she might be screaming, but couldn't tell above the tumult raging beyond the walls of this building. It resembled thunder mixed with the squealing of a million cats, each blast followed by a whoosh of displaced air. Dust cascaded from the ceiling, along with some larger chunks of debris. Still, Layla found she couldn't move, couldn't spare herself the task of witnessing Rehsa's end.

The most violent reactions had calmed now, leaving her on her back. A black tide continued to leak from her mouth, ebbing and flowing as her face shifted in form. Cheekbones swelled and relaxed. Her chin grew narrow, then broad. For an instant, Layla saw Eylsa again, then Romer, quickly followed by a rapid flicker of others she didn't recognise. The shifting parade of faces abruptly ended, becoming the inhuman, predatory visage once more as Rehsa's back arched for a final time. Her spine fractured with a loud crack before she slumped, broken and unmoving. With all life gone, the vestiges of the human she had pretended to be seeped away. Her skin thinned, paling into translucence to reveal the distorted skull beneath. It was not so different from a gamma, extended teeth and a prominent jaw, the eye sockets larger and more oval than seemed natural. Before she dragged herself over the edge and into the water, Layla knew Stave had been right. This thing had been an imitation of Rehsa. For all its schemes and pretensions, in the end, all it wanted to do was feed.

Chapter Twenty-Six

Layla ducked under the steel door to surface in a world of smoke. Water clogged the mask's filters, forcing her to take it off and suffer the acrid, oil-tinged miasma. Coughing, she dumped out as much liquid as she could and replaced the mask, dragging in air that retained more than a tinge of burning fuel. Looking around, she saw that the floodwater extended into the billowing clouds to all sides. According to her memorised plan of the refinery, the straightest route to the Redoubt lay to the right. Her various aches and pains flared in angry punishment as she struggled through the water, the most of acute of which lay in her right hand. Holding it up, she found it swollen and bruised. From the agonised throb of all but her thumb and index finger, she could tell the rest were probably broken.

The combination of pain and fatigue caused her to fall several times before she cleared the water. With her feet finally on firm ground, she allowed herself a brief pause until a bright blossom of flame in the roiling smoke compelled her into a stumbling run. Seeing trees up ahead burst into flames, Layla veered left, then did so again when the fire quickly spread. Behind her, the refinery's death agonies had taken on an almost orchestral majesty. The high-pitched notes of combustible gases blazing through a vast matrix of pipes counterpointed the percussive rumble of exploding tanks and buildings. As she ran, her stumbling gait banished by mounting fear, the ugly symphony was joined by the increasing roar of burning vegetation.

Heat built at her back as the fire chased her, growling and ravenous. She sprinted through woodland, leaping obstacles and ducking branches. Several times, the undergrowth ahead was too thick to navigate, forcing her to go around. The edges of her vision were crowded with firefly-like embers, the heat now so intense she wondered why her skin didn't blister. Then, through the swirling haze, she saw a wide expanse of tarmac. Hurtling towards it, she stumbled at the edge of the forest, rolling across a hard, cracked surface. Scrambling upright, she spared a single glance at the inferno consuming the trees, a wall of flame twenty feet high, bright beneath the black sky it had created. Seeing steam rise from the tarmac as it began to boil, she turned and ran on.

Inevitably, as the heat dissipated, the strain began to tell and her pace slowed. Faltering to a walk, Layla surveyed her surroundings, discovering the expanse to be a vast car park. Scattered with rusted wrecks, it surrounded a huge building that appeared to have been constructed entirely of glass and steel. The structure sprawled over several acres, most of its windows shattered or gone, and rising from its centre, the dome she recalled from that first hour outside the walls. Once, it must have shone bright in the sun, but now its curved girders were naked and buckled. A tall sign over what she assumed to be the main entrance read: HIGHPOINT MALL. One look at the dark interior instantly dissuaded Layla from venturing inside, and she kept her distance from the structure as she skirted it. The smoke obscured a large part of what lay beyond, but she could make out the familiar silhouettes of tenement buildings. She was closer to home than she thought.

A resurgent roar dragged her attention back to the fire, seeing it race along the overgrown walkways running through the car park. Within seconds, flames blossomed on the outer reaches of the huge building, the wind driving the inferno into the vacant windows and doorways. Backing away, Layla saw a burning figure burst through an open doorway. It sprinted into the car park and rolled on the ground, desperately trying to extinguish the fire eating its flesh. Several more followed, some slumping down into immobile, flame-wreathed husks. But others succeeded in smothering the flames, about twenty in all, and, as they rose, smoke rising from their scorched flesh, Layla made out the overlong limbs and elongated skulls of a beta pack.

A feeder's sky, Layla thought, eyes flicking to the black clouds above. Any hope they had missed her scent evaporated when she saw them all adopt the same predatory crouch, every one swivelling their charred, smoking bodies in her direction. She ran.

Despite her pains, her overtaxed muscles, and the breaths she was forced to drag through the mask's filters, she knew this was the fastest she had ever run. Across cracked roads and through the remnants of destroyed houses, she ran. The distance to the tenements seemed to take both a few seconds and an hour. Pelting along the broad thoroughfares between housing blocks, she worried she would run into the barrier of the collapsed junction. Fortunately, her route from the refinery had taken her into a district well clear of the ruined roadway. It also meant a greater distance to the waste ground separating the tenements from the wall. She pushed the mental calculations away and concentrated on maintaining her speed. *Fast as you are, they're faster.* She knew the truth of Taxo's words by now, but still, they hadn't caught her yet.

Her body finally gave out a hundred metres short of the last row of tenements. She could even see the wall through the tattered buildings. *So close.* The words repeated in her mind as the last vestige of strength fled her legs, sending her into a painful collision with the ground. *So close. So fucking close.* She tried to force effort from her body, but it was like she had tripped some kind of internal shut-down switch.

For a few seconds she could only lay there, one cheek pressed into the cracked pavement, chest heaving and heart hammering as if it wanted to escape the cage of her chest. It was the sound of the feeders' rapid, clawed feet that roused her. Flopping over, she raised herself up onto her elbows, watching them materialise out of the grey haze. They all seemed to be limping, suffering the agony of their burns to maintain the hunt.

A wounded animal still needs to eat, Layla concluded. Wincing, she reached for her ankle, then grunted in pain when her broken fingers failed to grasp Nehna's knife. Using her left hand, she managed to get it free, thumbing the switch to extend the blade. She rolled onto her side and tried to stand, but her legs were still unequal to the task and she collapsed again. Snarling wordless defiance, she waved the knife at the leading feeder as it closed on her, its face a mass of charred, blistered flesh. One eye had been boiled away and the left side of its maw seared down to the bone. Layla was struck by the clear, unmistakable animosity blazing in its remaining eye. This thing didn't just hunger for her. It hated her. *One of Rehsa's pack?* she wondered. *Come to avenge their fallen queen . . .*

The feeder was less than three feet away when its head exploded in a blaze of white and red. For a confused second, Layla thought it had been struck by lightning, then she heard the gunfire. More white flashes followed, tearing up paving stones and eviscerating feeders. Three were cut down by the second burst, two the one after that, blasted apart by white tracer bullets that raised sparks wherever they struck concrete. The sole surviving feeder turned and attempted to flee, only to be caught by a final salvo that left it a twitching red mess.

"Looks like titanium works just fine, sweets!"

Layla's gaze snapped to the diminutive figure perched on an exposed upper floor of the tenement ahead. Riann laughed, brandishing the machine gun before tossing it aside. "Never could resist a party!"

She had her hood down, revealing a face made feral by the joy of killing, teeth extended and skin paler than ever. Unmistakably a feeder, and Layla could see the wall to her back. The distance was too great to make out the guard post, but the gunfire would have drawn attention. She could also hear the faint, repeating blare of sirens.

Heart pounding with fresh alarm, Layla dragged herself to her feet and staggered towards Riann, waving her arms. "Get down!" she screamed, the words too muffled by the mask to reach Riann's ears. Layla tore it off and screamed again: "GET DOWN!"

She didn't hear the shot. The sniper was too far off for that. But she did hear the whine of the bullet and see the red plume as it tore through Riann's chest.

She took a single, unsteady sideways step, then fell, tumbling head over foot to land on her back. Layla sank to her knees, finding she had no strength left to even cry out in despair or rage. After a few gulps of smoke-laced air, she managed to stand and walk a faltering course to Riann's side.

Like Rehsa, the onset of death had heralded a shift in features to an inhuman state. Unlike Rehsa, Layla could see the human soul shining amid the fading glimmer of life in Riann's eyes. Crouching, Layla took hold of Riann's hand, watching her gasp and choke out her final few breaths. Incredibly, Layla saw a semblance of a smile curve the lips around her over-long teeth, and she said something, a name accompanied by a spray of blood: "Tricks!"

Layla looked into her eyes and nodded, then watched them dim as Riann gave her final gasp.

Rising from the body, Layla fixed her sight on the wall and started to walk home.

Chapter Twenty-Seven

The line of customers outside the Electric Palace Theatre wound its way through the Municipal Arts Centre and beyond. What surprised Layla most wasn't the number of people, but their patience. Day and night since her return, as word spread regarding the theatre's new disc, they came from all districts of the Redoubt to see it. There were no arguments or fights, no attempts to jump the line. Layla ascribed it partly to the regular crusher patrols. Large gatherings of citizens always made them nervous, but there was a lightness to the mood of this unshrinking procession, a sense of comradeship even. It was like they viewed standing in line as part of the experience, and didn't want to spoil it. Ever the enterprising soul, Taxo had recruited vendors to walk the line selling drinks and cakes, supplied at a reasonable rate by the local bakery. He had also been obliged to hire help to keep the projector running, and even then it had to be limited to no more than four hours at a stretch. A few days ago, its bulb finally burned out. The "Closed for Repairs" sign had sufficed to summon a tech from City Admin with a replacement. It seemed officialdom was keen to sustain this useful new diversion.

Looking down from her rooftop perch, Layla recognised several faces. Seeing the movie just once wasn't enough for most, and she understood why. It was everything Taxo always said it would be. The bombastic tones of the score accompanying the climax throbbed from the auditorium below, Layla finding herself mouthing along to Ripley's line as she stomped from the shadows in the cargo hauler. When she first got back, Taxo insisted the debut screening be only for them. They sat in the middle row and watched it together, Taxo crying all the way through. Although, by the end, so was she.

"One thing that bothers me," she said now. "What happened to Burke? I mean, I guess the alien killed him, but it seemed kinda anticlimactic. A piece of shit like him deserved a nastier comeuppance, narratively speaking."

Turning to where Strang rested on a deckchair, she watched him place his bookmark before closing his copy of *Nicholas Nickleby*. "The scene got cut from the theatrical release," he said. His voice was raspier than it used to be, but free of any cough. "But in the director's cut, Ripley finds him in the reactor, impregnated with a baby alien. She gives him a grenade, and he blows himself up."

"Oh." She turned back to the crowd, adding softly, "Have to look out for that next time."

She knew this would have brought a disapproving frown to Strang's brow, but he said nothing. Since her return he had asked no questions, though she saw them nag at him with increasing insistence as his condition improved. But still he didn't ask, and she loved him for it.

"Anyone home?"

She tensed at the sound of Dresh's voice, but forced a tight smile of greeting as he climbed the ladder to the roof. "Made it then?" she said, coming to clasp his arm, a brief expression of affection that summoned a pang of guilt. But anything more would have been cruel. Always taller than her, it seemed that Dresh had grown several inches in the space of a few weeks.

"You look well enough for it," Strang said, rising from the deckchair to clap a hand to Dresh's shoulder. "The Outside agrees with you."

"According to Nehna, it was the quietest crossing in history." Removing his pack, Dresh opened it to reveal a dozen or more books. "Courtesy of the Spark Town library. The batteries were where you said they'd be too," he added to Layla.

Strang's face lit with a mix of gratitude and joy at the sight of the books, clouding a little as he caught Layla's weighty glance. "I'll, uh, leave you to it," he said, making for the ladder. "Got shelves to organise."

"He seems a lot better," Dresh observed when Strang had descended the ladder.

"Hardly a cough in over a week," Layla said. Moving back to the roof's edge, she wrapped her shawl more tightly around her shoulders. Since her return she seemed to feel the cold more, something Cuhla had been quick to notice and rectify with the gift of a freshly woven shawl. She was there below, arranging her stool and uncasing her cello in preparation for the night's performance. The people in line always appreciated it.

"Sorry I wasn't there for your return," Layla told Dresh. "People gawp at me now. I don't like it."

"It's fine." He came to her side, Layla feeling the weight of his eyes on her. "Lotta disappointed folk there. No winnings if everyone comes back. Thought there was gonna be a riot at one point."

"Everyone?" She turned to him, finding a confirming grin but the same weight to his gaze.

"Didn't catch sight of a single feeder. Nehna couldn't believe it. Your fire's still burning fierce, by the way. Choking on smoke was the worst thing about the whole crossing. We had to keep the masks on most of the time. They reckon it's claimed about a third of Old City. Probably explains the absence of feeders."

"There's plenty more sleeping out there. They'll migrate in when the fire burns itself out."

"Which means we should make the most of the time we have. Venture further afield. With Harbour

Point gone, we need to find other settlements to trade with."

She heard the meaning beneath the words, coloured by a harder note than she expected. It sounded almost like judgement, or disappointment.

"I told Nehna I was done," she said. "And I meant it."

"You know things. Learned things out there that no one has before . . ."

"And it's all in the debrief. Watch the vid."

"I did. We all did. Alphas that can change their face . . ." He trailed off into a sigh, shaking his head. "Things are quiet out there now, but you're right, it won't last. To keep them out, we'll need everybody."

"Keep them out," she repeated softly, unable to keep the caustic disparagement from her voice. "That's not the real problem with this city, Dresh. Maybe you can keep the bad things out. Maybe you can't. But you definitely can't stop the rot from within. One day the walls are going to fall, and it won't be the feeders that bring them down. The only thing that'll save us is to stop living in a prison."

"And how do we do that? We need the walls or we die. It's just a fact."

Only as long as the feeders are out there. She didn't say it, just like she hadn't said a lot of things during the debrief. She'd told them all about Spark Town and Harbour Point, and Stave and Rehsa, especially her power over what she called the lesser breeds and her peculiar facility with faces. But when it came to Riann, she'd told them nothing. At first, she hadn't been sure why, just a vague unease that hardened into clarity when Mayor Flak arrived. He insisted on a private audience with her, sitting across the table with his hands clasped tight, brows drawn in a serious and purposeful frown. But it was a mask, the facade of a scared and mostly self-interested man. She saw it in the way his eyes, nervous and guarded, flicked over her face, and she smelled it in his sweat. She wondered how a few days in the Outside could have sharpened her senses so much, but didn't doubt what they told her. He reeked of fear. Nor were his questions particularly insightful, concerned mainly with if she was absolutely sure there was nothing left of Harbour Point and the veracity of all the disturbing news about Rehsa's abilities. When he left, she had no doubt: someone like him couldn't be trusted with Riann's story. But then, who could?

"I heard from Luce's people," Dresh said, breaking what she realised had been a long silence. "Her sister had the baby. A girl. All fine and healthy. They said to say thanks, again."

Layla just nodded. Before agreeing to the debrief, she had first insisted on going home to hand the amoxicillin over to Taxo. After that had been the visit to Agri-Unit Twelve B. Although barely a year Layla's junior, Una had seemed painfully young, a child with an absurdly swollen belly. But she bore the news of her sister's death with surprising fortitude, just a few tears when Layla handed her the tank of nitrous oxide. She didn't ask for details, for which Layla had been grateful.

"Flak's going to announce another Selection next week," Dresh said. "Be really good to see you there."

Various rejoinders came to her lips, none of them pleasant. Looking up at his judgemental but still earnest face, she wondered if he had, in fact, grown up at all in her absence. "I'll think about it," she muttered, wearied by the prospect of another argument. There was no point. "Thanks for bringing the books."

"Least I could do. Him and Taxo kept me fed after Thorn . . ." He trailed off into a sniff. "Anyway. Better get back. They've got a whole celebration planned at the village, which you'd also be welcome at, by the way."

A sideways look was enough to discourage further persuasion, and he touched a hand to her shoulder before making for the ladder.

"Dresh," she said, when he began to climb down. "What I said during Selection. It wasn't fair, or right. I'm sorry."

He gave her a grin, but it was muted, the judgement still lingering in his gaze before he descended from view. Turning, she watched him exit the theatre and make his way past the people lining the walkway before disappearing into the gloom of the arts centre. *Bye, Dresh*.

* * *

When the final showing ended and the audience drifted away, she waited an hour before going to the vent where she had hidden her pack. She hauled it out and rechecked the contents: ration packs and water enough for two weeks, making it heavier than she liked, but it couldn't be helped. She then extracted the item she had obtained at Velna's that morning. She had gone to the shop armed with the two additional pill bottles she hadn't handed over on her return. What she wanted would be expensive. But Velna refused to take any payment and produced the item without hesitation. Drawing it from the holster, Layla was gratified to find it the same model as Riann's pistol. Its magazine was only half full, but Layla still had the titanium-tipped ammo Riann had given her. Before clipping on the holster rig, she removed the bandaged splints from her fingers. After six weeks, they were mostly healed, but stiff and discoloured. Gripping the pistol proved a painful but bearable experience and she was confident she could fire it accurately.

Descending the ladder, she looked in on Taxo and Strang. They had begun sharing a bed again when Strang's cough abated, though she wondered how Taxo could sleep through Strang's grating snores. She stood in the doorway watching them for longer than she should, fighting the urge to wake them, explain what she was going to do and why. But she didn't. Leaving like this was cruel and cowardly, but also necessary. One word from either of them and she wouldn't ever leave.

There had been a time when venturing out at night was an absurd notion. Now she made her way through the darkened maze of street and shelter, unconcerned by the furtive figures in the shadows. A few darted into her path, then quickly retreated at the sight of her face. Being famously dangerous had its advantages. Picking the lock on the hatch to the Undercut took longer than usual, thanks to her aching fingers. Simply throwing a rope over the wall would have been easier, but there was always the chance a crusher might try to stop her, and she didn't need the commotion. Besides, there was something she needed to do.

Once through, she turned on her flashlight and began the long downward climb. Like much else in the Redoubt, the Undercut appeared to have both shrunk and lost its air of danger in her absence. She heard distant scuffling in the dark that might have been the dogs, but if they caught her scent, they wisely steered clear of her path.

Finding the pillar took a while, since the subterranean landscape had changed again. The vertical funnel that had taken her there before was now choked with subsided debris. Fortunately, a shift in stratified rubble had revealed the top of the pillar, enabling her to find a path to its base. By the time she crawled through to the metal grate, dawn light had begun to paint the grass beyond a pleasant shade of gold. The car wreck beyond seemed unaltered.

Layla sat and ate a protein bar, waiting for the sun

to fully rise. Then, taking a hammer and chisel from her pack, she used a couple of well-placed blows to collapse the tunnel to her rear. Removing one of the bars from the grate required more effort, but she managed it, kicking the metal rod away and crawling through. *There's something about the Outside that hooks you*, she remembered Romer saying as she raised her face to the sun, wondering why it felt warmer here than it did behind the walls.

Drawing the pistol, she picked up the freed metal rod and threw it at the car wreck. The reaction was instant, the door slamming open and the feeder's claw flashing out. She could see it nestled amid what remained of the back seat, eyes glowing and teeth shining in the gloom. It paused as the sunlight kissed its skin, letting out a hiss of discomfort that she knew would soon be overcome by hunger. The tattoos on its forearm were more discernible at this distance, confirming a reluctant but inescapable conclusion. Even so, she forced herself to look closer at its face. Like Luce, there was still enough resemblance there to recognise this thing for who it used to be.

"Did we really share dreams?" she asked it. "Were you calling to me like Rehsa called to Stave?"

The feeder had no answer for her. Baring elongating teeth, it tensed for a lunge, driven by hunger to suffer the pain of sunlight.

"Goodbye, Thorn," she said and shot the feeder once in the head. The titanium-tipped round pulped the front and rear of its skull, filling the wreck's interior with a red spatter as it slumped into the rusted bowels of the vehicle.

"Can't kill you all, can we?" she asked the dead feeder, watching a final twitch flutter its arm with its familiar web of ink. "But maybe, just maybe, we can cure you. Riann was a feeder, but she was also human. Human enough for it to matter, anyway. It's something. Somewhere to start."

Holstering the pistol, she drew the straps of her pack tight and started walking. The column of smoke that had been a feature of the skyline for over a month leaked an ugly stain into the sky, and she didn't relish the prospect of navigating the charred ruins left in the fire's wake. She had to hope the inferno had spared Riann's cabin, or at least the basement. She had a dog to find, after all. After that, there were many maps to study and, she suspected, a very long road towards an always uncertain future.

Acknowledgements

Many thanks to my agent Paul Lucas for his encouragement throughout the writing of this novel and his efforts in making sure it saw the light of day. Also, heartfelt thanks to my editors James Long at Orbit UK and Daniel Ehrenhaft at Blackstone Publishing for taking a chance on this second step outside my usual genre stomping grounds.

extras

A list of the Orbit imprint
orbit-books.co.uk

about the author

A. J. Ryan is a pseudonym for Anthony Ryan, who lives in London and is the *New York Times* bestselling author of the Raven's Shadow series, as well as the Raven's Blade, Draconis Memoria and Covenant of Steel series. He previously worked in a variety of roles for the UK government, but now writes full time. His interests include art, science and the unending quest for the perfect pint of real ale.

Find out more about A. J. Ryan and other Orbit authors by registering for the free monthly newsletter at orbit-books.co.uk.

if you enjoyed
THE FEEDING
look out for
THE BLACK HUNGER
by
Nicholas Pullen

John Sackville will soon be dead. Shadows writhe in the corners of his cell as he mourns the death of his secret lover and the gnawing hunger inside him grows impossible to ignore.

He must write his last testament before it is too late. The story he tells will take us to the darkest part of the human soul. It is a tale of otherworldly creatures, ancient cults and a terrifying journey from stone circles of Scotland to the icy peaks of Tibet.

It is a tale that will take us to the end of the world.

14 April 1921

I do not have long now. I can feel it. It has crept over me so slowly that, at first, I was hardly aware of it, but it's in my flesh now. A burning, tingling feeling, like when I was bitten by a spider as a child. Spreading through my limbs and my body, inexorably and painfully. I am outwardly in good health, despite the wound's grey festering. But I know, and my minders know, that there is no forestalling the inevitable result. And I am always hungry.

The asylum is cold and grey; its stone walls seem to emanate a deeper, more lasting cold than the frigid wind and rain outside my barred window. The darkness is absolute, at all hours of the day. I have a private room at least, and do not have to mingle with the other inmates. That is a small mercy. I interact with no one at all, except my minders, and their clumsy attempts to get the truth from me are hardly companionship. I will never know companionship again. Garrett is dead.

I know what it is you want from me. And I will give it to you in my own time, and on my own terms. If this is to be my last testament, then damn your urgency. I do not fully believe you can stop what is coming now, anyway. But I will help you try. I will tell you what happened. You will have your intelligence, but I will tell my story. And Garrett's.

You don't know who Garrett was. Or, rather, you don't know who he was to me. No one did, so far as I can tell. No one even suspected until the end: for a decade. I'm astonished at having hidden a best friend, a brother, a lover in plain sight for all those too short years. And now I will never see him again. Now that you know, I find I do not much care what you think. I have days left to live, if I'm lucky, and have no time or patience for your disapproval or the disapproval of God, or the law, or society at large. How can you punish me now? You talk of sin, but not of love. You talk of disgust, but not of beauty. And the love we had for all those years was beautiful. And perhaps it would have been even more beautiful had it been allowed to flourish in the light. God, if He is interested at all in what Garrett and I did when we were alone, now has bigger problems than us.

My name is John Sackville, and I am the only son of the Earl of Dorset. I have no children, and so the line will die with me. I was born in 1888, and I was the only one of my parents' children to reach adulthood. There were three boys and a girl before me, but they had died of various childhood diseases before I was born. By the time I was born, my parents were in their middle forties, and had long since resigned themselves to childlessness. I was an unexpected blessing that they seized upon fiercely, and I was the recipient of their entire affections; of all that was best in them.

I grew up on my father's estate outside Lyme Regis. Most of my father's peers had great, rambling estates and elaborate country mansions full of pompous grandeur. My grandfather let his father's ornate baroque palace go to ruin not long after he inherited it, and moved his family into a small manor house within our gift in the little village of Dalwood, just over the hill from the decaying old mansion. It was a quiet, unpretentious place. Clean and comfortable, and certainly spacious, but without grandiosity or pompous ornament.

This was in keeping with my parents' beliefs, for my grandfather had become a secret Quaker, and though my parents kept up the outward formalities of attendance at the Anglican Church, quietly, behind closed doors, they practised a kinder, gentler version of the faith of their fathers. Perhaps this is why they never judged me, even though I suspect, indeed am almost certain, that they knew.

My father had no interest in London, or politics, or society, or anything but managing his estates and raising his family and keeping to his religion. He kept an enormous diary and would spend the mornings beavering away at it in his study. He was also an amateur naturalist, and would go on long walks around the countryside, through the fruit orchards, often with me in tow, spotting birds and pressing flowers. My parents loved their version of God, loved each other, and they loved me, dearly. We could have spent our entire lives in Dalwood and never felt the need to leave.

And it was a pretty place, nestled in a glen, with enormous oak and chestnut trees shading a brook that flowed under a yellow stone bridge. The air was redolent with the smell of fruit from the orchards all around. All the houses, built in the same warm yellow stone, would glow in the late afternoon summer sunshine, and the light would flash and dance through the leaves of the trees in a wind which carried a faint tang of the sea. The packed earth roads would be warm under my bare feet as I skipped across the bridge looking for chestnuts and oddly coloured rocks. By winter candlelight, as frost glazed the ancient windows, my mother would read me stories by the roaring fire in our parlour, and I would doze off to Walter Scott novels and old collections of Arthurian folk tales, my head in my mother's lap. The village had a timelessness, as though nothing had changed there for hundreds of years, and nothing would change for hundreds of years to come. At Christmas I would be allowed a glass of elderberry wine, or golden cider from the local orchards, and we would make Christmas pudding from the fruits of our own trees. My mother would always remember where the coin had been placed, so invariably my portion contained it. Perhaps it was the accumulation of luck that allowed me to pass in polite society all these years. Perhaps it was what led me to Garrett.

We were near the same age, though Garrett was about a year my senior, which made him seem so much older at an age when nine months is an eternity. I first met him when my father engaged him to give me swimming lessons in the river that ran near our home. He had been born the son of one of my father's tenants, a thin, taciturn, black-haired man, with a dusting of a moustache, and a wife he did not seem to care for very much. Garrett and I grew up playing together in the village and in the fields and forests around it, and my father never made the slightest effort to curtail the friendship. Throughout our childhoods we were hardly aware of the class difference between us. That cruel truth would be made plain to us later. In those early days it was hardly more than my gentle mockery of his ponderous, cumbersome West Country accent, which he never lost, in later life, despite everything that happened.

He grew up stocky, with flaming auburn hair and bright blue eyes that would crinkle into his face when he smiled, which he did often. He had dimpled, pudgy cheeks, a thick beard that came to him early, and no discernible resemblance to his father of any kind. By the time we were both fourteen, it was rather obvious. And to hide his shame, Garrett's father would beat him with a belt, imagining all sorts of crimes that deserved such punishment. I found out this secret pain one evening the summer I turned fifteen. We were playing around in the vine-covered, collapsing ruins of my family's old estate, and he broke down in tears and confessed everything his father was doing to torture him. He sat on a low stone wall and he buried his face in his hands, weeping in that choked, broken way some men do, as though they would rather die than be seen to weep. I put my arms around his shoulders, and I kissed him once on the forehead. It seemed the natural thing to do. He looked up at me in shock, and I realised what I had done. But before I could cover my instinctive action with some plausible indifference, he was kissing me. His cheeks were wet with his tears, his lips were dry and cracked and his face rubbed mine raw with its thick, bristly stubble, already grown back from the morning's shave. But I kissed him back with all the passion I could muster from my frail frame.

It took us months to figure out the mechanics of love for men like us. Mostly in the ruins of the old estate where we knew we would never be disturbed. I would take him inside me, and my knees would be covered in red lines from the grass where I knelt. He would take me into his mouth, afterwards, when he was spent, and finish me then. But often I didn't need him to. It was enough to have him inside me. Sometimes, as though he felt guilty, it would be his turn to kneel. And I would do it because I knew he enjoyed it, too. But I was happiest when I was beneath him. And afterwards we would lie naked in the grass in the gathering summer dusk, a blanket discarded beside us, bathed in each other's sweat and with our arms draped around each other. I felt safe. I felt home.

My father had avoided sending me to boarding school as a child, as most children of my class were forced to do. The Empire relies for much of its strength on brutalising children in the system of organised violence and torture that we call the Public School System. The children are torn from their parents' sides, and thrown into a world of cold showers, casual cruelty and crushing loneliness, where they learn the delicate ropes of hierarchy and obedience, when to give, when to take, when to punish and when to accept punishment. They are stripped from love and safety and forged in the crucible of brutal conformity and rote Latin learning into good little psychopaths who can be trusted with the governance of the Empire. He put it off for as long as he could (most children were sent away before they were ten) and I had a succession of wonderful governesses and tutors, but eventually it couldn't be postponed any longer. I cried when my father called me into his study and told me that I had to spend the next four years at Rugby School, far away in Warwickshire. He embraced me, and dried my tears, and told me that I would be home for Christmas, and that all would be well, and that he and my mother would always love me.

"Is there anything I can do that might make it easier, John? Anything at all?" I shook my head and sniffed. "Perhaps you'd like Garrett to come with you? You're allowed one servant, after all. I suspect he would do the job well, and he would remind you of home." He looked at me rather significantly when he said this, and I felt a sinking feeling of discovery. But to this day I do not know if he knew or suspected anything at all, or if I merely imagined it. I suspect the former.

"Yes. I would like that."

I told Garrett that evening as we sat together, dangling our legs over the little stone bridge in the centre of the village. I wanted to hold his hand, as I sometimes did when we were alone in the ruins, but we knew enough even then to know from the fiery sermons of the vicar that we could not do so where we might be seen. I was terrified that, despite everything, he would balk at going so far from the only home we'd ever known, but he only smiled and looked in my eyes, and said:

"I'd go anywhere, sir, so long as it's with you." When he called me sir it was with a quiet, gentle mockery that only I understood, and an ironic knowledge of how things really stood between us. It made my heart sing with the hilarity of it.

And so we went to Rugby. I lived in my rooms, and Garrett lived in the servants' quarters, but he was with me in the evenings. We couldn't do anything untoward. There was no privacy to be had. And Garrett and I learned quickly under the cruel mockery of the other students and the other servants to hide in public whatever intimacy we possessed from our childhoods.

But sometimes Garrett and I could contrive to be alone with one another. And after a while, with his pay Garrett rented a little room above a pub in town from a landlady who didn't ask questions, and I would give him some of my allowance from Father to help with the rent, and we would be alone on Saturdays and Sundays. Sometimes for the whole day, if we were lucky. Garrett would tell me casually about the mockery he faced from the other servants, but after so many beatings from his father it did not faze him in the slightest, and he mocked their pomposity and their crude Essex accents to me as viciously as they mocked him, to my raucous laughter. He was a talented mimic, and had a devastating wit.

I didn't need to study. Mother had already drilled me in Latin and Greek, and I was well ahead of the other boys in my form. And when one day when we were sixteen Garrett expressed an interest in what I was learning, I began to tutor him myself, and smuggled him some textbooks from the lower forms, and before long he proved an astonishingly quick student, to whom languages, ancient and modern, came with uncanny ease. He eventually became a considerable classic in his own right. I admired him more and more as the years went by. I always will.

"If you'd been born with land, you'd be the talk of the school," I wrapped my arms around his neck and pulled him away from his Virgil for a kiss. He smiled up at me.

"If I'd been born with land, I'd have been born far away from you, and I would never have known you at all, sir. There can only be one Lord of the Manor."

"You don't have to call me that when we're alone." I grinned.

"Don't I ... sir?" he grinned again. Then he pushed me away. "I guess that's just the way of it. God doles out the titles before we're born, and the rest of us suffer what we must."

"I wish it wasn't this way." This was the first time we had ever addressed the subject directly.

"Wishing won't make it so, now, will it, sir? We have to live in the world we've got. And we're happy enough, far as I can see. I could be in the workhouse, or back on David's farm." He shuddered. He had stopped calling his father anything but David a few years before.

"Still, it's bloody stupid that you are where you are, and we are where we are. You'd have a brilliant career ahead of you."

"Well, your career will just have to be brilliant enough for the both of us." He stood up and pushed me against the wall. "As long as you and I always know the score ... sir." His breath was on my neck, and I was pinned against the coarse oak boards, panting with anticipation. He whispered in my ear:

"*Pedicabo ego vos et irrumabo*, sir." Then he flipped me around, and with a quick pull at both of our belts he was in me, and I forgot all the injustice, the deception, the risk. He was in me, and that was all that mattered. It's all that ever will. And you can keep your judgements to yourself.

Rugby, it turned out, had its share of degenerates like us. Lock that many vulnerable boys and corrupt old masters into a cloistered prison for long enough, and things will happen. But it had none of the tenderness and respect there that it had with Garrett and I. It was transactional. It was about power, and dominance, and cruelty. My relatively advanced age, my late arrival at the school and my title shielded me from the most dreadful duties of "fagging", as they called it. But the younger boys had it tough. Organised rape has been a principle of building male hierarchies since Sparta. You learn, and are meant to absorb forever, that there is no place so private that your superiors may not intrude there. I was disgusted by it and took no part. Garrett became jealous at the mere suggestion that I had and flushed red with embarrassment and anger when we talked about it. I promised him that I cared only for him and would never avail myself of any privileges such a corrupt system might offer me. And I never did, for the four years I was there. The younger boys treated me with a great deal of respect for it, and by the time I left school I had everyone's grudging admiration, if never their love, for my scholarly achievements, and for how I conducted myself.

I had one truly great teacher, Master Hornby, who has some bearing on my story. He was a stern old Northerner with massive, flared eyebrows and a shock of white hair over a glowering face. He was kind to me, in a gruff sort of way. I believe he saw how lonely I was, and he offered me scholarly companionship, along with a few other boys from the higher classics forms. We would get together on Thursday evenings to read Ausonius and Jordanes and Ammianus Marcellinus and some of the other, more obscure, late Roman authors.

I was drawn to late antiquity. There was a tremendous sense of possibility in everything I read from the third and fourth centuries AD. You could see the old world dying and a new one being born right on the page. The sad, aristocratic poets desperately aping Virgil and Cicero and awarding each other meaningless honours from a dead Republic as the barbarians set up camp all around them struck me as being inexpressibly tragic. Their ornate Latin was cloying and sweet, like Turkish Delight. Then there was the more muscular prose of the early Church Fathers; their fanaticism clear as a funeral bell, their language full of deadly purpose to exterminate the old, demon-haunted world and to usher in the Kingdom of Christ. As someone who often felt he might have been more able to be himself in the old, demon-haunted world, I rather resented it, though I admired their discipline and tenacity. Besides, one can only read Virgil and Cicero and Caesar so many times before one begins to tire of it. The problem with the classical texts is that there are only so many of them. There's the later scholarship, I suppose, but most of it is worth less than the paper it's printed on.

Hornby also taught Oriental Studies, though he had few takers for it. When he saw how bored I had become with Latin and Greek and the dead classics, he called me to his office one evening, and offered me a cup of tea, and changed the course of my life forever.

It was early evening, and the winter light was blood-red as it spilled through the window of his third-floor study, and a fire crackled under the mantel as we sat in high-backed chairs by the fire. He was blunt.

"You need a challenge, Sackville. Tell me, what do you know of India?" I told him that my mother had read me the *Thousand and One Nights* when I was young, which I supposed came from Persia, but that the strangeness of them, and the sense of a whole other cosmology underlying their construction, meant that I remembered them vividly.

"Good enough. How would you like to learn Sanskrit? And then modern Hindustani? Perhaps Urdu if we have the time. It's a much more elegant language. And perhaps Tibetan, which has a power all its own. We have some time before you go to Oxford, and I think I can prepare you in what time we have."

"For what, sir?"

"For Oxford, boy. You'll go mad reading the Western classics. Your father has taught you well. There won't be much you haven't read. I'm recommending you to Dacre Winslow at Pembroke. He's one of the foremost scholars on Buddhism in the Western world. I believe you and he will get along famously."

"Thank you, sir."

"I realise that you probably just want to go back to Dalwood and manage your father's estates with him," I grimaced slightly. I increasingly did not think I would want that. Garrett and I could never maintain discretion for long in Dalwood. Everyone would be desperately waiting for me to marry, and father children, and I dreaded the idea. "But I do believe it would be a terrible waste of your talents, John. You are capable of much more."

"Thank you, sir. I will do my best."

And for the rest of that last year of sixth form I focused on the basics of Sanskrit; its curious music and its even more curious elegant, ornate Brahmic script. I was fascinated from the very beginning. After two years I was able to construe, in a very basic sort of way, the Mahabharata and the Ramayana and the Upanishads and the four Vedas. I picked up a smattering of Urdu and Hindi, but I always struggled with Tibetan, finding its complex system of honorifics difficult to penetrate. Garrett was far better at it than I was.

Before I left for home for the summer, I received a letter from Dacre Winslow cordially introducing himself and informing me that, at Master Hornby's express recommendation, he would be delighted to take me on as a pupil at Pembroke College, assuming I had not already accepted another place elsewhere, for the Michaelmas term of 1906.

Enough has been written of the beauty of Oxford. You can find adequate panegyrics to dreaming spires in any threepenny paperback. I don't propose to add to their number. Go and see it for yourself if you're so inclined. It won't disappoint. For me, it will always be the scene of some of the happiest days of my life, but what is that to you? Make your own memories.

Of course, Garrett came with me, and my rank and title got me a lovely set of ground-floor rooms on Pembroke's Old Quad, with an adjoining servant's quarters, so Garrett became my scout, and he and I essentially lived together for the entire three years, in and out of college. In Rugby we had had our little rooms. But in a college it was much harder to find time to be alone together. My windows left little room for privacy. Mostly when we made love it was in Garrett's tiny, windowless servant's bedroom, and the room would stink of us for hours afterwards. But it was a delicious smell.

Garrett grew into a great bear of a man in those years. He kept his auburn hair and beard closely trimmed. His face was round and apple-cheeked, and when he smiled it was a great toothy grin that split his face like a peach, and his eyes would crinkle and disappear. He was thick and burly with a broad chest, a hairy belly and big heavy arms and legs like tree trunks. It was the kind of weight that gives the impression of immense strength, and not of ill health. And, God, he was strong.

The other freshers were noisy and boisterous and frequently broke the windows of those unfortunate enough to have rooms on the ground floor. I avoided them, and for the most part they avoided me. I formed a small coterie of like-minded friends, and a few of us would get together on Saturdays for a luncheon, which sometimes, I'll admit, got a little boozy. Once or twice I hosted one myself in our rooms, and Garrett would serve the food and pour the drinks for Yarmouth, Jones, Portishead and I, poker-faced and unsmiling. My eyes would follow him around the room, of course, but no one ever seemed to notice.

I did make one friend who has some bearing on my story, beyond vacuous reminiscence of Oxford days. I met him through my tutor, that first Michaelmas term.

Dr Dacre Winslow turned out to be in his late forties. Thin, tall, with a pleasant, long face and receding brown hair, he affected a little gold watch chain, but otherwise dressed much as you would expect a don to do: soberly and conservatively, all shabby gentility. His office was across the Old Quad from my own rooms, on the first floor, and at our first meeting I could look down and see Garrett clearing away the plates from breakfast in the morning sunlight. There was some preliminary chatter about how I was settling in and what I thought of the college, but once we were both comfortably seated on a pair of leather armchairs by the window, he cocked his head and smiled at me.

"So. What would you like to do?"

I was taken aback, and it must have shown on my face. Dacre narrowed his eyes and waited for my reply. The seconds ticked by on the grandfather clock in the corner of the study. I digested the implications.

"You mean we can do anything?"

"Yes, within reason. The Orient is rather large. Shall we look at ancient Persia? The Gupta Empire? The Mughals? Han China? Heian Japan?"

I hadn't expected this at all. I was eighteen, and used to being told what to do and what to study. I had expected it to be like Rugby, where a rigorous, pre-determined course of study had existed for centuries before I got there and would exist for centuries afterwards. I hadn't grasped that university meant intellectual freedom. It yawned like a dizzying abyss before me. I had to choose and did not know where to start.

"Well, I suppose I would like to look at Vedic India, and perhaps the Jain and Buddhist reformation."

"Reformation?" I waited for him to laugh in my face. Instead he looked thoughtful. "Well, yes, I suppose it was not unlike a reformation. A time of upheaval and change, certainly. I see your point. Though it's a rather more complex situation, and we have far fewer sources to hand." That was unexpected. "Well, that will certainly make my life easier." He drew a piece of paper from a folder on his desk.

"This is the reading list I usually give to first years. How is your Sanskrit? Passable? Good. It will improve as we go." There was a knock on the door, and Dacre glanced at his watch. "Oh, impeccable timing. Come in!"

A boy about my own age entered the room. I was taken aback to see that he was of oriental extraction. He was tall and well-built, with short black hair, cut in European fashion, and a lithe, athletic body hidden beneath a Savile Row suit. His face was aristocratic, fine-boned, but friendly and pleasant, with heavily hooded eyes.

"Dr Winslow, I hope I'm not interrupting?" He glanced at me, cool, offhand.

"Not at all, Sid, please come in. I was hoping to introduce the two of you." He entered. He was carrying a manuscript, which he handed to Dacre, who accepted it casually, with a nod of thanks.

"The translation is done. I trust you'll let me know if it's useful."

"Yes, thank you, dear boy. This is John Sackville, the Lord Dalwood," he said, indicating me. I stood up, hand outstretched.

"Pleased to meet you," I said with a smile. He shook my hand. "And you are?"

"Sidkeong Tulku Namgyal," he said. "But you can call me Sid.

You might have a bit of trouble pronouncing the whole mouthful."
He smiled, diffidently.

"Ha! I'm sure I'll get the hang of it. I haven't seen you around college yet. Where have you been keeping yourself?"

"Oh, I'm a year above you. I'm studying engineering and natural sciences, so I don't think you'd have seen much of me, if you're working with Dacre."

"Right, you two can leave now, and get better acquainted," said Dacre, and with a little wave of dismissal he turned his eyes to the manuscript Sid had handed him. We left his office, and descended the staircase to the Old Quad, and turned and regarded each other for a moment. There was an awkward silence.

"Pub?"

"Yes, pub." And so we went down St Aldate's to the Head of the River, and got ourselves some cider, finding a table overlooking the River Isis, watching the traffic flow back and forth across Folly Bridge. And that was how we began.

"So where are you from, then?" I asked.

"India," he said. He offered no further explanation.

"Yes, but where in India? My guess is somewhere in the Himalayas? Maybe one of the princely states?"

"You're a sharp one, you," he said, smiling ironically. "I suppose you mean that I don't look like the rest of the Indian students here."

"Well, I wasn't going to say so in so many words," I stammered.

"It's all right, it was a good guess." He took a long sip of his cider, and looked pensive, like he was weighing up his response. "Yes, I'm from Ladakh. My father is a merchant there."

"Quite a successful one, if he's able to afford to send you to Pembroke."

"Yes, he does quite well."

"And you're mostly studying the sciences?"

"Yes, it's a matter of practicalities. I need to be able to return home with something useful to offer my people. There is much to learn from the British. If we're ever to make something of India, or to become independent, we need to learn all we can from you, as long as this awkward arrangement of ours persists."

"Makes good sense you wouldn't be taking Oriental Studies," I laughed. "What would there be for you to learn?" I cringe to think of how awkward and ham-fisted my attempts at humorously bridging the gap between our worlds was, but Sidkeong was accommodating, and he shot back with jokes of his own.

"Quite. I'll have to go back to Ladakh and set up an institute of European studies, see if we can unravel the riddle of you people," he grinned. I laughed.

"It is rather an awkward arrangement, as you say."

"Who's that professor who came out with that tripe a few years ago about how the British Empire had been acquired in a fit of absence of mind?" Sidkeong asked.

"Ugh, I believe it was John Seeley," I said. "What a facile thing to say."

"Too right," said Sidkeong. I admired the idiomatic fluency of his English. Even his accent was purest Oxbridge. If it weren't for the colour of his skin you'd have thought he was just another young English gentleman taking his ease by the river. "I don't think anyone but the British could possibly believe that you had anything other than full presence of mind when you brought half the Asian continent under your sway. But presence of mind is a tricky thing, that I'm not sure any European really has."

"I suppose that's the Buddhist in you?"

"Indeed, you people seem to think that if you pray very hard to Jesus, he'll just give you all the answers, and grant you your wishes like some sort of Arab djinn." I barked with laughter.

"And there's more to it than that, you'd say?"

"I would. Perhaps if you knew how to meditate, you wouldn't have absent-mindedly stumbled around the world snapping up territories and dispossessing people." His voice was heavy with sarcasm.